Into the Blue

Into the Blue

Rebecca Gault

Five Star
Unity, Maine

Copyright © 2001 by Rebecca Gault

This novel is a work of fiction. Names, characters, places, and incidents are either the product of the author's imagination, or, if real, used fictitiously.

Five Star First Edition Romance Series.
Published in 2001 in conjunction with Rebecca Gault.

Set in 11 pt. Plantin.

Printed in the United States on permanent paper.

Library of Congress Cataloging-in-Publication Data

Gault, Rebecca.
    Into the blue / by Rebecca Gault.
        p. cm. — (Five Star first edition romance series)
      ISBN 0-7862-2929-2 (hc : alk. paper)
      1. Divorced mothers — Fiction. 2. Americans —
Germany — Fiction. 3. Westphalia (Germany) — Fiction.
I. Title. II. Series.
PS3557.A947 I5 2001
813'.6—dc21   00-049066

To my German teachers and professors, for showing
me the way,
To kindred spirits in Bavaria and Westphalia, for
friendship and inspiration,
To my family, for their love and constancy,
And to the Magus, for directing my sights once again
To the Land of the Blue Flower.

Farewell

Farewell, it cannot be but so!
Unmoor thy ship, unfurl thy sail,
Leave me in my castle when you go,
In this deserted house where spirits wail.

Farewell and take with thee my heart,
And my last ray of light sublime,
For sunshine too must needs depart,
As all in nature has its time.

Leave me aboard my seaside world,
Keening on the craggy shelf,
Alone but for a magic word,
An alpine ghost, and my own self.

Abandoned, yes, but not yet fazed.
Shaken, shocked, but not undone,
For there remains the holy gaze,
That warms me like a loving sun.

As long as still at forest's edge
Songs whisper sweet from every tree,
From every cliff and every ledge,
Bright elfin eyes still wink at me,

As long as I still hold the power
To reach my arms into the blue,
The vulture's cry at twilight hour
Will raise in me my wild muse.

Annette von Droste-Hülshoff,
1797–1848
Translation by the Author

Chapter One

"Mommy, Mommy, I can't find my ticket! Now they're not gonna let me go on the bus!" the little boy wailed as he pulled out piece after piece of paraphernalia from the backpack at his feet.

As if infected by his anxiety, his older sister began to look frantically through her belongings as well. "I don't have mine either! Now we'll have to go back to stay with Daddy."

"No, I'm staying with Mommy. We're gonna have fun in Germany—she said so! It's, it's . . ." the boy struggled with the word. "It's 'chanting, that's what!"

"Yes, Germany is enchanting, Chris," corrected his mother. "You'll see. Come on, we'll get on the bus, and then Professor Heinrich will pick us up, and everything will be fine. And don't worry about those tickets—here they are. I put them in my bag, remember?"

One month after the completion of her graduate studies, Rachel Simmons and her children, five-year-old Chris and eight-year-old Lisbeth, had landed in Europe to embark on a great adventure, her long-delayed "junior year abroad."

But it seemed that it might take forever to get to their destination. From the airport in Luxembourg, their European port of entry, they had to take a bus to the city of Wuppertal in the German state of Westphalia. And there Professor Heinrich would pick them up and take them to Münster, the city that would be their home for the next several months. This March in Europe was cold and blustery, and they had all thought it would be spring.

"I'm freezing, Mommy!" exclaimed Lisbeth.

Lisbeth's jacket was too light to offer much protection from the wind, so Rachel quickly removed her own full-length green cardigan and wrapped it around her daughter. But the child's backpack jutted up from under the sweater, giving her a dwarflike, hunchbacked appearance, much to her little brother's amusement.

"Look, Mommy—it's Rumpelstiltskin!" Chris shouted, causing Lisbeth to cry.

So began the quarreling that lasted all through customs and baggage claim. Continuing their bickering until they spotted their bags, the children then helped to drag the suit-cases from the conveyor belt onto the luggage cart. Finally, with everything loaded, kids' backpacks piled on top of the suitcases, and Lisbeth's Barbie doll seated atop them like a queen on her throne, they were ready to board the bus that would take them to Germany.

It was only nine o'clock in the morning, but Rachel was already exhausted. Their "great adventure" certainly wasn't too much fun yet—but then again, they hadn't yet arrived in the fairy-tale land of her dreams. Just a small group of passengers boarded the bus with them, and Rachel hoped she could catch up on the sleep she'd missed on the plane.

Indeed, she nodded off mere minutes after they were seated, sleeping so soundly that she almost missed the moment they actually crossed the border into Germany.

She felt the difference, though, felt the magic, and woke up. "Look, guys!" she said excitedly to the children. "It's Germany! See the signs? Those are German words! And the trucks—see how different they look from those at home?"

They were driving now on a highway parallel to the romantic Rhine, the river so often the subject of her favorite music and poetry. Rachel strained for a glimpse of something wondrous, but saw only large commercial steamers and barges slowly moving down the current of brownish water. Well, she reminded herself, they *were* some distance from the south of Germany where so many castles overlooked the river from their craggy hilltops.

Just then Rachel spotted the twin towers of Cologne's famous cathedral. "Look at that, kids—der Kölner Dom!"

"I'm hungry, Mommy," responded Chris, unimpressed by the sight of the massive Gothic building.

The bus driver had stopped to allow a few passengers to disembark, so Rachel asked him if he would watch the children while she ran to a snack stand on the street in front of the cathedral. She stopped for a moment, staring up in awe at the lofty spires, ornate carvings, and gargoyles peering down at her, wishing she had time to explore. She ordered a few *Würstchen*—grilled sausages that came with hard rolls—and some soft drinks.

"Siebzehn Mark? Ja, danke," Rachel responded to the vendor, giggling as she counted out the coins from the German currency she had in her change purse. Funny how even mundane activities could be thrilling—speaking German, ordering food, introducing her children to some of the country's indigenous fare.

After their snack, the children's temperaments improved, and the rest of the ride passed smoothly. They gazed out the windows as the bus drove through the area surrounding the industrial city of Düsseldorf, and soon they arrived at Wuppertal, where they were to meet Professor Kurt Heinrich.

The bus arrived ahead of schedule, so they waited at the stop in front of the train station for their ride. Lisbeth started wiggling and whining. The soda pop that had seemed such a good idea in Cologne had worked its way through her system, and she was in dire need of a restroom. "Mommy, I have to go really bad," she whimpered.

Rachel faced a moment of indecision, uncertain whether she could safely leave their belongings—too cumbersome to carry—out here on the street. But with Lisbeth's increasing discomfort, she had no choice but to take both of the children by the hand and run into the station—and no *Toilette* to be found! Unbelievable.

They went back to the luggage while Rachel tried to think of another solution. She took a deep breath and gently smoothed Lisbeth's hair to soothe her as throngs of seemingly unconcerned travelers passed by them. Is it something about the way we look? she wondered. She peered at their reflection in the glassy walls of the station. A slightly harried, thirty-something mother, in jeans and sneakers, uncontrollable strands of coppery hair blowing in the wind. The spilled soda pop on the front of Chris's jacket didn't make him any less cute, and even in the oversized sweater, backpack removed, Lisbeth was still a pretty little girl. Surely there was no truth to her ex-husband's vitriolic assertion that Germans didn't like kids or foreigners.

"When are we going to find a bathroom, Mommy?" Lisbeth asked.

"Soon, honey, soon. Imagine, we've come all the way from America, and we can't even find a bathroom!" Rachel teased, hoping to take Lisbeth's mind off her discomfort for a moment while she mustered up the courage to interrupt one of the passersby.

But just then she heard a familiar voice call her name. "Frau Simmons! Rachel! *Hier!*" It was Professor Heinrich, gesturing to her from a black Mercedes. She waved and beamed at the middle-aged man who looked to her at this moment like a knight in shining armor. In true courtly style, he leapt out of his metallic steed and strode to her side, rescuing the damsel in distress.

Relieved, Rachel gave herself and her family over to his care. Pointing out a hairstyling salon on the corner, the professor suggested that she would likely find a bathroom there for her daughter, and within minutes, that problem was solved. He loaded their bags into the trunk of his car and checked that his passengers were comfortable and safely buckled into their seats.

From the front seat, Rachel turned around to glance at her children now sitting quietly in the back. They seemed calm and happy, so she turned to face the professor once again. "Thank you so much for coming to meet us, Herr Doktor," she said warmly in German.

"Nichts zu danken," he replied—it's nothing. And then he reminded her that he had invited her, along with the other students in the last seminar he'd taught in the States, to call him by his first name, Kurt.

She looked at the man who sat next to her, his eyes now on the road. He had a nice profile, she thought, distinguished. Wire-rimmed glasses, bushy eyebrows above warm brown eyes, thinning brownish-blond hair, and a neatly trimmed goatee with strands of gray. The face of a man she could trust, a man she could be happy to call a friend.

Kurt had acted as Rachel's fairy godfather, arranging the scholarship from her department at the American university, making the required contacts with the German university, and tapping into a support system that allowed her to bring her children with her for this semester of post-graduate study.

He seemed to have a special empathy for her. Of all the faculty, he had been the most understanding about her situation, when she unexpectedly had to add the role of single mother to those of graduate student and teaching assistant. While Rachel was studying for her Master's exams back in the States, he was busy in his hometown of Münster, Germany, making the arrangements for her and her family to experience the adventure of living and learning abroad.

As much as she would have liked to forget that stressful period, she knew she never would. With just one week remaining until her last comprehensive exams, she had little time to orchestrate plans for what was called the summer semester in Germany, frantic as she had been preparing for her tests. Leaving Lisbeth and Chris in the hands of a capable, loving neighbor, Rachel was spending ten to twelve hours a day at the university library while also recovering from the 'flu, courtesy of the capricious weather changes of the Midwest.

As she sat hunched in her little cubicle surrounded by books, Rachel heard the avuncular voices of the authors Goethe, Schiller, Brecht, and others, joining in a polyphonic chorale across the ages and the ocean, their words tantalizing and confusing her overloaded brain. She had to disentangle the voices and remember each author's specific place in the literary canon, along with their works and their significance.

Strangely, only one woman appeared on her required reading list—the Westphalian poet Annette von Droste-Hülshoff. And as she picked up a volume of her poetry, Rachel suddenly heard a soprano voice soaring above the male chorus like a flute obbligato, its breathy presence winding, turning, and swirling, brushing the edges of her consciousness, suggesting myth and mystery.

"Das Leben ist so kurz, das Glück so selten," whispered the poet—"Life is so short, happiness so rare."

But Rachel hadn't the luxury of time to unearth the poet's secrets, or to savor her words—she just had to read, read,

read, and try to place every work in its chronological and literary perspective. Doubts surfaced. Would she be able to complete her readings and reviews? Would she be able to remember names, dates, plots, connections? The pressure mounted as the exams drew nearer.

Though she had longed to complete the studies she'd interrupted for marriage and childrearing, times like that week made her wish they were simply over. Those two years of study toward her master's degree entailed a lonely struggle, especially when Brent, her husband, left.

Brent had tried to help at first, picking up the kids from day care and school, even staying to help make them dinner occasionally. But he soon grew tired of the effort, and the girlfriend for whom he had left their marriage became jealous and demanding. So Rachel persevered with the help of her neighbor, Sharon, letting her ex-husband revert to his previously established visitation schedule of Wednesdays and every other weekend.

Tonight would probably be a repeat of last night, she had reasoned one evening in the library. She'd get to Sharon's after dark, be brought up to date on Lisbeth's homework and Chris's antics, take their tired little bodies home, and put them and herself into bed. No ceremony, no stories, and they had long since discontinued even the most perfunctory of evening prayers. But maybe instead of suffering a fitful, restless night, she'd sleep peacefully straight through until morning, dreaming about what awaited her and the kids on the other side of the exams.

In spite of the formidable tomes staring at her from the shelves above her desk, she had indulged in a flight of fancy.

She visualized walking with her children in a sunny marketplace in a town square in Germany, the three of them munching on delicious crusty rolls. Her arms were full of freshly cut flowers and an assortment of ripe fruits and vegetables just purchased from the open-air vendors. Her daughter was wearing a German *dirndl*—an aproned dress with puffed sleeves—and her son ran around in short gray *lederhosen*—leather pants. All around them was the cacophony of the marketplace, and the children joined in, chatting in fluent German.

But then, from around the corner of a flower stand, from beyond the borders of her imagination, a new figure emerged on the scene. As if through a haze, Rachel saw a man staring at her, his gaze full of meaning that she could not fathom. She did not know who he was or how he came to be there—she had not invited him into her vision—but she was unable to take her eyes off him, though his features were unclear. The sounds of the other shoppers and the children faded away, and she was aware only of this man who now walked toward her. She watched, mesmerized, as he reached into his pocket for something, enclosed it in his hand, and extended it to her. . . .

"How was your flight?" Kurt's question brought Rachel back to reality. This *was* reality, she reminded herself. She was actually here, in the land of her dreams.

"It was fine. The kids slept most of the way. As soon as the lights dimmed for the movie, they were out."

"And what about you? Did you watch the film or sleep?"

"I'm afraid the movie didn't hold my interest—it was a silly comedy about mixed-up lovers—but I couldn't sleep either."

Sitting between her son and daughter, butterflies fluttering in her stomach, Rachel had kept on the earphones and tried to watch the movie, but changed channels to listen to the strains of an orchestra playing a piece she couldn't quite place. The strings swelled and built to a crescendo, carrying her along with the yearning melody. And the silences, as powerful as the melody itself, made her conscious of an emptiness within her.

Then she recognized the music—Wagner's overture to *Tristan und Isolde*, a dramatic opera based on the medieval legend of eternal love and star-crossed lovers, a love so strong that it vanquishes death. Quite unexpectedly, tears came to her eyes. Then, angry at herself for her emotional reaction, she quickly yanked off the earphones and closed her eyes tightly.

"I tried to get a little sleep," she explained to Kurt, "but I had so many things to think about. My mind raced, and I couldn't really relax."

"I hope you were not worried about your stay here. I know it was of some concern to Mr. Simmons, but everything will work out well for you and the children."

"Oh, I think you convinced him of that."

Initially reluctant to let his children leave the country, Brent had acquiesced after a lot of persuasion from Rachel and a lengthy discussion with Professor Heinrich about the living and school arrangements for the family.

And Rachel sensed another factor in his decision. Brent was getting married in the spring, and although he wouldn't admit it to Rachel, she knew that he welcomed some time alone with his fiancée.

A wedding—a second chance for him to recreate the fairy tale, this time with a new heroine. Rachel still felt the pain of her failed marriage and wished she could call her ex-husband a villain or a monster, but she knew he wasn't really evil. Theirs was just one of those typical young marriages, each partner trying to make the other responsible for his happiness, for fulfilling her dreams.

And now that the marriage was over, Rachel could admit

to herself that she hadn't been madly in love with her husband. They had been friends, partners, and parents, but never soul mates—if there truly was such a thing.

Before their flight left, she had looked over at Brent as he stood with the children near the airport's observation window, watching the planes. His head was bent to his son's, and Rachel marveled at their physical likeness, although Chris was yet to grow into the proper figure of a man. His father exemplified something from *GQ*. His light brown hair was professionally styled into a casual but dignified cut befitting a rising executive, the stocky form that had served him so well as a college athlete now health-club trim and outfitted in a Ralph Lauren sweater, khaki pants, and Italian loafers.

Rachel could hear bits of their conversation as Brent pointed to a plane on the ground, describing something technical, far beyond the children's comprehension. Chris was trying to pay attention, but Lisbeth had turned her face from the window and seemed to be staring into space.

"Now what are you doing, Lizzy—off in la-la land again?"

Rachel bristled as she heard Brent address his daughter. Not only did she hate the nickname he used for the child, but that particular expression brought back unpleasant memories.

Rachel had tried to be an attentive and loving wife, but since her own solitary, often lonely childhood, she had entertained herself with fantasies and daydreams, even cocking her head as though she were listening to distant music. Her mother had teased her for wool gathering, but Brent would say derogatorily that she was always in "la-la land." As if under a spell, she still sought something, but did not know if she would ever find it. Certainly marriage hadn't been the answer.

Still, the end of that marriage had changed her. No longer so idealistic, she was determined to be responsible and practical, relegating fantasy to the realm of the intellect only—to the study of German culture. As for this trip, it wasn't about chasing fairy tales, she silently answered to Brent's frequent criticism. It was to broaden and deepen her knowledge of language, literature, and civilization that would help her in her teaching career.

"I hope you know what you're doing, Rachel," Brent had said to her just before she and the children got on the plane. "Maybe you'll find what you're looking for, flying off into the blue, who knows? But the kids—you think a few months abroad will mean anything to them? They hardly even know any of the language, for godssake."

As if to defend her decision even now, a good ten hours after that conversation, Rachel turned around once again to check on the children. Chris, with his slightly matted dark-blond curls resting against the seat, and Lisbeth, with her copper-tinted long brown waves framing her face, looked like painted cherubs.

What *did* they expect, she wondered. While her head might be spinning with romantic visions of charming villages, centuries-old churches and castles, breathtaking scenery, of a land imbued with the spirits of writers, artists, philosophers, and musicians, the children could be anticipating a glorified Disneyland with rides, balloons, and cartoon characters reciting the German nursery rhymes and Christmas carols she had taught them. Still, no matter what any of them expected, they were here, and it would be a real-life adventure for them all.

"Yes, Kurt, we're going to be just fine here," she said confidently, flashing him a smile.

As the Mercedes sped along the famous German Autobahn, Rachel enjoyed watching her first fleeting images of the scenery.

"Well, what do you think of our fair countryside?" Kurt asked.

"It's beautiful, so open and so . . ." She looked for a more poetic word but fell back on her first impression. "So flat!"

Kurt laughed. "Yes, it's quite different here from the image most tourists have of Germany. This part of the country is not as visually dramatic as the Alps of southern Germany, or along the lower Rhine. It is a low-lying region, with fertile soil. That's why you see so many farms."

Rachel was charmed by the landscape. Across the wide expanses of green acreage she spied what she recognized as examples of typical northern German architecture—stucco-frame barns and houses adorned with window boxes and gardens, surrounded by carefully tended plots of land. Cows and sheep grazed in the fields, and here and there, breaking up the land's flatness were occasional beech trees, their branches swaying in the breeze.

"I didn't expect it to be so peaceful."

"Yes, here in Westphalia it certainly is that," Kurt answered. "In some isolated areas, the atmosphere can be lonely, even austere, but we appreciate the sense of serenity here, even in the more populated areas." He smiled at her as she settled back into her seat again with a barely audible sigh.

"Mommy, Mommy!" came a shrill voice from the back seat, interrupting Rachel's relaxed state. "Look—a windmill!" exclaimed Chris.

"Awesome!" said Lisbeth. "But, Mom, don't German people have electricity?"

"*Ach, Kind,* of course we do," responded the professor. "We're really very modern! You'll see that it's not so different from America. We have everything you're used to—we even have a McDonald's in the city!"

That wasn't something Rachel necessarily cared to hear; though she expected the kids to be happy and comfortable, she didn't want them to expect all the so-called comforts of home.

She turned to Kurt, hoping to elicit information that would give the children an idea of what was unique to the region, features they could start to recognize as typically German. "I've read that there are at least a few castles in this area. Is that true?" she asked him.

"Oh, yes. Now, these aren't like the huge ones you have seen in the movies or in your fairy-tale books," he said, addressing the children. "And they're not on mountaintops, since we don't have any mountains here."

Still, Lisbeth was interested. "So are the castles here just like big houses?" she asked Kurt.

"Some of them are very big indeed," he answered. "And, yes, many of them are houses that families still live in. Others are museums. What makes the castles of Westphalia special is that they are *Wasserschlösser*—water castles."

Chris started to laugh. "A castle made out of water?"

His sister refined the question. "You mean a castle that's *in* the water?"

"Well, I believe you would call them moated castles in English. They are circled by moats of water, as though resting on an island. By having deep canals around their homes, the owners could make sure they were protected from their enemies or unwelcome strangers who passed by."

Enjoying the children's interest, Kurt continued his explanation, starting to sound like a tour guide. "In fact, one of these old castles is very close to here. It's where our most famous female poet, Annette von Droste-Hülshoff, was born. It even bears her name, Hülshoff Castle."

He turned to Rachel. "You remember her, don't you—the Westphalian poet who wrote about our beautiful countryside?"

Rachel smiled her assent. Of course she remembered her —the soprano voice she had heard above all the basses and tenors of the male writers as she had studied for her exams: "Life is so short, happiness so rare."

Why, she asked herself, couldn't she get that phrase out of her mind? Nor could she rid herself of a tingle of excitement, a hint of intrigue, an odd feeling that perhaps her stay here was somehow connected to the writer.

The Mercedes turned off the Autobahn onto a two-lane highway. "I have a little surprise for you," Kurt said, and they drove for a few more minutes until he stopped the car. "Look, here's the castle I was talking about—Hülshoff Castle," he said rather proudly. "I know you're all tired, but at least you can take a quick peek. Look over there, children—do you see all the water around the castle and the other building?"

Feeling an odd frisson of excitement in the presence of the poet's birthplace, Rachel looked back at the children, but their eyes had a glazed look, and they fidgeted in their seats. Overload, definitely. "Thanks so much for showing us the castle, Kurt. We'll have to come back soon and explore it and the grounds."

Kurt seemed a bit disappointed by the inattention of his young passengers, Rachel noticed. He pursed his lips and turned the car around while she sat in silence, unsure what else she could say.

But he had apparently decided to direct his attention from the children to their mother. "You know, Rachel, if you register for my seminar, Poetic Realism, you will have an opportunity to become acquainted with this castle as well as the other estate in Münster where Frau von Droste-Hülshoff, or

Frau Droste, as we call her, lived. My research assistant and I have special permission to use the library here, and we will have a class meeting at the Rüschhaus—the House in the Rushes—her home for twenty years."

"Oh yes, I'd like that," she said, enthusiastic about the prospect. She did want to learn more about this particular poet.

Rachel then tried to change the subject, hoping to engage Kurt in lighter topics that wouldn't require scholarly explanations, but that wouldn't insult him either. "So, you have an assistant? Does she just help with your research—or does she teach undergraduate language classes as I did in the States?"

"First of all, my assistant is a he, not a she, and his name is Michael Obregón. Quite a fine young man, actually, with the promise of becoming a decent scholar and professor himself one day. He has already completed his *Staatsexamen* and receives a stipend for helping me with my research and seminars, not for teaching, as at your university. His family has known mine for many years, and his father was a history professor at the university."

"Well, I guess I'll get to meet Michael soon."

"Most certainly. I expect him to sit in on my seminar, so you'll become acquainted with him then. And as a family friend, he is often in my home, so you will probably encounter him before the beginning of the semester. In fact, he may be there today. And we do have to stop by my house to pick up the key to your apartment."

Rachel wasn't sure why she was feeling so uneasy. The professor had offered her his help and his friendship, and everything had been going well, and then the kids had acted like, well, kids, and he'd seemed disturbed.

He bragged about this research assistant, probably one of those serious scholarly types, like so many graduate students

21

who devoted themselves to books because they didn't have a life. She could see him—scruffy, with shaggy hair and taped glasses, wearing a moth-eaten old sweater and baggy pants with sandals.

Still, a polite response was called for. "I'll look forward to meeting your assistant," she said, trying to inject a hearty tone into her voice despite the fact that she was starting to feel very tired.

Kurt began talking then about his plans for the seminar. "Our study of nineteenth-century literature will begin with that well-known image of German romanticism, the blue flower, which came to symbolize the suppressed longings of a generation reacting to the constraints of a well-ordered Classicism."

His voice droned on as though he were in a lecture hall, and Rachel's mind wandered. *Suppressed longing*—how erotic that sounded. It was a good thing that she had decided to be practical and give up all thoughts of marriage or even of relationships—love and attempts at intimacy only led to frustration and heartache. She wondered if the professor had engaged in any romances since his wife died. Probably not, since she knew from comments he'd made in the States that he'd had a daughter to raise.

By now the scenery outside the car window had changed, and Rachel realized that they were entering Münster itself, their new home. Now that she had a glimpse of the peaceful backdrop, she was looking forward to becoming acquainted with the city.

Kurt pointed out some of the local historical sites and places of interest. "We're taking a little detour so that you can see a bit of your new hometown," he explained as he guided the car down a narrow, crowded street. "All roads lead to the center of the city, which was a busy trade center even in antiquity."

The excitement of entering town was lost on the backseat passengers, who had fallen asleep, but Rachel was thrilled to see all the old buildings, shops, and throngs of pedestrians.

"Look at all those shoppers and all those arched doorways. They make this street look almost like a cloister!" she exclaimed.

"It's not surprising you should say that—the city's name comes from the Middle Ages, when it meant *monastery*. This curved street is called the Prinzipalmarkt, and it leads to the market square in front of St. Paul's Cathedral. Even now, hundreds of years later, these shoppers are much like their predecessors in the Middle Ages, when people from all over came to trade their wares at the market."

"But the place doesn't really look that old. It's not dark or crumbling, and, while it doesn't look exactly modern, it certainly seems newer than the Middle Ages."

"Münster was devastated by World War II, when bombs flattened many of the old buildings. But through careful reconstruction and historically accurate restorations, the city has recovered," he explained. "Now the buildings once again stand as monuments to what one could call the three spheres of Münster: the religious, economic, and intellectual."

"And here's the cathedral, seat of the intellect and the soul, and the marketplace, where the open-air market is on Wednesdays and Saturdays," Kurt continued, pointing to his right.

Rachel looked in the direction he indicated, seeing a magnificent Gothic cathedral with a large, paved expanse in front of it—the market square. "I can't wait to sample all the wares at the market! To buy fresh produce and staples from nearby farms, instead of plastic-wrapped products from chain grocery stores—that will be such fun for the kids and me."

Then she recalled the daydream of a German marketplace

that had come to her while she was studying for her exams. Her kids, the local colors and sounds—and then that man who had suddenly appeared in the picture. She could still see him, although his face remained unclear, walking slowly toward her, offering something to her in his closed hand.

She shivered involuntarily, causing Kurt to look at her with concern. "*Ach, du Arme,* you poor thing. Enough of the tour. It is chilly today, and of course you're tired after your long trip. Let's retrieve the key for your apartment and get you settled."

Though still oddly affected by the image in her mind, Rachel smiled with gratitude as they headed out of the center of town.

"I promise not to extend our little tour, but I must point out to you that there, across the street, are the main buildings of the university," said Kurt almost apologetically. "But you can see more at a later date. You've plenty of time."

They drove through residential areas, mostly apartment buildings interspersed with a few private homes, until they reached the neighborhood where the professor lived.

"Oh good, we are in luck—Elke is home," Kurt announced. "And that's Michael's bicycle. You can meet them both!" Kurt pulled up in front of an attractive single-family brick house with carved wooden window boxes.

In most circumstances, Rachel would have been happy to meet two new faces—especially Kurt's teenaged daughter, about whom he had often spoken when he was in the States. But now all she could think about was her ever-increasing fatigue. It was like a heavy cloud descending on her, threatening to close her eyes, bow her head, and overtake the rest of her body. And the kids were still asleep in the back seat.

As if reading her thoughts or, probably more accurately, her body language, noting her slumping posture and half-closed eyes, Kurt assured her, "We'll go in, pick up the key, and I'll introduce you to Elke. It will take but a few minutes, so you can leave the little ones in the car."

He came around and opened the car door for her, and as they walked up to the house, Rachel was struck by how orderly everything was—neatly clipped grass, regimental rows of flowers in the freshly painted window boxes, and framing the front door, starched snowy white curtains behind shiny glass bearing no fingerprints. The impression of orderliness intensified as they entered the foyer with its dust-free elegance.

"Elke!" called Kurt, and from the back of the house came a slender girl with long blond hair.

"This is my daughter, Elke. *Liebchen,* I'd like you to meet our new exchange student, the woman I've told you about. This is Mrs. Simmons."

"Oh, please call me Rachel," she said as they shook hands. The girl merely nodded, not replying. Probably wasn't too sure of her English, thought Rachel. She was sometimes unsure of her German, especially in new situations.

Rachel gave the girl an encouraging smile, but Elke didn't seem especially receptive. She was tall and fair, like her father, but whereas his eyes were brown, hers were gray, and nowhere near as warm. Such a pretty girl, but with a distinct coolness about her. Must be shy, Rachel thought.

But suddenly the girl spoke in perfect British English. "I am very happy to meet you, Mrs. Simmons. I hope your trip wasn't too tiring. May I offer you some coffee and *Kuchen?* We often have a little *Kaffeestunde* in the afternoon."

Kurt beamed. "My daughter bakes the cakes herself. She learned from her mother and grandmother."

Rachel felt a bit little flustered. How could she decline gracefully? "Thank you so much, but the children are still sleeping in the car. Maybe I could take a rain check?" Noticing Elke's bemused expression, she silently chastised herself. Elke was probably wondering what in the world a rain check was. In the current context, the Americanism sounded like something to eat!

But the girl seemed to understand. "Yes, another time would be better. Well, I must go finish my tasks in the kitchen. It was very nice to meet you, Mrs. Simmons."

As she walked away, Rachel admired her shiny, straight, neatly cut blond hair. It fell to her shoulders and flowed in a smooth, slow swish just like the models' hair in shampoo commercials on television back home.

"I'll go upstairs and get the key for the apartment. I'll be right back." Kurt left the room, taking the stairs to the left of the foyer.

In the few minutes of his absence, Rachel looked around. It was funny how people and their surroundings often matched, she thought. Everything here was in shades of gold, ranging from dark, almost topaz tones to the nearly ivory hues. Just like the family that lived here: dad, daughter, and mom as well. At least, she assumed that was Kurt's deceased wife in the photos on the wall opposite the staircase.

Looking physically very much like the girl Rachel had just met, this woman had a sunny presence that seemed to radiate from her framed image. Photographed in a field of wild flowers, she looked toward the camera with a gorgeous smile, her honey-blond hair glinting in the sunlight. A smaller framed photo above showed the whole family from a much earlier time: a younger, lighter-haired, beardless Kurt Heinrich with his arm around the lovely woman, who held a rosy-cheeked, towheaded toddler on her lap. A golden family.

She heard heavy footsteps on the stairs, which surprised her. Kurt seemed lighter on his feet than that. But then she realized she was hearing two people descend. Someone was behind the professor.

"And yet another introduction, Rachel," he said. "May I present my research assistant, Michael Obregón." Kurt stood aside, and a tall, lean, but well-formed young man stepped forward. He had dark hair curling around his ears, a cleft in his chin, and a sober expression as he walked toward her, extending his hand.

As he approached her, a swirl of confusing sensations overtook Rachel, her thoughts becoming disjointed. Kurt's assistant wasn't supposed to look like this. He was supposed to be a sloppy, unkempt scholar. And she knew she'd never seen this man before, so why did he look familiar? And he didn't even look German but dark, foreign, exotic. Like his unusual last name. And why was he gazing at her that way, with those intense blue eyes? Half remembering, half imagining something, all of a sudden Rachel felt woozy. She closed her eyes, trying to quell her dizziness, but she could feel her body listing to one side, against the wall. Her knees buckled, and she slumped in a heap to the floor.

Chapter Two

"Rachel! Rachel!" Someone was calling her name, just as at the train station, which seemed so long ago. But now the voice was more insistent. Through half-closed eyes, Rachel saw the concerned face of the professor above her, who seemed to be studying her for signs of life.

"Are you all right?" Kurt asked when he realized she was conscious again. "Here, let me help you." Not waiting for an answer, he carefully slid an arm under her shoulders and tried to raise her head.

"No, I—I'm all right, really," Rachel said weakly. She sat up and looked around. Just a few feet away was that man, Michael. And next to him, hand on his arm, stood the professor's daughter, Elke. Both were scrutinizing her as she sat on the floor.

Deeply embarrassed to have caused such a scene, Rachel tried to apologize. "I guess all that travel—you know, jet lag —just caught up with me. I'm so sorry."

Kurt helped her to her feet. "Not to worry. You haven't had enough sleep, and you probably haven't eaten, either. International travel often affects me that way, too."

Rachel appreciated his corroboration of her lame excuse. Who knew? Maybe it was the truth. Maybe it was just jet lag. But something inexplicable also seemed to be in play. She didn't have any idea why, but the appearance of Michael Obregón had profoundly upset her equilibrium.

Even now, standing across from the young couple, Rachel

could barely look at him. Elke was saying something to him in a barely audible tone, but his intense gaze was still directed at Rachel. And when he spoke, she had another surprise.

"Are you all right, Frau Simmons?" he asked in beautiful but faintly accented German, which had a slight but distinctly melodic cadence.

"Yes, yes, quite all right," Rachel assured him and everyone else. By now she just wanted to remove herself from the scene.

She apologized again, exchanged polite good-byes with Elke Heinrich and Michael Obregón, and allowed herself to take Kurt's arm as they walked toward the car, where her children still slept in the back seat. As they made their way down the front path, she was conscious of the double gaze of the pair standing in the doorway.

Rachel felt much improved by the time she and the children arrived at the apartment building that would be their home for the next several months. Refreshed from their naps in the professor's car, Lisbeth and Christopher ran up to the front steps, excited to see their new living quarters. Kurt gave Rachel the key and went back to the car to bring in their luggage. When she opened the door, the kids rushed ahead, and she followed them into the furnished lodgings.

Their exploration didn't take long—it was a small apartment, after all. An entryway with a coat rack, a small kitchen with a curtained window to the right, and a living-dining area straight ahead. Rachel was pleased to see a large picture window running the length of the room, with a balcony overlooking the grassy yard below. She even spotted a couple of tiny brown rabbits cavorting around the bushes.

The living room had a comfortable ambiance. Beige carpeting, nubby brown sofa, a matching easy chair set at an angle toward the wall unit, which held a small, old-fashioned-looking television set and telephone. An evocative, impressionistic print of a young woman in a white dress hung on the wall above the sofa.

To one side was a dining room table with four chairs, upholstered in a geometric pattern of brown, orange, and green. Above the table hung another framed print, a landscape, wide green fields populated with grazing cattle, in the background of a village and its church, steeple rising into a deep blue sky.

Rachel walked down the narrow hallway, and straight ahead was the bathroom, which boasted a clawfoot tub but no shower, only a hand-held apparatus for washing hair or rinsing off.

To the right of the bath was a bedroom with a large wooden *Schrank,* a cupboard to store clothing. The curtain on the wide window was drawn, making the room seem dark but soothing. Lisbeth and Christopher had already snuggled down into the big platform bed's fluffy feather comforter.

"This is cozy, Mommy! I like our new house," said Lisbeth.

"Me, too!" exclaimed Chris.

Rachel had to concur after her cursory inspection. All these earth tones, though normally not her favorite color scheme, seemed just right here.

"I have to agree with you guys. It's like a snug little cave, isn't it?"

She heard Kurt's voice behind her. "Well, it seems as though *die Kinder* are making themselves at home already. *Das freut mich*—I'm happy to see that."

He had made several trips to the car, bringing in all of their luggage, and on his last trip, he entered with a crate full of bottles, which he carried into the kitchen.

"Germany is not exactly like the States," he explained. "We

don't drink from the tap here—you have to get bottled water. That will be difficult for you without a car, but I can help you. When you have finished these, let me know and I'll get you more."

With her visions of small specialty stores, open-air markets and fresh produce purchased daily in the European manner, Rachel hadn't really thought about major grocery shopping. She knew she could get by without a car, since Kurt had assured her that the bus service was excellent, but substantial purchases might pose a challenge.

Kurt then opened some cupboard doors and showed her the small refrigerator, which, he explained, Elke and he had stocked with milk, eggs, cheese sausage, butter, honey, and apples. Breakfast supplies—müsli and coffee—nestled in another cupboard, and he had even provided several bars of dark Swiss chocolate.

"Kurt, I don't know how to thank you," she said. "You're too kind!"

"It was no problem, believe me. I'm used to helping our exchange students. After all, your university at home takes care of our students as well. And—" his voice deepened, sounding more personal—"I'm very happy to help such a deserving woman. You're a good student, Rachel, and a good mother, and I admire your courage. I wish your experience in Germany to be fulfilling—for all of you."

Rachel smiled her appreciation, blushing slightly at his praise.

"So then, I'll leave you for now. Please try to relax, have something to eat, and get a good night's sleep. I am sorry I will be out of town for the holiday, but you have the telephone number of our *pension* in Italy if there is an emergency, and on the table I've left a map and some brochures so you can find your way around town."

It seemed that they had arrived in Germany at just the wrong time. Distracted with her preparations for their adventure, Rachel had not realized that their arrival would coincide with a national slowdown as the locals took their Easter vacation.

"Please don't worry. We'll be just fine. It will be fun to explore on our own, right, kids?" Rachel said, excited about getting acquainted with their new home.

"Yeah, Mommy—maybe we can find that McDonald's!" Chris said.

"*Ja,* that would be nice, Chris," answered Kurt. "And perhaps you will find some other things to your liking as well. I hope you have a good time this week, and I will see you as soon as I return."

Kurt bent and shook Chris's hand, then Lisbeth's, before turning to their mother. He took her hand in a firm clasp, giving her a warm smile. "*Schlaft schön*—sleep well," he said softly, and then he departed, leaving the family on their own in their new home.

They spent the rest of the evening doing exactly as Kurt had advised—snacking and relaxing before bedtime. They even turned on the television, watching a show the children didn't understand but seemed to enjoy anyway. Curled up on the sofa next to them, Rachel felt cozy and content. But she also felt an underlying unease. She kept remembering the strange occurrence of that afternoon. It was so humiliating to lose control that way. Thank goodness for Kurt's chivalrous behavior; at least he had tried to preserve what little dignity she had left after collapsing upon meeting Michael Obregón. The more she thought about it, the less sense it all made.

And then awakening to see Elke and Michael, standing side by side, the fair ice princess and the tall, dark, oddly familiar stranger. They were quite a pair—and they did seem to *be* a pair. Kurt had said that the two families were close, but Rachel wondered if he was aware of the romantic connection between his daughter and his research assistant. It was certainly obvious to her; she had seen the intimate way Elke rested her hand on Michael's arm, the way she leaned into him as they stood watching her.

In the States Kurt had described his daughter in the context of childhood antics, family outings, and school achievements. Elke was in her last year at the *Gymnasium,* and high schools in Germany were different from those in the States. The last two years here were more like the first two years of American college, preparatory for higher studies at a university, so the students were nineteen or twenty when they graduated. At almost twenty, then, Elke was no insecure American teenager, but a young woman who seemed to know who she was and what she wanted.

Elke was obviously smitten with Michael, the dark young man with those compelling blue eyes. What an unusual presence he had. Rachel became anxious just thinking about him. Even now, she could feel herself tensing. Better not to think about it, she decided, and resolved to forget about him and that whole incident.

But after settling the children in for the night, and tucking them under the feather comforter, Rachel found her thoughts turning once again to the mysterious Michael.

How silly she was being, she thought, undressing in the darkness. Michael Obregón was just part of the new and unknown environment here in Germany. Even in her few short hours in Germany, she had hints of what was to come: medieval architecture, the marketplace, windmills, moated castles, and interesting people. Despite her fatigue, she was excited to see how this adventure would unfold. Rachel kicked her rumpled travel outfit into a corner and pulled her nightgown over her head. In the stillness of the cool night air, she felt the silky gown caress her body, and she noticed how it outlined her curves in the moonlight that seeped through the curtains. An unknown fragrance, redolent of herbs, flowers, and forest, wafted its way through the open window, as though welcoming her home.

Early the following morning Rachel was awake and refreshed, ready to become acquainted with her new surroundings. She dragged the sleepy children out of bed, helped them find clothes from their suitcases, fed them breakfast, and prepared them for the day's adventure.

Then, armed with a bus schedule, a handful of brochures in English and in German, and a satchel of what she secretly considered bribes for the children—lollipops and little toys —Rachel and her children took to the streets of Münster, their destination the marketplace at the city's center. It was a beautiful, sunny day, and the people, young and old, wandered among the stalls of wares.

"Look over there—how cute!" Lisbeth exclaimed, having spotted cages with small animals for sale—guinea pigs, rabbits, and chickens. She took her mother's hand, dragging Rachel over to see and pat the creatures. Of course she and her brother instantly started begging for a pet, but Rachel explained the no-animals rule of the apartment building and promised they could come visit their furry friends at the market on weekends.

After playing with the animals, they wended their way among various stands and made a few purchases. Rachel was pleased at her ease with both the vendors and the currency. At one stand she bought a loaf of crusty rye bread, a few vegetables at another. Then she stood in awe before a flower stall, reveling in all the colors and varieties of fresh blooms.

She was vaguely aware of someone next to her having the proprietor arrange an incredible profusion of flowers into a bouquet. Intent on selecting her own assortment, she didn't notice the conclusion of her neighbor's transaction and was surprised when his bouquet appeared right in front of her eyes. As she stared into the glorious petals, she heard a voice saying in German, "For you, gracious lady."

Shocked, she looked up toward the speaker. Oh, no, not again—and not here! Inserting himself into her family's enjoyment of the marketplace was that striking but unnerving young man, Michael Obregón.

"I hope you are feeling better today?" he asked, using the formal form of address. Rachel knew that in this culture it was the correct, polite way to speak to someone you didn't know well, but she felt a little annoyed. Students usually spoke to one another using the familiar form, and Michael's politeness made her feel overly aware that, at thirty-four, she was his elder.

Once again nervous in his presence, she answered in kind —in proper, formal German. "Yes, thank you. I am so sorry to have caused a scene at Professor Heinrich's home the other day."

"Not at all. We were all just concerned about you and we hoped you had recovered from your strenuous trip. We should all have been more considerate of your need for rest. Please accept these flowers as a belated welcome to our country."

Rachel couldn't very well refuse the bouquet, so she nodded her thanks and forced a smile. But then she let her natural curiosity overcome the distance she should have maintained.

"Excuse me if I'm being too personal, but your last name . . . is Germany your native country?" she asked.

"Yes, Germany is my home, although I spent many summers with my grandparents in Spain. My father came to Germany years ago as a student, and he stayed here, becoming a professor of history. And then, long after his career was established, he met my mother. Her family has been in Westphalia for many generations."

Chris tugged at his mother's sleeve, weary of all the talk in German, and Michael looked down at the two children standing next to Rachel. He crouched so that he was at the boy's eye level.

"Aha! Elke told me that we would have two very special visitors from America," he said to them in English. "Welcome to Germany!"

"Who's Elke?" asked Lisbeth.

"What's your name?" asked Chris simultaneously.

"Elke is Professor Heinrich's daughter. This is a friend of theirs," interjected Rachel.

"My name is Michael, and I am very happy to meet you both. And what are you called?" When they told him their names, he very seriously shook their hands.

Rachel watched as first Chris's small, chubby hand, then Lisbeth's delicate little fingers were engulfed in Michael's right hand. And realized that she herself had yet to shake Michael's hand. She had ignominiously fainted when they were first introduced, and when he greeted her here at the market, it was with a huge bouquet of flowers. Now, looking down at his strong hands, she couldn't help but wonder how it would feel to have her own fingers held in his. Were his hands rough or soft? Would he have a firm, businesslike grip or a smooth, seductive clasp, in keeping with his sexy appearance?

As Rachel wondered, Michael stood up. "I have an idea," he said. "Have you tried the ice cream in one of our *Eisdielen?*"

36

"No," Rachel answered. "Is it special German ice cream?"

"It's not really German—it's Italian. Almost all the ice cream parlors here are owned by Italians who come to Germany for the spring and summer and go home to vacation during the winter. And—well, let me take you and you can judge for yourself."

Michael had continued speaking in English, so the children understood and were enthusiastic about his suggestion.

"Yes, Mommy, let's go!"

"Well . . . all right, but you must not pay for us." She couldn't think of how to refuse the invitation without appearing rude and disappointing the children.

As they left the marketplace, Michael leading the way, Chris sidled up to him. "I'm going to walk with Michael, okay, Mom?" he asked.

Michael, hearing Chris's question, slowed down and held out his hand. "*Ja, komm mal mit*—come along," he said to the boy.

Rachel watched the scene unfold, still uncertain why Michael unnerved her so. He was being kind, likeable, open, and kids were usually good judges of character. But something tugged at the edges of her mind.

The ice cream parlor turned out to be an even bigger hit than the marketplace livestock had been. Michael was right about the ice cream—it was wonderful. The *Eisdiele* offered all kinds of fanciful treats, mixtures of flavors, colorful garnishes, waffles or cookies on the side, and everything bedecked with fresh whipped cream. The children were delighted with their choices. Chris's selection was prepared to look like a fried egg on waffle "toast," and Lisbeth's looked just like spaghetti—both made of ice cream, of course.

Rachel enjoyed herself as well, savoring her bowl of assorted ice cream balls. And that real whipped cream! The children laughed when her last bite of the luscious, melting confection dripped down her chin while she searched to find her napkin.

"Allow me, gracious lady," Michael said in German, taking a handkerchief from his pocket and handing it to her. For a moment she was afraid that he might lean a little closer and wipe her chin himself and she wondered briefly how she should respond.

But Michael had turned away from her blushing face and was talking now with the children about Easter, who had told him about the bunny rabbits they saw from their balcony each night.

"Maybe one of them is the rabbit that brings the colorful eggs on Easter morning," he said. "Did you know that custom began long ago right here in Germany?"

"You mean the Easter Bunny comes from Germany, just like Santa Claus comes from the North Pole?" Chris asked, his eyes wide and trusting.

"Well, we can't always explain magic that precisely. Some people claim that German rabbits make special nests at Easter, while others have said that hens lay colored eggs on Green Thursday."

"But that's not right, 'cuz Mommy buys the eggs at the store and we color them. Then the Easter Bunny hides them!" exclaimed Lisbeth with the voice of eight years of experience. "What's Green Thursday anyway? Is it like St. Patrick's Day, when we all wear something green?"

"Green Thursday comes right before Easter weekend and tradition says that if the *Hausfrau* cooks a special kind of cabbage with nine different herbs, her family will stay healthy all year long."

"I never learned about any of these local customs in my studies," observed Rachel. "What else happens here at Easter?"

"We have quite a few Easter traditions, most of them dating all the way back to the time of the first Germanic tribes." Michael looked at the children.

"Lisbeth, do you ever help your mother sweep the floor at home? Yes? Well, one popular symbol at Eastertime is a simple broom. For instance, on *Karfreitag*—I think you call it Good Friday—it is the custom here to clean your house. If you sweep the dust from all four corners before the sun comes up in the morning, then no fleas or other insects can come to disturb the house."

"Mittens, my kitty, had fleas," Chris piped up. "If we could have brought him here to Germany, then maybe a magic broom would have gotten rid of the fleas. But my daddy has him now."

"And your daddy is taking good care of him," Rachel assured him. She was intrigued by Michael's knowledge of German folklore and wanted to learn more—and she most definitely wanted to avoid any discussion of her ex-husband. "So, what else can you tell us?"

"On Easter Saturday, it was once customary to put out all the fires in the fireplaces, then scatter the ashes around the outside of the house and barn, to protect the buildings and their inhabitants from being struck by lightning and catching fire."

"And, back to the broom," he continued, "it is also connected to the ritual hilltop Easter bonfires. Young men would make torches of birch rods topped with straw, like upside-down homemade brooms, then coat the tops with tar, so they would burn for hours and fill the whole mountain with light. Then they would make a huge bonfire in the middle of a clearing and everyone—men, women, and children—would sing a resurrection song. After that, they would go back down the mountain to wait for the dawning of Easter."

Michael had a wonderful way of telling stories. He knew just when to pause for effect, how to shape his narrative to hold the interest of his listeners. The children seemed enthralled at everything he said, and Rachel wanted to know more about what was behind the traditions he described.

"Why the burning brooms, why the fire, and what about the lightning? What do—or did—these rituals have to do with the celebration of Easter?"

"The traditions originally honored the god of lightning, Donar, and his consort, goddess of the hearth, Freya. She is also called Ostara, and she gave us the name for the day we celebrate as *Ostern* in German and Easter in English. Of course, Christianity took over the pagan customs or changed them and established others in their place."

"Michael, may I ask you a question?" Lisbeth asked politely in the pause in the conversation. Encouraged by Michael's grin and nod, she proceeded. "What's the 'section song that you said the people sang on the mountaintop?"

Michael looked puzzled for a moment, then he responded. "Oh, you're speaking of the *resurrection* song." Realizing that the girl and her brother did not understand the term, he explained, "The resurrection—when Christ rose from the dead."

The children still looked confused.

Embarrassed, Rachel admitted, "I'm afraid I haven't done a very good job of educating them about religion. My husband was Jewish, although hardly a practicing one, and I . . . lost touch with my own Protestant background a long time ago, after my mother died."

Uneasy again, she looked around, realizing that they had been sitting at their table for quite a long time. Their leftovers had melted and some of the flowers in her beautiful bouquet were starting to wilt.

"Thank you so much for entertaining us, Michael, and for being so kind," she said, "but we've taken more than enough of your time. We really must be going."

The children got up from their chairs and pushed them in. "Yeah, thank you, Michael," they agreed.

Grabbing Rachel's hand, Chris looked at Michael and then up at his mother. "Mommy, can he come to our house for Easter?"

Michael spared her the awkwardness of responding, explaining that he was expected at the home of relatives in the country.

"Then can you come see us on the Green Day?" Lisbeth pleaded. "We don't have any other friends here and Mommy's professor friend went on vacation to Italy."

Now Rachel was really embarrassed, with her children implying that they all were lonely. True, they hadn't yet met any other children, but she had talked to her cousin, Emma, in Geneva, who had said she would try to come with her family for the Easter weekend, although that was still a week away.

"I would be happy to come visit on Thursday, if your mother approves. And perhaps I could bring the green cabbage, a specialty of *my* mother."

Rachel felt cornered and uncomfortable, but for the sake of the children, she was obligated to extend a formal invitation. She wrote their phone number and address on a scrap of paper she found in the bottom of her satchel and handed it to him.

It was arranged, then. He would join them for dinner on Thursday, in just five days. They said good-bye at the door of the ice cream parlor, and this time, Rachel had no choice but to shake Michael's hand. He had extended his hand to the children and then turned to her. It happened so fast that she scarcely should have registered any sensation. But that simple, brief formality sent a shiver through her, though the touch of his fingers was firm and warm.

Rachel shakily arranged her purchases in her satchel, carefully placing the flowers on top, then walked with the children to the bus stop. The two seemed quite satisfied with their first day on their own. They had experienced the marketplace and had enjoyed a special ice cream treat. And Rachel had gotten through that latter interaction with what she hoped was barely discernible discomfort, but how on earth would she handle Thursday's dinner?

The phone was ringing as they walked into the apartment.

"Daddy!" cried Chris, running to pick up the receiver. But it wasn't Brent. The rosy excitement left Chris's face, and he assumed his polite, talking-to-grownups voice. "Hi, yes, we had a nice time today. Wanna talk to my mom?"

It was Kurt Heinrich, calling from his holiday quarters to see how they had enjoyed their first day. Rachel told him about her pleasure in the marketplace and the chance meeting with his research assistant.

"So Michael introduced you to our Italian ice cream? I'm sure that was fun for the children. And it was kind of him to give you flowers. You know, that's very typical of him—of his whole family, actually. Mediterranean charm, some call it."

Rachel had almost convinced herself that Michael Obregón had taken a personal interest in her little family, but at Kurt's words, she questioned his motives. Mediterranean charm—a practiced, cultivated quality, most definitely flattering, but probably not sincere. And she had invited the man to her home.

She talked with Kurt for a few more minutes, discussing the family's Easter plans and her cousin's upcoming visit, but she did not tell him that Michael was coming to dinner on

Thursday, uncertain what Kurt would think or say.

"Mommy, was that Professor Heinrich?" Lisbeth asked as Rachel hung up the phone.

Rachel nodded.

"He doesn't have a wife anymore, right? Well, maybe he wants you to be his girlfriend."

"Don't be ridiculous. He's a very good friend to me, to all of us but that's all, and that's enough."

"Well, Daddy has a girlfriend, so you can have a boyfriend. And maybe you'll get married, too!"

Rachel shook her head, rolling her eyes as Lisbeth giggled.

The rest of the evening passed much as the previous one had, with eating, reading, and a little television. No shows about romance, though—she made sure of that. While the children watched a nature show, Rachel sat next to them on the sofa and read.

She became engrossed in tourist information, reading the brochures Kurt had given her as well as a few other pieces she'd picked up that afternoon. Of all the attractions in the area—the city's historic buildings, in the churches, the zoo, even the open-air folk museum—she looked forward most to visiting Westphalia's moated castles—some of them haunted, according to local legend. They were said to have beautiful grounds, lakes, and fountains, amid misty landscapes of marshes and moors. The old castles promised mystery, enchantment, and perhaps a hint of revelation.

Still recovering from jet lag, Rachel and the children went to bed early. Almost as soon as she laid her head on her pillow, she was asleep. But her dreams took her back to the marketplace and the memory of a man who walked toward her with a mesmerizing gaze, threatening to disrupt the calm waters surrounding the undiscovered castle of her soul.

Chapter Three

The next few days passed quickly, with more exploring, reading and doing language exercises in the German workbooks Rachel had bought for the children, and getting fresh air at a playground several blocks from their apartment.

There they met a group of children who looked markedly different from those they had seen in the streets of the city, most with dark hair and olive skin, the little girls wearing tiny gold earrings. None were as impeccably clothed as the other children Rachel had encountered, but they all spoke German, and invited Chris and Lisbeth to join them as they clambered over the playground equipment.

Involved as she was with uninterrupted child care, Rachel was almost looking forward to their Thursday night guest. Except for short interchanges with bus drivers, shopkeepers, and a quick telephone call with her cousin to confirm arrangements for the Easter visit, she had felt rather isolated from conversation with other adults, which she had taken for granted at home.

Although her husband hadn't been much of a conversationalist, he had at least pretended to listen to her. She had neighbors for small talk, and, after entering graduate school, she had endless opportunities for deep discussion and the stimulating exchange of ideas, especially with her closest friend at the university, Julie Noble. Though steeped in the research and early stages of writing her doctoral dissertation, Julie always had time for a cup of coffee and sharing.

As Rachel cleaned house and prepared the ingredients for the meal she had planned, her thoughts went to the enigmatic Michael Obregón. She tried to imagine conversation with him, in English and in German, already feeling edgy. She wondered if he would bring any more tales of folklore and superstition along with his promised green cabbage and herbs. At least that prospect was intriguing; she loved hearing about local customs.

At promptly 7:00 P.M. on Green Thursday, the doorbell rang.

"Mommy, he's here!" called Chris. Both children ran from the bedroom toward the door, racing to see who would get there faster. This was their first guest, not counting the professor, and they had exerted extra effort in getting ready. Toys were put away, books straightened, hair combed, and hands washed. And Rachel, dressed in pants and a new cobalt blue sweater she had found in one of the shops in the city, felt her heart skip a beat.

"*Schön guten Abend, Kinder!* How are you this evening?" Michael greeted the children, handing Lisbeth a covered bowl. "This is the cabbage dish I promised to bring. Could you take it into your kitchen?"

He then looked up at Rachel and smiled. "And once again, for the lady"—and he offered Rachel a small nosegay of violets. "From the forest near my parents' home," he explained.

Rachel wordlessly accepted the flowers. Though wondering about his motives, she couldn't help but be pleased with the little bouquet. Blue flowers, so rare in nature—that's why the Romantic poets had made the blue flower emblematic of the emotions they expressed in their writing, a symbol of eternal longing for something just beyond the horizon . . .

Lisbeth's voice interrupted her mother's reverie. "Here, Mommy. Here's a glass of water that you can put the pretty flowers in." So Rachel placed the tiny bouquet into a juice glass and set it on the table.

"Well, Michael, from here you have a good view of our world," she said, standing as they all were in the living-dining room. "You caught a glimpse of our kitchen when you came in, and here's where we eat and do our lessons, and over there"—she pointed to the sofa—"that's of course where we relax and read or watch television."

She started to gesture toward the balcony and the grounds outside, but she noticed that he was staring at the framed print of the woman in the white dress above the sofa.

"Ah, die weisse Frau," he said, then turned his gaze to his hostess. "Rachel, surely you know about our legendary White Ladies?" When she professed ignorance, he explained that ghostly ladies, gowned in white, were said to haunt woods, caves, and castles in Westphalia and other parts of Germany. They might be members of families who had lost their ancestral home, novice nuns who had disappeared from a convent before taking their vows, guardians of hidden treasure, or, most often, maidens who waited endlessly for the man who held the key to their heart.

"Many times a White Lady has been sighted roaming the corridors of a castle, wearing a key ring at her waist, looking for the one who will come to save her."

"Oh, dear, the typical helpless female who needs to be rescued by a man, then?" Rachel couldn't hide the sardonic note in her voice.

Lisbeth interrupted before Michael could respond. "Have you ever seen a White Lady, Michael?"

Rachel expected him to answer in the negative—no rational adult would say he had seen a ghost, after all.

"Yes, Lisbeth, I have. Sightings are not uncommon in this area. But of course, to see them, you must believe they exist."

He looked at Rachel, and she wondered if he expected her to disagree or if he was simply waiting for her reaction. In truth, she didn't know how to respond. She was about to argue with him, but then again, she herself had loved fantasy and fairy stories as a child, though she wasn't at all sure it was a good idea to present myths as fact. Still, she couldn't quite quell the temptation to believe, even as an adult, so she said nothing.

"Perhaps later, after dinner, Lisbeth, I will tell you an Easter story about a White Lady—and especially for you, Chris, there's a story about the hunter who is forever hunting, even on Easter."

Chris was excited. "Is the hunter a bad guy or a good guy? I have some bad guys—wanna see 'em?" he asked, pointing to a collection of plastic action figures, complete with costumes and weapons.

Michael laughed. "You'll see. You can tell me if he is a hero or villain when you hear the story, all right?"

Rachel excused herself to check on dinner, and Michael went over to the bookcase where the children stored their toys on the lower shelves. As she tended to her cooking, she could hear her children's high-pitched, excited chattering, punctuated by Michael's lower tones of amusement or admiration.

She took the roasted chicken from the oven, draining the juices for gravy. Studded with slivers of garlic and sprigs of fresh rosemary and thyme, it smelled wonderful. She hoped her attempt at creating a real meal here in this miniscule kitchen would meet with Michael's approval, especially since his girlfriend, Elke, had an excellent reputation for baking.

All preparations complete, Rachel sprinkled chopped parsley over the chicken and roasted potatoes and carried the platter into the dining area.

With the main course now wafting its invitation to dinner,

it didn't take long until the rest of the table was set. The children rushed to bring the plates, glasses, and silverware from the kitchen, and Rachel carried in the remaining components of the meal—mineral water, a bottle of wine, gravy bowl, and dish of herbed cabbage. When everyone was seated, she retrieved two small candles from the bookcase, placing them on either side of the bouquet of violets, lit them, and sat down.

Rachel started to serve her guest, but she noticed that he had closed his eyes as though invoking a blessing, so she quietly began to serve the children. She wondered about the apparent contradiction between praying and his beliefs in ghosts and superstitions. It was all quite confusing. Oh well, just one more reason to be leery of him. He was just too unsettling.

The meal proved a great success. Michael raved about her cooking, and judging from the excellence of the cabbage dish, and his explanation of the ingredients, it was clear that not only was his mother a wonderful cook, but that he had a discerning palate. Or, on the down side, maybe he'd simply expected that all Americans ate only hamburgers or microwaved frozen dishes?

She remembered Elke and her father's bragging about her culinary skills. She probably cooked for Michael all the time. Rachel could just see her, serving him solicitously, bending over him, hand on his arm. So Michael was likely just practicing his Mediterranean charm, flattering her with his compliments on her cooking.

After dinner, as promised, Michael regaled them with tales of the White Lady and of the hunter. But instead of beginning his stories with "Once upon a time in a faraway land," he set them in real places, the first near a town called Damme, as if the events he described had really happened.

"Long ago a cave in Damme housed savage robbers. The robbers needed someone to care and cook for them, so they captured a girl from the country and dragged her off with them. No one knew what had happened to her but sometimes people from her former village saw the figure of a woman in the mist and heard mournful cries in the wind, and they wondered.

"The girl was there a very long time before she asked just one favor—that she be allowed to go into the nearby town to attend church on Easter. The robbers let her go, as long as she promised to return and tell no one where they were, threatening her with death if she betrayed them. So she did promise, and she went to the Easter service. Afterward, she met an old woman carrying a basket of vegetables. The crone asked why she was tearful on such a joyous day, and the lonely girl related her story.

"The old woman gave her three handfuls of peas, telling her she should drop them along behind her as she returned to the cave, to mark her way back and ensure that she would be able to return to church. So the girl walked back to the robbers, scattering the green peas behind her.

"But she did not realize the townspeople who had attended the service would use the peas to follow her trail to the cave. There they discovered the robbers and freed the girl to live in the town and to attend church not only on Easter but every Sunday. And the people covered the entrance to the cave with heavy boulders to trap the evil ones inside forever."

"And did she turn into a White Lady after that?" asked Lisbeth.

Michael shrugged. "The villagers had seen a White Lady in the mists around the cave during the years when she was imprisoned, but when the girl joined the townfolk, she appeared quite normal. She eventually married and had children and grandchildren and was no more different than anyone else. But some people still claim to see a White Lady near the cave, and on holy days, they say you can hear the groaning, grumbling sounds of the robbers' spirits."

"I wouldn't be afraid of those bad guys!" Chris proclaimed. "If they escaped, I would just get them with my laser gun!" He mimicked how he would shoot them with his invisible weapon's rays.

"Chris, you know how I feel about guns," Rachel gently chided him.

"Obviously, you are very brave, Chris, but even brave men must be careful with their powers. Now I'll tell you about a man who was not careful and about what happened to him."

Again, Michael's story was set in a real location, an area south of Heiden where there once stood a castle inhabited by a man who so much loved to hunt that he went hunting every day, even on holidays.

"One Easter, the man donned his hunting clothes and gathered his weapons. Along came a rabbit, so he shot it. Then another one came, and another, and still more, and he shot them, and he thought he had found them all. But then came one more. He tried to get it, but he had run out of arrows, so he quickly returned home to get more. When he came back to where he had seen the rabbit, he saw nothing. He was very disappointed and vowed that he must find it, that he must have it, and that he would never stop hunting until he did. And as soon as he uttered those words, a strange thing happened. The hunter was lifted into the heavens, and now he hunts without ceasing."

Chris's eyes sparkled. "You mean he never comes home to eat?"

"And he couldn't see his family ever again?" asked Lisbeth.

"No, *der ewige Jäger*—the Everlasting Hunter—just keeps hunting, and the grand castle where he lived is gone, though you can still see a small hill forming an island surrounded by a canal where it once stood."

"Now, see what happens to people who just do whatever they want and don't listen to reason or conscience?" Rachel took advantage of the moral of the story. "Now it's time to listen to your mother and get ready for bed—let's go get you washed up and your pajamas on."

Much to her surprise, the children didn't argue. They went into the bedroom and got out their nightclothes while she cleaned up the dishes. Refusing Michael's offer to help, Rachel put away the leftovers and carefully washed and dried the bowl he had brought.

She emerged from the kitchen with it, and saw the candles on the table still casting a soft light. But where was Michael? He wasn't at the table or on the sofa and she could see the children brushing their teeth in the bathroom. Then she spied him standing on the balcony, gazing out at the foliage bordering the lawn below.

She placed the bowl on the table and went into the bathroom, sweeping both children into her arms. "Okay, let's get you guys into bed now. You have a big day ahead of you tomorrow, too. We have to get ready for Aunt Emma, and Uncle Rob, and your cousins—and the Easter bunny!"

"But wait, we have to say goodnight to Michael!" exclaimed Lisbeth. She wriggled out of her mother's arms and ran with her brother toward the living room just as Michael entered from the balcony. As though by tacit agreement, they stopped short and then extended their right hands. *"Gute Nacht,"* they said in unison, to which Michael

51

responded, "*Gute Nacht,* Christopher, *gute Nacht,* Lisbeth."

Then they rushed back into the bedroom where their mother waited at the door. She tucked them in lovingly and, a bit nervously, went back to rejoin her guest.

Returning to the living room, Rachel noted that Michael had re-filled their wine glasses.

"I shouldn't have too much," he said, "even though I am not driving. You know, we are quite strict about driving after drinking in Germany. But I have no car and ride my bicycle everywhere."

"Even at night?" Rachel asked, surprised, used to a life in which it seemed like everyone had at least one car. She had noticed the multitude of cyclists speeding along paths all through the city but hadn't thought about a bicycle's being anyone's sole method of transportation.

"Of course. I have a light in front. A bicycle is quite convenient and often faster than traveling by auto or bus, especially in the city. From my apartment in the student dormitory it takes only about a quarter of an hour to reach most of the university buildings. In fact, you should think about getting a bicycle yourself. Kurt told me you have just been going on foot or with the bus."

"But what about the kids—Chris doesn't even know how to ride a two-wheeler yet!"

"The children will be in school soon, right?" he asked.

She nodded.

"All right, then, if you have a bicycle, you can get to your classes more quickly, and instead of depending on bus schedules, you can go wherever you want, whenever you want. You can even carry packages in the basket or on the handles."

"I hadn't thought of that," she admitted. "Maybe it would be a good idea. But I don't have a lot of money to spend—can I find a used bike?"

"*Ja,* I'm sure you can." He paused. "In fact, I think Elke has a bicycle you could borrow. She doesn't use it too often now that she has a car and of course, she could ride her mother's old bike if she needed to."

"No, I have already been too much trouble for that family. I would rather find an inexpensive one to purchase instead of borrowing one from someone else."

She couldn't let him see how the mention of Elke's name bothered her.

"All right—we can look in the advertisements in the paper and on the kiosks around the university and I'm sure we'll find something suitable. Then we will have to make a bicycle trip into the countryside—maybe to Hülshoff Castle."

"Speaking of the castle, Kurt drove us by there on our way into town on our first day. We didn't really see much because the children were too tired—and as you could see, so was I." Attempting to turn her embarrassment about that incident into a joke, she forced a laugh.

Michael merely nodded, looking serious, so Rachel continued. "But anyway, my cousin Emma and her family are coming from Geneva for the Easter holiday and I wanted to show them some of the local sights. They will have their car, so we can go anywhere. Do you think we should visit the castle?"

"Oh, yes, you will like it very much. And then there is the *Rüschhaus,* the smaller estate where Annette von Droste-Hülshoff spent so many years. It's more personal. I prefer it, but it's your choice. Of course, if you have time, you could visit both of them and even some of the other *Wasserschlösser.*"

"There's that word again. It sounds so right in German, but 'water castles' in English sounds funny—the kids couldn't figure out what they were until Kurt told them about the moat surrounding them. I can't wait to explore them all."

They sat sipping their wine on the sofa, in relaxed silence for a few minutes, the light Riesling serving to relax Rachel a fraction.

Michael asked her about her cousin and her family and how she happened to be in Geneva. Rachel explained that Emma's husband, Rob Patterson, was a computer expert who worked for an international concern. They had lived in several cities in the States and in the South of France before the job took him to Geneva. Their three children were now bilingual, as Rachel hoped Lisbeth and Chris would be, having attended international schools.

Emma was twelve years old when Rachel was born and married and moved away from their hometown in suburban Illinois while Rachel was growing up. Still, she remained close to her cousin, despite the age and geographical distance, she explained to Michael.

"That's something I can understand," he replied. "My older sister, Anna, left home early when she married a Spanish man. She didn't even go to the university because she was so much in love with him. He has a very successful import-export business and she helps him in the office now that their children are older. I wish I could see more of them."

"Is she much older than you, then, like my cousin?"

"Well, I'm twenty-five and she's thirty-four. But we used to joke that we were the same age."

"What do you mean, the same age?" asked Rachel, trying to conceal the edge to her voice. He had hit a sensitive area— her own age. She was, in fact, the same age as his sister, nine years older than Michael.

"Look," he said, taking a pen from his pocket. "Do you have a piece of paper?" She grabbed a book from the shelf and found a folded piece of paper that had served as a bookmark and handed it to him.

Michael smoothed the paper and then drew two simple equations on it: 25: 2 + 5 = ? and, under it, 34: 3 + 4 = ? "Now you tell me, what's the answer to both of these?"

"Well, seven of course. But that's just this year."

"No, look—that's the magical thing about mathematics, and especially with the number nine. Anna and I are nine years apart, but every year, the sum of the two digits of our age is the same. Look here." And he showed her how the numerals worked through all possible combinations, with the sum remaining equal. "So you see, it's just the way you look at it—it's all a matter of your perspective."

"Michael, did you know that I am as old as your sister?"

"No, but it does not make a difference. Do you think people can be friends only if they are the same age?"

"Not really. But I am so much older than the other students here. I already have children, and won't have anything in common with them besides the classes we'll be taking."

"I think and hope you will find out that age is not so very important. I know other women with children, and it is not uncommon for adults to return to the university after they have been working for a while. Last semester there were even two seniors in one of my seminars."

"And I mentioned my parents," he continued. Well, my father is almost twenty years older than my mother, but they loved each other when they met, and I believe even more so now. And my sister and I are not their only children. I also have a younger brother, Paul, who is just sixteen."

Feeling somewhat reassured, Rachel listened to Michael as he told her more about his family. And she described her childhood and early adulthood as well, although it sounded rather colorless compared to his. His life had been filled with multi-national people and extensive travel, whereas she had experienced most of her adventures in the realm of books.

She felt disconcerted when the topic turned to marriage, but gamely attempted to explain how it had been with Brent. How she had met him right after her widowed mother died, while she was working at a dead-end job as a proofreader to pay debts—her own college loans and the medical bills incurred by her mother's long bout with cancer. She had been flattered by Brent's attention. Appearing at a time when she was vulnerable and lonely, he had seemed to her to be a brave knight, sent to rescue her from her prison of solitude. So she married him, hoping for a happily-ever-after.

"I want to think of marriage as forever," Michael said. "But that must be a very old-fashioned notion today, in Germany as well as America."

"That's what I thought, too," Rachel said sadly, and then she turned the focus away from her: "So you think then that you will marry someday?"

"Oh yes," he said emphatically. "It is my destiny."

Destiny seemed an odd word to use, Rachel thought. He must be referring to his family's relationship with the Heinrichs. Their parents had probably arranged a marriage between him and Elke when they were children.

Curious but weary, Rachel stifled a yawn, which wasn't lost on Michael. "Oh, it is getting late. I must be going," he said politely. He rose from the sofa and Rachel followed suit, walking over to the table to fetch the bowl he had brought.

Michael paused at the door. "Thank you so much for inviting me—or I rather think the children invited me, didn't they? I had a very nice time."

"It was my pleasure. You are the first guest we have had in our home here, and I hope you will come again." To her surprise, Rachel found she meant her words.

Michael looked down at her, and she felt even smaller than usual, coming barely to his shoulders without the shoes she had kicked off while they sat on the sofa. She handed him his bowl, and he put it under his left arm.

His dark-fringed blue eyes sparkled as he smiled at her and then he took her hand. *"Es war eine echte Freude, Mütterchen,"* he said, and slipped out the door, leaving Rachel to ponder his words and the touch of his hand.

In the following days, through the preparations for Easter, Rachel returned often to that moment of leavetaking at the door. That the evening had been a real joy was nice of him to say, but *Mütterchen*—little mother? She didn't know whether she should feel complimented or insulted. Maybe he was teasing her about being too much of a mother, or maybe he really did think of her as an older woman, even though he had gone through that little number exercise with her to convince her that the years between them did not matter.

And his touch. The sensation of his warm, strong hand on hers lingered long after he had left. It hadn't seemed anything like a formal handshake, like the one at the ice cream shop, but something entirely different, something more . . . intimate. A slight pressure of his fingers, and a sudden, compelling warmth that she had felt through her whole body. And once again, she felt an exciting tingle run through her, like ripples from a pond . . . or a moat.

Rachel tried to explain her feelings to her cousin a couple of days later. Emma was amused and teased her about having found a boyfriend, which Rachel vehemently denied.

"You don't understand. I'm not looking for romance," she protested. "Besides, Michael Obregón is hardly suitable. Even if he didn't already have a girlfriend—my professor's daughter, no less—he's far too young for me. What would people think?"

"All right then, if you insist, we'll discount Michael for now. Who else is interesting in this town?" Emma asked, with a swing of her beautifully coifed hair. Though she and Rachel had similar features, their appearance was different. Emma was always impeccably made up, foundation concealing the freckles that had not faded with time, while Rachel's freckles danced mischievously across her nose and cheekbones. And her ginger-colored hair, unlike her cousin's well-behaved auburn locks, was always unruly, even when she tried to contain the strands with a hastily created ponytail.

In response to Emma's question, Rachel described some of the neighbors, the international community of children and parents she knew so far only by appearance and polite greetings in passing.

"And of course there's Professor Heinrich—Kurt." For some reason she blushed when she used his first name, which Emma picked up on immediately.

"Aha! Kurt is it? And is he married?" she asked with a smirk.

Rachel explained that he was a widower with a teenaged— she corrected herself—young adult daughter and that he was a kind, considerate man who had offered his friendship to her family.

"Don't forget, Rachie, I've lived in Europe for a long time. People here don't offer their friendship as casually as in the States. If this professor has asked you to call him by his first name, and he's available, as you say, he might have something more than mentoring in mind," Emma said with sisterly authority.

Rachel didn't feel like arguing the point. She knew that Emma had a different orientation to love and marriage from her perspective of almost twenty-five years of marriage. Rachel couldn't imagine it. So many years with one man, even after three children—and still in love. She remembered when Emma had confided in her that when Rob was out of town, she longed for him to return and was unable to rest until he was back home sleeping next to her.

She could see the affection in their easygoing relationship with one another. Though Rob was a successful, hard-working businessman, he clearly adored his family and loved spending time with his wife and their children—nine-year-old Angie, twelve-year-old Matt, and fourteen-year-old Janie.

As Rachel and Emma talked on the balcony, she looked at their children playing soccer in the yard below. Since yesterday, Good Friday, she had hardly seen her children, so involved were they in playing with their cousins.

It was growing dark, and Rachel realized she was getting tired. She had given the relative privacy of the fold-out sofa in the living room to her cousin and her husband last night, while she slept in the bedroom with wall-to-wall children, Emma's three on the makeshift bedding on the floor and her own two with her on the bed. Tonight would be more of the same—a giggling pajama party, she was sure, and they still had to make up Easter baskets for the kids.

Emma volunteered to get all five children ready for bed. She called them to come in and took charge of the washing up, changing, and settling-in process. While Rob sat reading a magazine, Rachel rested for a few minutes on the sofa. Her thoughts wandered back to other Easters, from her daughter's first year—complete with stuffed bunny, to which Brent had halfheartedly objected—to other celebrations with family and friends.

That first year without Brent had been the hardest, but then Julie and some of her other friends had come for the day, which helped. Rachel rarely attended church services on Easter, which sometimes made her feel guilty, but at least she didn't feel like a hypocrite.

She thought about Michael's stories from Thursday night, of the young woman who wanted so desperately to go to church on Easter and who wouldn't break her word even to those who abused her. Her faith and sense of responsibility had been rewarded by the charity of the villagers who rescued her. And then the tale of the faithless hunter who refused to recognize the dictates of society and religion and was condemned to eternal wandering and hunting. In folklore and in fairy tales, virtue was rewarded and wrongdoing punished. Faith and responsibility *über alles*.

Once again, Rachel felt a sense of guilt. Yes, she acted responsibly with her children and tried to raise them to know right from wrong, and they were kind, good-hearted children. But Rachel could not give them any kind of religious guidance, because she had no religion. Though not willing to call herself an atheist, she had not found comfort in any organized church and, unable to classify her beliefs, often felt as though she were just . . . nothing.

That night, after spending a couple of hours with Emma and Rob preparing the children's Easter baskets, Rachel woke up from an intense dream, her heart pounding. In the dream, she felt herself rising from the hearth of a large fireplace, becoming lighter, floating in the air, then drifting slowly to the mist above a mountaintop, swirls of white enveloping her body. Just below her, she could see the glow of a bonfire. She could even feel its heat, and she saw a crowd of people around the blaze, their faces reflecting its light. Then dark clouds of smoke rose from the center of the conflagration, surrounding her, and preventing further observation of the scene below.

Suddenly the dark clouds parted with a burst of light and a loud thunderclap, and a dark figure approached her with his hand extended, as though inviting her to dance. But before she could respond, the figure disappeared.

Then she heard the faint but recognizable tones of a Bach chorus, as though villagers were singing a song of resurrection. But it, too, faded away as the first rays of dawn shone through the curtains and she slowly became aware of her bedroom and the children sleeping all around her.

Within a few hours, Rachel's dream of confused spirituality was superseded by a madhouse of shiny paper, cellophane grass, sticky candy and bits of chocolate, and little wooden and ceramic bunnies and chicks.

So much for all of our housecleaning on Friday, she thought wryly. Lisbeth had been especially insistent about sweeping, especially in the corners, remembering Michael's explanation of the Eastertime custom, even if she did not get up in time to sweep before daybreak.

Still, no fleas or other unwelcome intruders marred what turned out to be a beautiful day. All the children, even the older ones, had enjoyed finding colored eggs and treats and after they had amused themselves with all the Easter trappings, they played cooperatively and even helped clean up the carnage. Then, supervised by Rob, they took off for the playground, which was deserted on the holiday, while Rachel and Emma prepared their dinner.

Toward the end of the day, when the tiny apartment began to feel confining, they decided to take a car tour through the streets of the city. The usually bustling shopping area was almost empty, which was fortunate, since Rob made a wrong turn and they found themselves driving in the pedestrian zone. Even with her limited knowledge, Rachel enjoyed playing the role of tour guide, describing some of the sights.

"You know, this may sound silly, but this city reminds me of an elegant lady," she observed. After reading brochures and listening to Kurt's narratives, as well as exploring a bit on her own, Rachel saw the city of Münster as a grande dame, a fine, well-bred dowager schooled in the arts, proud to display her illustrious history and culture.

"Lady Münster has led a tumultuous life, the poor dear," Rachel continued in a dramatic, storyteller's tone. "She has witnessed much violence and has had her faith tested, even converting under duress to another religion for a while, but essentially, she has remained Catholic. She even survived the devastation of World War II with a little reconstructive surgery, a bit of a facelift. Now look at her—she is dressed up in a lovely ball gown, and reigns over the entire countryside."

"That's sweet, Rachel. You always were so good at making up stories when you were a kid. The way you tell it, I *can* visualize the city as a lady . . ." Emma responded.

"Look at that church, Aunt Rachel. Do you know anything about it?" The oldest of the cousins, Janie, pointed to the tall Gothic spire that towered at one end of the curved Prinzipalmarkt.

"That's the Lambertikirche—St. Lambert's Church. A watchman lives at the top of the tower, and he rings the church bells to announce the time. And do you see those large cages up there, hanging from the steeple?" The children nodded.

"Those cages date back to a fascinating period. In the 1500s a religious group called the Anabaptists overtook Münster, and anyone who didn't convert to their religion was driven out of the city. But they were finally overcome by troops sent from the Catholic bishop and then the three leaders were executed, their corpses displayed in those life-sized cages hanging from the spire. It was supposed to be a warning to the people, to make them keep the order of society and the Church."

"Yuck, you mean the bodies just hung in those cages and rotted?" asked twelve-year-old Matt from the rear seat.

"I think so," answered Rachel.

"Gross!" exclaimed Lisbeth, Janie, and Angie, simultaneously.

"Did the warning work?" asked Rob.

"Maybe," she answered. "My professor friend tells me the city is still mostly Catholic—almost two-thirds of the population."

"Are we Catholic, Mommy?" asked Chris.

"No, honey, we're not . . ." Rachel's voice trailed off. All this religious stuff lately—surely they could be *something*. She resolved to give it more thought.

Later, after all the children were sleeping, Rachel discussed her confusion with her cousin. Emma and Rob had no problem practicing their Protestant faith. Their children had been baptized, they attended Sunday school at home in the States, and went to church often, no matter where they were.

"But do you believe in God?" Rachel asked.

"Yes, of course. Why not?" answered Emma. But for Rachel, "Why not?" was a question, not an answer, and it never would be one. She wanted to know, wanted to believe in something, to know it beyond the shadow of a doubt.

Well, she could only profess her complete belief in one thing, the joy of a loving family. And she felt that in full measure the entire weekend, surrounded by her children and the family of her cousin.

The poignant realization of how much she had missed Emma, her only remaining relative, came to her, of all places, when they visited Hülshoff Castle. The children enjoyed exploring the spacious, beautiful grounds, delighting in the ducks and geese swimming in the moat around the castle.

An English-speaking guide gave them a tour through the interior, and the adults were interested to hear about the earlier inhabitants, the von Droste-Hülshoff family: Annette, her sister Jenny, her brothers, and her parents, as well as the childhood nanny, Frau von Plettendorf, who had been like a second mother to Annette.

Hearing about the poet's childhood and her closeness to her sister—the guide mentioned that the poet had even spent her last days with Jenny, dying far away from her beloved Westphalian homeland in Meersburg Castle, which towered above Lake Constance in southern Germany—made an impression on Rachel, reminding her of her love for Emma, the cousin who was like a big sister to her.

As the day grew to a close and twilight approached, Rachel and her children, along with Emma's family, gathered to walk toward the parking lot. And she heard again the voice of the poet: "Life is so short, happiness so rare."

Chapter Four

"I don't know how you do it, Kurt!" Rachel exclaimed as she left the elementary school with the professor. "You always know how to make everything work out perfectly!"

Once again Kurt had saved the day. It was mid-April, a couple of days before the start of the university's "summer" semester, and, if it hadn't been for Kurt's intervention, Rachel never would have been able to get both children settled in their school.

Reassured by Kurt's take-charge attitude, Rachel calmed any fears she had about leaving Chris and Lisbeth at the school by themselves. He made sure that they found their classrooms and that they were properly introduced to their teachers. Then, with a wink, he promised them a special treat after they returned from class—a German custom, he explained. So with the children comfortable and excited about their upcoming surprise, Rachel left the building with a smile.

"It's no problem, you know," Kurt responded to her praise. "And I really do have a surprise in mind that I think they will enjoy. Do you know our custom for the first day of school?"

"No, I don't. Things like that aren't in our literature texts, you know."

"Let me tell you about it then," Kurt responded with a grin. "As we both know, learning is reward enough. But sometimes it is nice to make an experience sweeter with something that tastes sweet—and that is why little children receive a *Schultüte* on their first day of school. It is a cone-shaped container filled with candies and treats."

"Do you buy them, or do the parents make them?"

"We buy them nowadays. In the fall there are always many different and colorful varieties in the shops, filled with all sorts of delightful sweets, but of course we are now in the middle of the school year. I doubt that we can find any proper *Schultüten* in the stores. But I know there is one in my storage room from Elke's first day. So, if it is all right with you, we can take a ride to my home to get it."

"It's so good of you, as always. Are you sure you have the time?"

"Oh yes, Rachel. I enjoy making time for you," he paused briefly. "And your family."

Walking into Kurt's home, Rachel couldn't help but remember her mortifying experience of several weeks ago. She walked quickly through the foyer into the living room, as though afraid of a repeat performance.

"Please sit down and make yourself at home, Rachel. I will go to the storage and come right back," promised Kurt.

Once again, as on that first visit, Rachel surveyed her sur-roundings—all the lovely gold colors, brass, gilt accents, lush ivory fabrics on the upholstered pieces and draping the win-dows. Elegant and perfect, mirroring the perfection of the golden family. And even now, Frau Heinrich's presence seemed to shine on her husband and daughter.

Kurt came up the stairs from the basement carrying a huge colorful paper cone. "I found it, still as good as new!" he exclaimed.

"My goodness—it's almost as big as Chris! How will we ever fill it up?"

"That's our next adventure—let's go into the city and see what we can find."

They drove downtown and went to several department and confectionery stores, choosing hard fruit candy, lollipops, whimsically wrapped chocolates, and little marzipan figures to fill the cone. Then Kurt insisted on stopping for lunch, telling Rachel that she simply must try some of the authentic Westphalian cuisine at the famous restaurant *Pinkus Müller*.

Seated at a table covered with a blue-and-white checked cloth in front of a gold-tinted leaded glass window, Rachel was charmed by the atmosphere. Kurt suggested the sausage platter, one of the local specialties and the equally popular dark beer. It was so comfortable in the restaurant, a true example of that almost untranslatable German word, *gemütlichkeit*, she thought.

"Kurt, I don't know what to say. I'm just so . . ." She felt a lump in her throat, unable to express how happy she was that everything was starting to work out and how grateful she felt for all his help in making it possible.

He smiled tenderly at her, the corners of his eyes crinkling above the beer glass he had just sipped from. "No, Rachel, the pleasure is certainly all mine," he said as he put down his glass and rather awkwardly patted her hand where it rested on the table.

Just then the waiter came with their order, to Rachel's relief. Although Kurt's spontaneous gesture was probably only a response to her expression of emotion, she'd caught a glimmer in his eye that reminded her that he was undeniably a man. She wondered if there might be some truth to Emma's suspicions about his offer of friendship.

She tried to remain calm while she sampled her Westphalian platter with its variety of sausages and meats, but was unable to finish the order. She wasn't sure whether it was because the portion was so large or because she had become nervous about Kurt's possible expectations. But once they left the intimate atmosphere of the restaurant and walked back into the light of day, she realized she did not have to be worried. Kurt was again polite and proper in every way, with no presumption of closeness.

In the next few days, with Kurt's help she officially enrolled as foreign student at the university, and selected her courses, all of which were meant to broaden her already-completed graduate studies in the States. In addition to a class on pedagogy, she selected a Danish language class, a twentieth-century literature lecture series, and Kurt's nineteenth-century Poetic Realism seminar. She briefly wondered if it would feel strange to sit in his class with all the other students now that they had become friends.

But walking into the classroom for his seminar, she was accosted by a wave of emotion that had nothing to do with the professor. Instead, what shook her was the presence of Michael Obregón, sitting in earnest conversation with a female student, his handsome face in profile, a lock of black hair falling onto his forehead, dark lashes curling up toward his heavy brows. She tried to slide inconspicuously into a chair near the door, but her satchel dropped to the floor with a thud, and he looked up—right at her.

"*Grüss dich,* Rachel," he said with a smile. Here in the university environment he used the familiar form for *you* instead of the formal form he had used when they first met.

"*Darf ich vorstellen?*" he asked. Without waiting for a reply, he introduced Rachel to his companion, Beate Neubert.

"Oh, you are from America?" Beate said. "How interesting. I went to New York City last year. Manhattan is magnificent, is it not?" Beate had initially frowned in annoyance at the interruption, but now she became animated, raving about particular museums and galleries.

"Well, I don't really know New York very well. My home is closer to Chicago."

"Oh, I see. Known for its gangsters, isn't it?" Beate said with a laugh. A group of students then came through the door, and she waved to one of her friends, sparing Rachel the need to respond.

Rachel sat quietly in her seat, wondering what the seminar would be like and whether everyone would be as forthright as the woman she had just met. Within a few minutes Kurt entered the classroom, suggested that introductions be performed throughout the entire group.

Since this was a small seminar, he explained, he wanted to make sure the students were acquainted with one another. They would be doing some research together, and they were expected to be active participants in discussions, unlike in the larger lectures, so the success of their learning experience depended in large part on their interaction. Rachel detected the influence of Kurt's American teaching experience in his informal tone with the students, and was relieved to see that a couple of the other students returned that familiarity. He was the same with everyone after all, she thought.

Professor Heinrich asked his assistant to distribute the syllabus to the class. Avoiding Michael's intense blue eyes as he handed her a copy, Rachel quickly scanned the page. She saw that they were expected to turn in a paper and give an oral report on it in addition to the reading assignments. She also noted that they would have several sessions at the *Rüschhaus*—the House in the Rushes—where the poet Annette von Droste-Hülshoff lived—and the first meeting there was scheduled for the following week.

Kurt began discussing guidelines for the oral report.

"Please look at our syllabus and the authors we will be discussing during this seminar. Now, it isn't binding at this point, but I would like to hear if you have a special interest in a topic or author today so I can have some idea of where the research pursuits of the class lie."

"Let's start with you, Heike," he said, nodding to the young woman at his right.

Most of the students were quite specific about their favored topics. Writers' names—Storm, Raabe, Fontane, Grillparzer, Stifter—arced across the room.

These students already seemed to be so well-versed, not only about the authors and their works, but they were also acquainted with major theoretical perspectives, something that had never appealed to Rachel. Eschewing theory, she had always preferred a more subjective approach to literary analysis, based on solid biographical and historical research. And now it was her turn.

"Rachel, have you chosen the subject for your paper?" Kurt asked. Without conscious thought, she stammered that she would like to research Annette von Droste-Hülshoff, though she wasn't yet sure of the focus for the report.

She wondered if the others thought it was absurd for a foreigner to write about this famous poet, their regional and national treasure, but no one seemed to evince any outrage. Far from it. An earnest young man with shoulder-length hair said she would certainly find a lot of resources for her subject here in Münster, and Michael's friend, Beate, suggested several recent feminist studies that might help her to establish her topic.

The seminar that had seemed so intimidating at the beginning of the hour had a much different feeling by its close. Invigorated by the enthusiasm of the class and the well-meaning suggestions many had made, Rachel thought she just might really enjoy herself here. She was already looking forward to the next session, to be held on Thursday, and she could hardly wait for class on the following Tuesday, which would be held at the poet's home.

As the group began to disperse, Rachel gathered her books and satchel. As she got up from the table, she felt Kurt's gaze on her. She gave him a smile, but seeming uncomfortable, he nodded quickly and looked away.

Michael, once again engaged in animated conversation with Beate, looked over at her and smiled.

"Hallo, Rachel! We're going out for coffee. Would you like to come with us?"

"Oh . . . well," she looked down quickly at her watch. She had just enough time to join them and still get home before Chris and Lisbeth arrived home from school. "Thanks, that would be nice."

They strolled down the sidewalk three abreast, chatting idly on the way to the Kiepenkerl café in an area called the Spiekerhof. Situated in a tall gabled building, with flower boxes adorning the windows of the upper stories, the café had red-and-white striped awnings and umbrella-sheltered tables surrounding the statue of an old-fashioned country peddler that lent the establishment its name.

Spotting a group getting up from their places, Michael strode quickly ahead to claim their table. Standing behind one of the red plastic chairs, he gestured with a flourish for the women to take their seats.

"Right under the statue, Michael. Good choice," said Rachel as she seated herself at the table.

"Why so, Rachel? Do you like statues in general, or just this one?" asked Beate, amused.

"Both, actually. I find myself taking a lot of photographs

of statues when I travel. I think they say a great deal about the history and culture of an area."

"Yes, of course, this one speaks of Münster's history, but don't you find it a little . . . kitschy?" Beate asked.

Rachel looked up at the likeness of the peddler in his long smock, neckerchief, cap, breeches, and hobnailed boots. A basket with local wares was strapped to his back, and his left hand supported a long pipe, which he smoked contentedly, as though anticipating a fine day of trading in the city.

"Not at all. I find him quite delightful. And look— someone has placed a little bouquet of flowers in his hand."

"I agree with you, Rachel. I find that statuary can give us insights into the spirit and people of a locale," added Michael.

"Not I. I prefer modern sculpture, especially in that most fascinating city, New York." Beate sighed. "In the garden alone of the Museum of Modern Art, you can find—"

The waitress interrupted Beate's recitation before it began. Michael ordered coffee and *Erdbeerkuchen*—strawberry torte—Beate merely mineral water. Rachel was tempted to order ice cream, remembering her afternoon with Michael and the kids at the marketplace, but decided on a simple cup of coffee *mit Sahne*—with rich cream.

Beate lit a cigarette and inhaled slowly. "So, I gather you like our fair city. Have you had a chance to explore the rest of Münsterland?"

"Not too much yet. I don't have a car, but I'm looking for a bike. Then maybe I can get out into the country and see more."

Michael touched her lightly on the wrist. "Don't forget, Rachel, I can show you some special places here that most tourists and newcomers never find."

"Some of our haunted Westphalian castles, no doubt,"

Beate said, blowing a plume of smoke toward Michael.

Rachel ignored the cynical tone in Beate's voice. "Oh Michael, do you really believe there are haunted places here?"

"Of course. Westphalia is filled with them. Haunted castles, magical caves and enchanted lakes."

"Rachel, didn't you know that our friend Michael has had a long-standing reputation for being the most romantic student at the university?" Beate rested her cigarette in the ash tray and smiled indulgently at him.

He ignored her comment and continued.

"I have often thought that there is a special sort of magic here. A magic of place, as if there is a presence just waiting . . ."

Rachel looked at him intently, fascinated, as Michael Obregón gave voice to the lore of her childhood, when she had immersed herself in fairy tales and legends.

"Like Excalibur in the Arthurian tales, the sword in the stone waiting for the rightful owner to claim it?" she asked softly, wistfully.

"And we mustn't forget our famous Frederick Barbarossa, the medieval king who sleeps in his mountain in Thuringia, waiting to return to rescue his people . . ." said Beate with a sarcastic laugh.

"Exactly," Michael said, responding directly to Rachel's observation. "Nature holds her secrets close, waiting for those who understand the mystery."

As though Beate had vaporized into the puffs of smoke from her cigarette, Michael and Rachel were absorbed in their own conversation. Their eyes met and locked in a moment of perfect understanding.

But the waitress returned with a large silver tray holding their drinks and pastry, Beate put out her cigarette, and the spell was broken. Rachel silently sipped her coffee, observing the café's other patrons and listening to the fragments of desultory conversation between Michael and Beate. Finally, she glanced at her watch.

"Sorry, I have to go. Children, you know," she explained to Beate.

"Ah yes, Michael told me about your two. That must be difficult for you. Well, we'll see you again. *Tschüss!*" She gave a wave of her hand and as soon as Michael rose from the table, she took his fork and attacked his strawberry torte.

Michael stepped toward Rachel, extending his hand. "Thanks for joining us, Rachel. We'll have to talk more about exploring Westphalia. You'll be going to the Heinrich's on Sunday, right?"

Rachel nodded, surprised that he knew.

"All right, then, I'll see you there. Perhaps we can take care of your bicycle then." He shook her hand, gave her a warm smile, and turned back to join Beate at the table.

"Now what have you done to my cake?" Rachel heard him fondly accuse Beate with a laugh as she walked away from the Spiekerhof.

Rachel had almost forgotten that she and the kids were expected at the Heinrich's home that weekend. Although she appreciated the invitation, she wasn't looking forward to taking her Lisbeth and Chris into that pristine environment. Despite her short acquaintance with the girl, she didn't imagine that the elegant Elke would be patient with two rambunctious children. She would have to make sure that she dressed them appropriately and coached them in proper decorum.

When Sunday afternoon came, Rachel was glad she had prepared herself and her little family for the occasion. Lisbeth's wavy hair was freshly braided and tied with red ribbons, matching her floral-patterned dress. Chris wore khaki pants and a red and blue striped cotton sweater. And Rachel had abandoned her usual student uniform of jeans and sweater for a white jersey dress and navy blazer. Sheer hose and navy pumps completed the outfit, and she had twisted her wiry, coppery hair into a roll at her neck. They were ready in plenty of time for Kurt to pick them up, since the buses didn't run as frequently on Sunday.

"Meine Gute, Rachel, you look lovely!" Kurt exclaimed when she came to the door. His eyes shone as he looked her up and down admiringly, making her feel self-conscious, but pleased with her efforts. It had been a long time—years—since she had felt the slightest bit attractive. And here was this sophisticated man whose gaze reminded her that she was indeed a woman, apart from being a mother, teacher, or student.

When they arrived at the Heinrichs' home as bidden, Elke greeted her effusively, complimenting her on her appearance. Then she turned to the children, and complimented them as well. Relieved, Rachel dispensed with her worries about how her children would be received—Elke seemed to genuinely like them.

The other guests, the Schmidt family, had been delayed, and while they waited, Elke entertained Lisbeth and Chris with a box of toys she had brought up from the storage area just for them. They were engrossed in the contents: beautifully clothed cloth dolls, hand-carved puppets, realistic-looking stuffed animals with trademark buttons in their ears, and a little wooden train—and didn't look up when the doorbell rang.

Kurt led the new visitors into the living room and introduced them—Herr Schmidt, Frau Schmidt, and their two children, who were roughly the same ages as Rachel's.

Markus was seven years old and Susi was almost six. Impeccably dressed, they walked quietly and confidently into the room and shook hands with everyone. Their parents, Stephan and Caroline, were equally charming, modeling the composure their children exhibited. Stephan was an instructor at the university in the English department and had spent many summers in Britain, so everyone in the family spoke English, which, as Rachel was reminded while the children played, was not "American." The Schmidt children spoke with an accent that sounded more British than German, giving them an even greater air of precocious formality.

How different the mood of this group was from the exuberant atmosphere of the playground near the apartment house where her children played. Instead of five adults in the room, it was as though there were nine, with four of them merely smaller in stature than the others. And that serious mood prevailed even when Elke called them all to the table for the promised coffee and cake. She had made a chocolate-hazelnut cake and a mixed-fruit torte, which she served with a big bowl of rich whipped cream. Chris and Lisbeth ate quietly and neatly, speaking when spoken to, using their very best manners. Rachel was proud of them, but she wished they would act more like the children they were.

"Frau Simmons, how are you finding your experience in Germany so far? Is it all you expected?" asked Caroline.

"Please call me Rachel. We haven't been here very long, and we have all just begun our schoolwork, but my classes at the university are quite good, and the teachers and the staff at the children's school seem very kind and caring."

"Yes, the school is excellent, but one wonders how the other children behave—you know, those in the all-day school."

Rachel was confused. "Don't Markus and Susi go to the same school?"

"Yes, but they attend the traditional school in another building. The all-day school your children attend was created only recently for the children of working and single parents," Caroline explained.

"Frau Schmidt, do you mean to say that the children who attend the all-day school have behavior problems because of their family situation?" she asked, unable to hide her incredulity. Surely the woman couldn't be implying that children of working or divorced parents were inferior to those in "traditional" families like her own.

Elke had sensed Rachel's irritation and tried to smooth the conversation. "You need not worry, Rachel, your children are lovely."

"But it is true, Rachel," Caroline insisted, "that some of those children have difficulties in meeting the expectations of the classroom and can be quite disruptive. You must make sure your dear ones are not affected by negative influences," she continued.

Now Kurt jumped in to defend his American student. "Ach, Caroline, you needn't be concerned about that. I am very impressed by Rachel's capabilities as a mother. She would not let any unsuitable influences enter their lives. And you should know that I myself took the children into the school on their first day and everything seemed just fine."

Rachel flashed him a grateful smile. Once again he was there for her. The edge of anger she had felt dissipated, and she began to tell some of the stories her kids had shared with her about school that week. She described the other children living in the apartment building, many of whose parents were doing postdoctoral work at the university, and then she spoke of the children at the playground. Fresh from her experience of the previous afternoon, she talked enthusiastically about the scrappy Guido, tiny Maria, and their older friend, Ramona.

Caroline arched her eyebrows expressively. "I know the neighborhood near the playground you are speaking of, and you must watch out for those children. Their families are refugees, Gypsies, and even the little ones are not to be trusted."

Rachel remembered that Michael had mentioned his father's Spanish Gypsy heritage . . . where was he, anyway? He had said he would be at the Heinrich home today.

"Or perhaps I say *especially* the children are not to be trusted," Caroline continued. "An acquaintance of mine who lives in the area allowed her children to play with some of the Gypsies, even invited them into her home, and they stole some of their belongings."

Rachel certainly did not want to tell this woman that she had invited the three children she'd mentioned into her home after they had played with hers. The so-called Gypsy children were so cheerful and spontaneous, and had enthusiastically embraced her children, figuratively and physically. The little one, Maria, almost five years old, liked to hug Lisbeth and Chris, giggling and chattering in German and another language that Rachel didn't understand. True, they had been fascinated by her kids' toys, but when she asked them, they had helped put them away and had left when she said it was time to go home. And, although Rachel hadn't thought to look, it didn't seem as though any of them had filled their pockets with a memento of their visit.

Attempting to fill the awkward silence, Stephan broke in, asking Rachel about her scholarly interests. When she hesitantly said she would like to learn more about their famous native poet, Annette von Droste-Hühlshoff, he responded with enthusiasm.

"Ah, our Annette. We are so close to her here—too close perhaps. I think it is very valuable to have the views of others to help analyze the work of a writer. Some of the most original research on your famous American writer, Edgar Allan Poe, for example, has been contributed by German scholars. As for Annette, her work reminds me most of your poet, Emily Dickinson."

The two professors, Stephan and Kurt, then launched into a long argument filled with comparisons of American and German nineteenth-century poets.

Elke and Caroline began to clear the dishes from the table, refusing Rachel's offer of help, so she went to the sofa where the children were playing with Elke's outgrown toys. At the bottom of the box she found a couple of books, including the German version of one that had been her children's favorite, *Aschenputtel*, or *Cinderella*.

"Do you know this story, Susi?" she asked.

"Mama does not approve of *Märchen*. She says they are too morbid and violent for us," responded Susi. Rachel was shocked, but couldn't tell the child what she thought of her mother's condemnation of fairy tales.

"Well, then, I'll just read the story to my children. You can continue to play with these toys if you don't want to listen, all right?"

Rachel picked up the picture book, showing the beautiful illustrations while she told the story in English, translating the German as closely as she could. All four children sat, seemingly enraptured, as the tale unfolded. As she read, Rachel herself was struck by the depth of the original version of the tale.

The tenderhearted girl was manipulated by the cruel step-mother, scheming stepsisters, and a heartless society. She found her friends in the natural world of plants, birds, and animals, and those creatures came to her aid when she needed them. The prince who met the mysterious maiden at the ball was struck by her character and beauty and would not give up until he found her again. When he rediscovered the little ash girl, who was really a princess, he took her away to be his wife and to live happily ever after. But, contrary to the Disney and other sanitized versions of the tale, *Aschenputtel* stressed the punishment of those who had done evil. One of the sisters had her heel chopped off and the other had her eyes plucked out by the birds who had helped the little ash girl, Cinder-ella.

Rachel wasn't worried about possible ill effects on her children from hearing the tale—they knew it was pretend. She counted on their ability to distinguish real life from make-believe, and trusted that they understood the messages of fairy tales on a subconscious, if not conscious level. That was something she believed in spite of the opinions of some modern psychologists and other well-meaning authorities— like Markus and Susi's mother, who had just come back into the room.

Caroline was far too well bred to comment, but her face registered severe disapproval of the storytelling. She gathered her children, making apologies for staying only a short time. The children hadn't had their naps that afternoon, she explained, and they needed their rest before the school week started again. Stephan joined his family in the living room, helping the children put away the toys and get their jackets. Everyone said polite farewells, and within a few moments, the Schmidt family departed.

No sooner were the four gone than the doorbell rang.

"They must have forgotten something. Could you answer the door please, Elke?" asked her father.

Rachel sat on the sofa with Kurt while Lisbeth and Chris

played in a corner of the room. Elke had run to the door, and they could hear her laughter and the deeper tones of a male voice. Caroline must have sent Stephan back while she waited in the car, thought Rachel. She quickly looked around the room to see what they had left.

But it wasn't Stephan who had come to the door. It was Michael. He walked into the room, a smiling Elke at his side. *"Guten Abend, Alle,"* he greeted them. "Hello, Rachel, Christopher, Lisbeth. And Herr Doktor Heinrich, how are you doing?"

Rachel gazed at him, perplexed. From his remarks the other day at the café, she had assumed he would join the rest of them during their Sunday afternoon *Kaffeestunde.* And apparently she wasn't the only one who had made that assumption.

"Michael has been very naughty, haven't you?" said Elke, turning to him and sticking out her lower lip in an exaggerated pout. "Now, you knew you were expected here at four, and here it is almost six!"

"As for that, I'm very sorry. I was delayed at the library, helping one of the students in your father's seminar with her research."

Elke whirled away from him and flounced dramatically onto the sofa, inserting herself between Kurt and Rachel. "I don't even know why you bothered to come, then, if you have to be so late," she remonstrated, arms crossed.

"Well, I was hoping we could talk about that bicycle of yours. You're not using it anymore, and I thought perhaps Rachel could . . ."

"My bicycle? For Rachel?" Elke was quite obviously miffed at Michael's inattention to her.

"We have a seminar meeting at the Rüschhaus and I wanted to make sure that Rachel had a way to get there," he explained.

He looked at Rachel, addressing his comments to her. "Elke's bicycle has a very good light, so it will be safe even on the return trip. But I would be very happy to come to your apartment and ride along with you."

"On the other hand, Rachel, if you don't mind going a little early, I could fetch you with my car," volunteered Kurt.

"Wait, wait. Thank you all, but I have already taken care of it." Rachel was overwhelmed with the sudden rush of male solicitude, uncertain whether to be grateful or worried that they thought her so helpless.

"On Thursday I saw a notice on the bulletin board at the university of a bicycle for sale for only 75 marks. I called the woman who was selling it, and that evening I brought it home. It's not much, but it works—with a basket in front *and* a light!"

"Now, Rachel, why would you do that?" Kurt asked. "You need not spend extra money, when it is something your friends could provide. And I'm sure Elke's bicycle is more dependable than the one you purchased." Kurt meant to be kind, but his tone sounded like a rebuke.

Michael, however, offered encouragement. "That's splendid, Rachel. I think you will be very happy with your freedom, the speed, and the fresh air. And we must take some outings into the countryside on the bicycle paths that I mentioned earlier."

"Oh, yes, Rachel, now Michael and I can take you to some of our favorite destinations!" added Elke with forced enthusiasm.

"Elke, how thoughtful of you, *Liebchen*," Kurt said proudly. "I'm sure Rachel would appreciate that." He turned to Rachel. "You know, my daughter is always thinking about how to bring happiness to other people, like her mother before her. Baking, entertaining, little gifts and surprises . . ."

He turned to his daughter again with a tender smile.

Yeah, I'll bet she likes to make others happy—especially her father and her boyfriend, thought Rachel. She had to admit Elke had been a perfect hostess—it wasn't really her fault that Rachel had not had a good time. But of course Rachel couldn't openly express those thoughts, so she resorted to safe platitudes.

"Elke, you certainly are thoughtful. We very much appreciate your hospitality. But as you know, tomorrow is another school day, so I'm afraid we'll have to be leaving soon."

"Yes, my dear, I can take you any time you wish," said Kurt.

"Rachel, about riding to the *Rüschhaus*. Should I pick you up on Tuesday at about six then?" asked Michael.

Before Rachel could answer, Elke interjected, "Michael, Rachel is not a child. She said she has taken care of her transportation. I'm sure she can find her way there."

By this time Rachel had frankly more than enough of all of them—of their entangling affections and of their assumptions or expectations of her. She had to agree with Elke on this one. There was no way she wanted either of them to accompany her on a simple bike ride. She had a map and she'd be fine, she assured them.

She said the proper good-byes, using her most charming if superficial manner, which seemed to satisfy Elke. Michael, however, looked at her in a strange way. As usual, his presence disconcerted her and she avoided his deep blue eyes, eager to be away from them all. She was relieved when Kurt delivered her and the children to their apartment.

Home once again in her refuge, Rachel felt secure, content, and safe. "Snug as a bug in a rug," her mother had sometimes said when she tucked her in at night as a little girl. But here she felt rather more like a snail than an insect. In this great Westphalian garden she was like a tiny creature finding her own path, eager antennae extending toward the unknown, marking her trail with a glistening testament of her explorations. And when it all became overwhelming in the garden, she could simply retreat into her sanctuary, her shell, her little snail home.

But why did she feel a sense of unease, as though in the shadow of a giant foot that could at any time crush her progress?

Chapter Five

"Blick in mein Auge—ist es nicht das deine? Du lächelst, und dein Lächeln ist das meine . . ." "Look into my eye—is it not yours? You smile, and your smile is mine, rich of the same passion and thought."

Rachel's eyes misted as she read the poet's emotion-laden verses, the lines describing oneness, the magnetic attraction between two people, despite barriers. And the closing lines of the poem by Frau von Droste-Hülshoff told of a *Zwillings-flamme*—a glowing twin flame.

How awful, how painful to love someone so much when there was little hope of having that love returned or recognized by society. The poet's beloved, a writer named Levin, was much younger than she—by almost eighteen years. And Annette was in such poor health, not ever expected to marry, certainly never to have children. She was fortunate at least to have been raised in an enlightened family, which allowed her to develop her writing talent, thus providing an outlet for the passions that had accompanied her throughout her life.

Perhaps the poet accepted her fate willingly—Rachel wasn't sure. But the woman's words addressed to Levin haunted her nonetheless: *Life is so short, happiness so rare.*

On this sunny afternoon at the end of April, Rachel sat on a bank of a water canal, amid the wild grass and rushes that had lent the neighboring house its name: *Rüschhaus,* Frau Droste's House in the Rushes. Taking advantage of a free afternoon, she had biked to this place where she could sit in relative silence, surrounded by the natural environment that had inspired the poet's works.

Rachel had taken her maiden voyage on the bike the Tuesday evening her seminar group had their scheduled meeting here, and since then she had returned several times to the House in the Rushes. She felt drawn to the poet and to the home in which she had lived for over twenty years, this country estate that had sheltered her and nourished her imagination.

Remembering that Tuesday evening, Rachel could feel again the sense of anticipation that accompanied her as she navigated her way to the House in the Rushes. That anxious, butterflies-in-the-stomach feeling that occurs upon meeting a loved one at the airport after a separation, or on answering the door in expectation of a long-awaited guest. Joining her class in the salon, Rachel's butterflies had been replaced by other feelings—curiosity, wonder, and a gentle excitement.

The house seemed imbued with the presence of the poet, even now, a century and a half after her death. It was as though the surroundings were a repository for the creativity and character of the woman whose spirit emanated from every corner of every room, as well as from all the elements of the natural landscape.

Through a special arrangement Kurt made with the foundation responsible for maintaining the house and grounds as a museum, the students were to be given a tour before their class session. Rachel joined the group just in time, finding herself at the end of the line, next to Michael. He smiled and nodded at her as the tour guide began her speech. Many of the others had probably already visited the house, but everyone listened in respectful silence as the guide led them through the rooms, explaining their use in the 1800s when the poet and her family had lived there.

It was new to Rachel, though, and she was fascinated by all of it, especially by the poet's personal quarters. The three small rooms were laid out in a row, one after another, connected by narrow doorways. The sitting room led to her bedchamber, which in turn led to a third room, where Annette's beloved nursemaid, Frau von Plettendorf slept. This last room now displayed the extensive collection of natural and arcane memorabilia the poet had accumulated.

"Just look at all that—isn't it fantastic?" whispered Michael, gesturing to the glass cases holding shells, fossils, tiny pieces of coral, geodes, and gemstones.

Rachel gazed at the collection in wonder, but was startled from her examination by the guide's mention of Annette's reference to her private quarters as a *Schneckenhäuschen*—a little snail house.

"That's what I call my own place!" she exclaimed in a whisper to Michael. She experienced the coincidence with a shock of recognition underscoring her spiritual affinity to the poet.

When the formal tour ended, Michael left her side to join Kurt and Rachel stepped into the large salon where the class was to take place. Who are you, Rachel silently asked as she approached the portrait that hung above the ornate fireplace mantel. The woman posed in contemplation, hands folded, as though dreaming of something far away. Dressed in a plain dark dress, accented with white cuffs and collar and a brooch at the neck, she appeared unconcerned with such mundane matters as fashion or physical adornment. Her slender neck and pale face rose from the shadow of her dress and dark backdrop like a water lily from a deep pond. Her hair was bound in two plaited honey-colored loops that framed her face, and a third braided circlet created a crown atop her head. Her deeply set blue eyes eternally sought something to the left of the frame's border, and her enigmatic Mona Lisa smile hinted at undiscovered mysteries.

Inspired by the atmosphere of that class meeting, Rachel renewed her research on the poet's life and work in earnest, drawing closer and closer to this woman from a previous century. She had even taken to referring to her as Nette, the affectionate nickname given the girl during her childhood. Annette had lived with her family in the larger moated Hülshoff Castle until the age of twenty-two, when her father died. Then she and her sister moved with their mother to the House in the Rushes, leaving the care of the castle to her brother and his wife.

Poor Nette, Rachel had thought upon hearing about the exodus of the female members of the family when she and her cousin Emma had toured Hülshoff Castle. But now, after visiting the smaller home, she could see how the environment was perfect to nurture the writer's creative gifts.

And the poems she wrote here! Rachel was moved by Nette's detailed descriptions of nature, her vibrant images from long ago, and the universal feelings of joy and sorrow, appreciation, longing, and love. Especially love. Encumbered by ill health, at the mercy of the inclement weather that often restricted her contact with others, Annette spent much of her time in isolation, especially after her sister married and moved to Meersburg. She treasured visits from friends, paticularly those of her young male soul mate, Levin Schücking.

Also a writer, Schücking inspired and encouraged her to the fullest flowering of her poetic talent. Critics and scholars, including Professor Doktor Kurt Heinrich, referred to the friendship between the two as a fruitful literary partnership, but Rachel heard the voice of a woman who spoke of love—heartfelt, real, and apparently unrequited.

She had been sitting by the water trench alongside the courtyard entrance to the house, and now she made her way to the other side, where the carefully landscaped gardens awaited her with their burgeoning growth.

A crowd of tourists had just descended the stairs, chattering in what sounded like Dutch, and she heard footsteps following her along the gravel path toward the main garden. As she reached the entrance, she was happy to see the endearing sculpture of a little cherub, one of four that graced the garden. This one represented the element Water. Reeds in his hair, supporting himself on an urn, he perpetually poured a stream of water from a shell in his hand, a fish cavorting at his feet. Opposite him, at the intersection of two garden paths, stood another cherub, signifying Earth. With a blade of grass in his hair, he leaned against a spade, a basket of fruit and a rabbit at his feet. Their brothers, Fire and Air, stood at the end of the garden, alongside the canal.

"Which one is your favorite?" Rachel heard a deep male voice ask her. She turned around.

"Michael! What are you doing here?" she exclaimed in surprise.

"I would think I am here for much the same reason as you. Why are you here?" He didn't wait for an answer. "Beautiful day, isn't it? It's good to have some sun after last week—rained every day, didn't it?"

"But you know the saying about Münster: it either rains or the bells are ringing," Rachel replied.

Michael laughed at her recitation of the popular slogan, so descriptive of the area's characteristically damp climate and the preponderance of churches, their bells chiming the hours throughout the day.

"My family came here often," he said, "as well as to the other water castles. On Sundays we would travel by bicycle or by car, visiting a different castle each week. My little brother, Paul, always wanted to visit his favorite statue, and insisted we choose our favorites as well. So we did, and we came to see them frequently."

"Which one was his favorite?" asked Rachel. She could guess the answer, based on her own little boy's choice during their visit the previous week. As she expected, Michael said his brother's special friend was Fire, the cherub dressed in a sturdy helmet, his arsenal of weapons strapped onto his back, a torch in one hand and a salamander in the other.

"Chris likes him too. I guess it reminds him of some of the action figures he plays with. It's kind of funny to see this chubby little guy dressed up in all the trappings of battle—but maybe no more disconcerting than seeing boys pretend to be grown-up soldiers or superheroes. Lisbeth chose Earth, because she liked the rabbit. How about you and your sister?"

"Our sister, Anna, was living in Spain at the time, so she wasn't part of the game, though she had, of course, visited the garden before. My father, however, chose Earth and my mother chose Water. I was always drawn to the one representing Air. It's as though the falcon on his arm and the heron at his feet could rise up at any moment and fly away, just soar off into the blue. And I've always liked the spiritual qualities of air as well."

"Its spiritual qualities?" Rachel echoed, intrigued by Michael's point of view. His orientation to the world, as well as the way he expressed himself, was so different from that of most people she knew.

"Air. The realm of ideas, wisdom, intuition. Did you ever think of all that is transported by air? Sounds, words, visions. Water, sunlight, and where they meet, a rainbow. And the air we breathe—if you think about the English words *inhale* and *exhale*, they don't quite convey the magic, but in German, *ein-atmen* and *aus-atmen,* express the connection to *atma,* the soul. But you do have other words in English that express the spiritual dimensions of air: *expire* and *inspire.* When we die, our spirit departs, but while we are living, spirit can visit us through our imagination or through reason, as inspiration, from the air."

"You have such an unusual way of expressing yourself, Michael. It makes sense, in a poetic kind of way, but I never would have thought about air in that way. Maybe this is a silly question, but where does your inspiration come from?"

Michael smiled, his blue eyes twinkling. "From the air, of course! It's difficult to explain why any of us believe anything —it simply seems like part of us. But I think many of my ideas about life come from my parents. My father's culture shaped his beliefs, and he has had a strong influence on me. There's something dark, rich, and romantic about the atmosphere of Spain. And my mother grew up in an isolated area of West-phalia, in the land of moors and marshes, far from so-called civilization. She became wise in the ways of nature and has taught all of us about growing things and the beliefs of those who work close to the land."

"You said your mother's favorite cherub was Water, and that's my favorite too. I like the little guy with the reeds in his hair—that kind of disarray is so typical of kids, getting into everything. And I used to love vacationing on Lake Michigan —just being near water is so comforting. Like this cherub, I played endlessly with shells on the beach. But I suppose his shell, as well as the fish and reeds all have a symbolic meaning?"

"Meaning is always subjective, Rachel. And sometimes we can't explain why we like something. It's just so. Surely you've noticed that."

"Of course. I'm often drawn to people, places, or things

for reasons I can't quite articulate. Like the Rüschhaus. I could list the things I like about it—the statues, the garden, the canal, the coziness of the house. But mostly I like it because of its . . . spirit," she admitted, "Annette's spirit. I like her. That sounds silly when I say it aloud, but . . ." Rachel was embarrassed to confess that she felt a kinship with a person who was no longer living.

"Ja, Rachel. *Seelenverwandschaft*—soul connection. It's a rare and beautiful thing, isn't it? When we feel a strong bond to another, we need to simply honor it, not explain it. It makes no difference if that person is a man or a woman, what age he or she is, or even if the person lives in the same time or place. 'Nettchen' is fortunate to have you as a friend."

Rachel couldn't believe Michael's ready acceptance of her empathy with the poet, as though she were a contemporary. And to suggest that she was lucky to have Rachel as a friend? It did seem as though Annette was speaking to her through those words written long ago, and Rachel felt that there was some kind of lesson to be learned from the connection. But if so, Rachel was the fortunate one, certainly not Annette von Droste-Hülshoff.

They began walking down a nearby path.

"That poor woman," she said. "I don't care how famous she was, she wasn't happy. Her family was good to her, and she had friends, but she couldn't have what she really wanted in life."

"And what was that, Rachel? I take it you're not among those who believe that she fulfilled herself through her writing?"

"Well, she did express much of herself through her poetry, and I think she felt a sense of satisfaction when her words were accepted by others. But it wasn't that she had a single-minded desire to publish. She had the desire and need to *create,* to give birth to her ideas, to share her view of the world, and to express in verse the beauty and pain of love."

"So although her works were published, and she was successful in her lifetime, which certainly isn't true for all artists, you still think she was unhappy?" Michael asked.

"Michael, you sound just like the rest of those scholars— those men, and even some feminist critics—with their theories about her place in the literary canon. Don't you read her words? I don't care what theory or history has to say about her situation. She is—I mean was—a person, a woman, with real and powerful emotions that she expressed honestly and openly."

Rachel held up the volume of poetry she had been carrying, as if the sight of it could help Michael become acquainted with the spirit of the woman she believed she had come to know. "I've been reading these words, her words, and they make me so sad."

"And why is that?" Michael asked in a gentle, compassionate way.

"Because of love, Michael. You know, that silly emotion that 'makes the world go 'round.' " Rachel tried to lighten the mood. "Everybody knows about her relationship with Levin Schücking, but it seems so misunderstood. It wasn't merely a friendship or a supportive literary association—it was love, at least on her part."

"Do you think he was in love with her as well?"

"I don't know. Maybe. I haven't read too much of his work yet. I do know some things about his life, though. He was introduced to Annette through his mother, an acquaintance of hers. I know he visited her often and that they corresponded. They discussed his writing and hers, as well as other topics and events in their lives. And they spent time together in Meersburg when she stayed with her sister and he was working as a librarian for her brother-in-law. And he finally married someone else. But all this is common knowledge, isn't it? Why bother asking me?"

"I'm asking you what you *think*, Rachel, not what you know from lectures or books. Of course I'm familiar with those facts, and I have read some of Levin's correspondence, and literary efforts. But I'm curious to know what you think for another reason as well—because Levin Schücking was a distant relative of mine."

"You're related to him? How?"

"Through my mother. Her name is Katharina, the same as Levin's mother, though she does not resemble that side of the family. Nor do I, as I take after my father primarily. But one hears stories, those that are not written in history books. I have my own ideas about the character of that young man who was involved with our Westphalian poet."

Rachel looked at him more closely, trying to detect any resemblance between him and the picture she had seen of Schücking in one of her research books. But had to agree with Michael's assessment—they looked nothing alike. The portrait of the writer depicted a young man probably about Michael's age, with a delicate, heart-shaped face, insignificant eyes, a little mustache, and nondescript wavy hair. Dressed with typical nineteenth-century formality, he seemed stiff, like a child playing dress-up. Michael's face was more squared, with strong cheekbones and compelling eyes and long lashes framed by his dark curls. Even without facial hair, his appearance was overwhelmingly masculine and gave the impression of strength. Not even his casual dress of jeans and pale blue sweater could diminish that air of self-confidence. No, there was no comparison.

During their walk through the garden, the two had come

to a small wooded area. Just ahead, between two trees, was a wooden bench.

"Look, Rachel. That bench is like the one where Annette would sit, waiting for visitors to arrive. She had a little looking glass—a type of binoculars, I think you would say today —through which she would watch to see if anyone was approaching."

"So what do you think, then? Did Levin care about her, or did he just use her to help nurture him and advance his own literary reputation? Did he know how much she depended on him, how much she wanted to be with him? Of course, a marriage between them wouldn't have worked, but it would be nice to know that he also felt something for her, that they were, in fact, the soul mates she thought they were."

"It's hard to know what he felt. I think he did have feelings of love for Annette, but he was undependable. And so she waited for him here, often in vain, day after day."

"But why, Michael, if he cared for her too? Why couldn't he show her?"

Michael shook his head, looking at the ground.

"And if they did love each other, what happened to that love? Did it just simply vanish when he married another? Tell me, where does love go when it departs?"

Michael raised his eyes and looked at her sadly. Once again, he shook his head.

"It's all so tragic," Rachel said softly. "Before you arrived, I was about to take a walk through the gardens to cheer myself up a little. I had just read the 'Levin' poems and then I read 'Carpe diem' and started thinking about seizing the moment. I thought about my own life and my family, and I realized how happy I was here, and I felt guilty that I don't always appreciate it, and then I realized that this too shall pass." Rachel stopped, breathless.

Michael nodded as though he understood, but remained silent for a few more minutes as they walked. Then he looked at her, his eyes twinkling again. "All right, let's talk of something else, something cheerful. Do you know what day it is today?"

"Yes, it's Friday, the end of the school week, the day I usually take the children out to eat. But today the school had an all-day outing, so I'm here instead. Or did you mean something else? Surely it's not another holiday already?"

"Well, perhaps not a real holiday, but it is an important time of the year. Tomorrow is the first of May, a very special day indeed. And tonight, May Eve, is also special—it's called *Walpurgisnacht*. Do you know of it?"

"Doesn't it have something to do with witches? I think it was in *Faust*, right?"

"Yes, you're right about that. It's kind of funny that Goethe, who was so interested in the feminine spirit—*das ewig Weibliche*—would describe witches in such a negative light. Our pre-Christian forbears embraced many pagan practices later often explained as witchcraft."

"I thought you were Catholic. You mean you wouldn't call witchcraft anti-Christian?" Rachel was confused, again confronted with the apparent dichotomy in Michael's beliefs.

"Well, just because something pre-dates Christianity, doesn't mean it's evil. And I don't think that women who engage in so-called magical practices are necessarily witches, and even if they are, then they aren't necessarily wicked women who worship the devil."

Michael described a few of the practices attributed to witches. Some seemed quite harmless, such as those involved in healing, others simply superstitious, and illogical to the modern mind. For instance, on the magical night before the official beginning of spring was when they would gather, at the top of the mountain, the Blocksberg, described in Goethe's *Faust*. There they would dance and carouse all night.

"And did these witches ride broomsticks to the mountaintop?" Rachel asked.

"That is what is claimed. Remember the brooms I told you about at Eastertime? Instead of the broom being used as a way to clean and bring order to the home, it is used in the lore of witchcraft as a means of escape for the woman from the bondage of her hearth."

What Michael said made sense. Because of her interest in fairy tales, Rachel could see a connection between stories like "Cinderella" and the actual situation of women in history.

"So the broom became a symbol of flight from earthly responsibilities to another realm. And of course it must have been threatening to men and their society if women's dreams and abilities took them beyond normal, everyday expectations."

"Yes, I think so. And that's where religion steps in to help. Our saints are meant to protect us against evil or frightening spirits and prevent bad fortune. The night before May Day takes its name from St. Walpurgis, who is said to protect the home, with all its human and animal inhabitants. As a further protective measure, people place twigs bound in the form of a cross in front of animals' stalls, or more commonly, use chalk to make the sign of the cross on doorways to guard against evil.

"And you mentioned that saying earlier about ringing church bells—did you know you can actually hear more bells on May Eve than at any other time of year? It is rumored that mysterious bell-ringing can be heard from underground sources, and farmers used to ring bells the whole of May Day to ensure the successful planting of their crops. So you see how pagan and Christian practices have intermingled.

Indeed, church bells ring to counteract evil and to honor the Virgin Mary, the most powerful female of all."

"So the Mother of God can overcome the frightening powers of the witch, right?"

Michael smiled. "You could say that. Society has always found it difficult to avoid dualistic thinking, especially in regard to women. Even Annette has been called both the 'Little Nun' as well as the 'Little Witch' because of the difficulty people have synthesizing the religious with the pagan, or nature-worshipping, elements in her works."

They had eased themselves onto the bench as Michael started to talk about May Day customs. Now they sat quietly for a moment, Rachel pondering the difficulties Nette must have faced simply by being a woman. How lucky she was to be free enough to pursue her long-held dream of coming to this country to study and learn through experience, even as the mother of two young children. She could read what she wanted, say or write anything—within reason, of course— and marry anyone she chose. True, her marriage hadn't worked out, but that wasn't the fault of her society. She could love anyone she wanted, but that wasn't going to happen.

"Why are you so pensive all of a sudden? What are you thinking about?"

Michael's deep voice interrupted her musing, and, surprised at herself, she admitted where her thoughts had taken her. "I was thinking about love, actually."

"In general, or in particular?" he asked.

When she hesitated, Michael didn't press for an answer. He seemed to know that she couldn't respond. So he brought up another piece of folklore, saying lightly that if anyone really wanted to know about love, May Day provided the perfect opportunity, because that's when the oracle of love spoke. Peasant boys and girls would bury a mirror, face down in the ground, at midnight and dig it up the next night at the same time. The vision in the mirror would then reveal the identity of the seeker's intended.

Once again Rachel marveled at Michael's knowledge of folklore. She wondered if he had ever tried the mirror trick himself, and what the mirror had shown him. Maybe a vision of Elke Heinrich? Or maybe a different girl every year? She had seen him around the university, talking to so many different women. Of course they would be drawn to him—he was so good-looking, interesting, and charming.

As they sat in silence, she heard a gentle humming. A bird twittered musically in the branches above them, and suddenly Michael began to sing. In a beautiful baritone voice, he sang a folk tune celebrating the coming of May. Surprisingly enough, it was a melody that Rachel had learned in the madrigal group during her undergraduate years, so hesitantly, softly, she joined in for the refrain about the greening of May, *"Der Mai, und der war grüne."*

Michael's eyes widened with pleasure. "How about this one?" He began another song of spring, a second one she remembered, though not very well, so he carried her over the weak spots. As their voices merged and drifted into the balmy spring air, Rachel felt a surge of joy. And as the song ended, Michael looked at her with a broad smile, clearly expecting one in return.

He saw instead her lower lip trembling and a puddle in her eye.

He murmured something in Spanish. Rachel didn't understand the words—just the tenderness they conveyed. And this made her more confused. He always confused her, this Michael Obregón. From the first he had unsettled her, though her children took to him right away. And here, now, she was becoming aware of an undeniable kind of connection between them, a subtle attraction. She stared at him, and it was as though she were being drawn into the depths of the sea. She could not resist the attraction pulling them together, and with one hand touching her hair and the other lightly resting on her back, Michael drew her closer.

When their lips touched, it was like nothing Rachel had ever experienced. Indescribable sensations suffused her entire body, as if she were drowning in her own emotions. She was lost—or maybe she was found. She felt transported to somewhere far, far away, yet she was more at home than she had ever been.

Elated but terrified, she pulled away from him, denying the incredible desire pulling her into the depths of the promise in his eyes.

"Michael, Michael, it's getting late. I have to go. The children will be home soon—I just have to go!" She avoided looking at him as she rose from the bench and backed away.

She knew he must think her ridiculous. He probably kissed all the girls—but she wasn't a girl. She was a grown woman, not a college kid. She was older, she had children, and was an American, a foreigner. This just wasn't right.

Not giving Michael time to respond, she turned and ran out of the garden to the front of the house where she'd left her bike. She thought she heard him call her name, but she stuck her book into the basket, jumped on the bicycle, and sped home.

She had been home for no longer than fifteen minutes when she heard the children's footsteps and rustling at the door. She enfolded both of them in a big hug.

"Chris, Lisbeth, my sweeties! How was your day? Mommy missed you!"

"It was okay, but I'm tired," answered her son.

"Mommy, Chris was a baby. He sucked his thumb on the bus and some of the kids teased him."

"And what happened?" asked their mother, concerned if her kids, as foreigners, were having difficulty being accepted.

"I just told the mean one, *'Halt's Maul und geh doch weg!'* " exclaimed Lisbeth. "And you know what? He did shut up and go away and left us alone for the rest of the ride."

Rachel was surprised by her daughter's vocabulary—she certainly hadn't taught her how to tell someone to shut up in German. But that spontaneous utterance revealed two positive things: that Lisbeth's language learning was proceeding nicely, and that she could cope with challenges in difficult situations. This daughter of hers wasn't going to be a docile little weakling, but would develop into a woman of strength and courage.

And that was something Rachel vowed to nurture—in both of her children. Because even though their mother was achieving many of her goals, so "bravely" as many people said, pursuing graduate studies, living abroad, Rachel often felt insecure and confused, worried about what people would think. And clearly she was weak. Otherwise, why would she have married the first man she ever dated, not because she loved him but because she felt alone? Lisbeth would be smarter. She would stand up to bullies, not be led into compromising situations, and not be afraid to stand on her own.

"Thank you for defending your brother," Rachel said as she helped them take off their jackets and hang them on the coat rack behind the door. "Are you guys hungry?"

"Yeah, what do we have to eat?"

As usual, maintaining a selection wasn't easy, given that Rachel's bicycle basket and handlebars could carry only two bags of groceries at a time. But there was fresh meat and cheese, that wonderful German rye bread, and the sweetened yogurt they liked. Rachel quickly placed an assortment on the tiny kitchen table and the children sat down and began to eat. Restless, she stood, her back against the window, as they told her more about their school field trip that day.

"Mommy, we saw another water castle—you know, like the one we saw with Aunt Emma? It was way bigger than that place where the cherubs are, too," said Chris. "It was really cool, because there it had a suit of armor in the hallway and some real weapons on the wall. But the teacher wouldn't let us touch them."

"And we went to this little town where there was a real tall pole right in the middle of the market square," Lisbeth added. "It had a little tree, like a Christmas tree, on top, and lots of long ribbons hanging around it. My teacher called it a *Maibaum* and said that people danced around it."

Rachel remembered circling around a maypole with her elementary school classmates during a spring festival, each taking the end of a ribbon, walking, dancing, bobbing up and down, weaving the bands around the pole until it was covered in plaited bands of color, but she didn't think the custom was common in the States anymore. This, too, then, was an Old World German custom, imported into America.

"You know what? Tomorrow is May Day—that's why you saw the maypole in the village. It's like the first day of spring here, and if it's nice out, we'll go somewhere to celebrate springtime, okay? How about that big garden in the city—the one with the restaurant. Maybe we can get some *Eis* afterward."

The kids agreed happily, but they seemed to be talked out after their outing. So, as they finished their supper and as she began to clean up, Rachel told them some of the country's May Day customs that she had learned from Michael.

The children were especially interested in the witches.

From what they knew, witches—those scary old black-garbed women—belonged to Halloween, and certainly had no place in the spring. Interestingly enough, though, they had both noticed the many chalk marks on houses and barns as they rode on the bus.

Hearing the voices of the other children from the building playing on the lawn below, they both said they wanted to go outside for a while, so they took the soccer ball and joined them, leaving Rachel alone in the living room.

Rachel decided to read for a while to unwind with a book and a glass of wine. Earlier that week she had bought a bottle of May Wine, which had a hint of special woodsy flavoring. By the time the children came in from downstairs, it was getting close to bedtime, so they went to get ready for bed.

She was surprised when they emerged from the bedroom, giggling. They ran into the kitchen and got a chair and dragged it to the front door. "What are you doing?" she asked from the sofa. With much scuffling and laughter, they closed the door briefly, and dragged the chair back into the kitchen, then rushed over to her on the sofa.

"Look, Mom. We made the chalk marks and now we'll be safe from the witches." Chris held out his hand to show her a piece of chalk.

Lisbeth opened her hand to reveal the pocket mirror she had taken from the small purse she carried for dress-up. "And here's a present for you, Mom. You can take it outside when it gets dark and bury it in the ground, just like you told us, and then we'll go dig it up tomorrow and find out who you're going to marry!"

"Oh, honey, Mommy isn't going to get married," Rachel said. "I'm happy that your Daddy and I were married and we had you, but it's not going to happen again."

"Why? Daddy's getting married again. He told us so in

that letter we got this week. He's going to get married to Stacey while we're here," Lisbeth pointed out.

"Yeah. And he's going to send us pictures. They're gonna buy a big house with lots of rooms, and we can each have our own when we go to visit!" added Chris.

That happily-ever-after thing again, Rachel mused. You'd think Brent would have learned his lesson after trying once. But maybe his bride-to-be was as starry-eyed as she had once been. Rachel knew she should at least pretend to be happy for her ex, for the sake of their children, but her powers of make-believe weren't that strong. So she just took another sip of wine and let the children chatter on, murmuring appropriate responses, while they played a card game at her feet. Lost in thought, she barely noticed when they put the game away and went back into the bedroom. She roused herself briefly to tuck them in, and resumed her place on the sofa.

As it became dark outside, her thoughts took her all over— into her own past, with Brent, and then much farther into the past, into the nineteenth-century world of two would-be lovers, Annette and her Levin.

She fell asleep still sitting on the sofa, and woke at midnight, hearing the church bells strike twelve. Bemused, she looked around the room, wondering what she was doing there, then remembered the May wine.

Her head spinning, she made her way to the bathroom where she washed up and got ready for bed. Forget the bath until tomorrow morning, she said to herself. She didn't think she could make it into and out of that tub tonight. So she grabbed a towel and turned the faucet on, filling the basin with hot water. She looked into the mirror through rising steam. What a mess she was—wild, disheveled locks, rumpled shirt, and unfocused eyes. She looked like a witch—and maybe that's what she was.

Who are you, she asked her blurry image, and as she peered into the mirror, she saw her face change. As if by the hand of some invisible hairdresser, her locks became tamed, braided into loops at her ears and a coronet at the top of her head. Her flushed features disappeared into an ivory countenance, her nose becoming less snubbed and more aquiline, and even her eyes seemed to change color from their usual topaz to blue. Her bosom was now decently covered by a tight-fitting dark garment with white collar, giving her the appearance of an old-fashioned schoolteacher—or a nun. She laughed then, saying into the mirror, "Oh, Nettchen, it's you!"

Then, remembering the fairy tale of "Snow White" she had heard since childhood, she asked the question: "Mirror, mirror, on the wall, who's the fairest of them all?"

And as she watched, she was astonished to see the feminine images merge into one, then disappear, only to be replaced by another face. It was hazy at first, but then she saw dark hair, a mustache. A man? How strange. His hair was slightly wavy atop a heart-shaped face, and his pale blue eyes seemed to stare right at her. Levin?

"What do you want?" she whispered. The face was unresponsive, and then it changed again. The waves became curls, the hair chestnut, a face broad, with ruddy cheeks. Brent? What was he doing here? His eyes looked at her sternly, but then his face changed as well. The eyes became brown, the hair blondish; the face was thinner, its lower half covered with a salt-and-pepper beard. Kurt's kindly eyes gazed at her for a moment, then he, too, disappeared.

And then another face appeared in the glass—black hair falling onto his forehead and curling at his ears, the hint of a five o'clock shadow covering cheeks and chin, but not quite concealing an adorable dimple; dark, bushy brows with full lashes above those deep blue eyes. Michael. He stared at her, into her, and she quickly shut her own eyes.

When she opened them again, she saw only a steamy mirror, much to her relief. She laughed at herself. She wasn't possessed, she thought, only—what was the word anyway—a bit tipsy. She finished her ablutions as best she could, with everything whirling around her, then threw on her nightgown and rounded the corner to the bedroom, dropping onto the comforter to welcome May Day in her sleep.

Chapter Six

The jangling of the telephone penetrated Rachel's consciousness, dragging her from a deep sleep. She stumbled into the living room and grabbed the phone.

"Hallo, Simmons," she said, trying to modulate her voice so that she wouldn't sound as terrible as she felt.

"Rachel, are you all right? This is Kurt," said the voice at the other end. Rachel surmised that her attempt at normalcy hadn't worked. The truth was, her head was pounding, she still felt dizzy, and she really wanted to go back to bed. She muttered something about being tired.

"I am sorry to disturb you so early on a Saturday morning, but I have an idea of possible interest to you. As you know, I am teaching a seminar on turn-of-the-century literature, and I scheduled an excursion to Bremen for some of the foreign students in the class today. One of our students had to cancel because of illness, and I thought you might like to come with us instead. Or perhaps you are not feeling well enough?" he inquired politely.

Rachel certainly did not want to tell him she had a hangover. She didn't even like to admit it to herself. Mind over matter, she told herself. I just won't give in to it.

"No, I'm fine, really, just a little tired. It is very nice of you to think of me for this outing, but I can't leave the children alone," she said, hearing them stir in the bedroom.

"That's no problem, Rachel. My daughter is so fond of your children, she has offered to care for them today. It looks as though it will be a beautiful day and she has offered to take them to the zoo. Really, she would very much like to spend time with them."

"I don't know. It would be wonderful to see more of Germany with you and your group . . ." she said, her headache making it difficult to be more decisive.

"Mommy, who's on the phone? Is it Daddy?" asked Lisbeth, who had come into the living room with her brother. She knew it was a Saturday, and their father usually called on the weekend.

"Kurt, could you hold on for a minute, please?" asked Rachel, turning toward her daughter. "No, it's not your father. He'll probably call tomorrow. It's Professor Heinrich. He has a suggestion for today, but I want to know what you two think. I told you yesterday that we might go to the park today and get ice cream to celebrate springtime, but Elke Heinrich would like to take you to the zoo and the professor has invited me to go on an outing with him and some other students."

"You mean you wouldn't go to the zoo with us?" Chris asked.

"No, honey, but maybe you can tell me all about it later," she answered in a placating tone, expecting complaints.

"Okay," he said, and his sister echoed her agreement.

"That would be cool, Mom. You can go on your field trip just like we did with our school. Maybe you'll even get to take a bus like ours," Lisbeth said.

Surprised at their ready agreement, Rachel turned back to the phone. "Kurt, the children think that would be a great idea. Lisbeth was wondering if we'll take a bus, as her class did on their excursion. No, just your car? Well, it must be a small group of students."

Kurt explained that there would be five of them in all—

Rachel, three other students, and himself as driver and tour guide. Again apologizing for the short notice, he then informed her that she would need to be ready within an hour, and that he would pick her up with the children at eight.

No wonder she was so tired, Rachel thought as she hung up the phone. No one should be expected to be wide awake this early on the weekend—even if they had behaved themselves the night before.

She looked over at the coffee table and the empty green bottle there, feeling chagrined. The children didn't seem to notice anything out of the ordinary, but she was embarrassed nonetheless. Drinking alone was simply not like her. What on earth was happening to her here in Germany?

"Okay, guys, we'd better get a move on, then. We all need to have breakfast and get dressed so we'll be ready when Professor Heinrich gets here."

As the children went back into the bedroom to find their clothes, Rachel took the wine bottle and glass into the kitchen. Seeing the piece of chalk on the kitchen table, she smiled, remembering how Chris had so proudly made the cross mark on the door as a hex sign against evil the night before. Walpurgis night, May Eve. Nothing sinister had happened, except for her slight indiscretion with that May wine, and May Day had arrived in all its glory. Seeing the sun shine in through the windows, she was sure it would be a beautiful day for all of them—if she could just get rid of her headache.

Rachel called to the children as she entered the bathroom, "I'm glad you had your baths last night, but I didn't, so I'm going in there now. When you're dressed, get yourselves some cereal and juice, and I'll be out in a few minutes."

She leaned over the tub to turn on the hot water, and, as the tub filled, she rose and opened the medicine cabinet above the sink, hoping a couple of aspirin tablets and the bath would help her return to normal. Closing the cabinet door again, she looked at the mirror, now fogged with the steam rising from the tub, reminding her of the previous night when she thought she saw all those faces reflected in the glass. But now she saw only her own face, slightly pale, messy hair, and tired eyes.

Rachel hung her nightgown on the hook at the back of the door, and lowered herself into the hot water into which she poured some herbal bath gel. She usually bathed at night, after the children were in bed. Sometimes she would turn out the overhead light and bathe by candlelight as a way to relax. She scrubbed, lathered, and rinsed, then lay back and closed her eyes, hoping that she might benefit from just a few moments of quiet contemplation.

Michael, she thought involuntarily. The memory of the previous day pulsed through her. She could feel his presence, his mouth on hers, the gentle yet compelling pressure of his hands on her hair and back.

She sank for a moment under the water, imagining those hands wandering, exploring, finding, and she felt a warmth carrying her into undulating depths, as though she were a mermaid whose lover pleasured her in an underwater grotto. Reluctantly, she rose again to the surface, caught her breath, and returned to the reality of her bathroom.

The water was becoming cold and the chill helped spur Rachel to activity. Throwing on her robe, she ran into the kitchen to see if the children had been able to get themselves a suitable breakfast.

"Mommy, you're not ready! Look, we're all dressed for the zoo. I put the yogurt and cereal away already, and I even got out some apples and juice packs to put in our backpacks," Lisbeth said proudly.

"Bless you, child. Thank you for doing all that while I took my bath. I'll be ready in just a minute." Rachel hurried back to finish dressing.

When the knock on the door came at exactly 8:00 A.M., they were all prepared and ready for their respective outings. The children were wearing jeans and T-shirts with American sweatshirts over them. Like the children, Rachel wore sneakers and jeans, but she had chosen a patterned blue and green sweater and a light cotton aqua jacket. Once again, Kurt's eyes indicated his approval of her appearance as he greeted the family.

"Good morning! I'm glad to see you're all fit and ready for a great day. And, Rachel, you look very well, not at all as tired as you sounded when I so rudely interrupted your sleep. I have left the others at my house, where they're having a cup of coffee with Elke while they wait for us. So let's go!" Kurt seemed eager and more animated than usual.

When they got to the Heinrichs' home, Rachel met the rest of the group: Geoffrey Hunter, who was from England, Lin Wen-Sha from China, and Terry Matheson, another American student. They had already had their coffee, so Rachel declined Elke's offer of a cup for herself.

"I'm sure we don't have much time to waste if we want to get to Bremen this morning and see the city. How far did you say it was, Kurt? About two hours?"

"Yes, it will take us about that long to get to the city itself, but we will make one stop on the way. There's something that may be of special interest to you and Mrs. Lin, as German scholars—one of our prehistoric markers, the *Hunnengräber*."

Rachel wondered why Terry's eyes widened as Kurt was talking. A student of international business, the young woman had admitted when they were introduced that her German wasn't very good. She whispered something to

Geoffrey, who burst out laughing.

"No, silly, it's *Hunnen*—the Huns, not *Hühner*—those are chickens!" he responded. He turned to the rest of the group. "Terry thought Dr. Heinrich was going to show us the grave of a chicken, and she couldn't figure out why!"

Terry took the teasing well, laughing at her own misunderstanding. She picked up her jacket and handbag, and the others followed suit. "All aboard for the chicken graves!" she joked.

Rachel turned to Elke, who was standing in near the kitchen door. "Thank you for offering to watch the children," she said. "Are you sure it won't be too much trouble?"

"Not at all. Your children are well-behaved and I would like to show them our *Allwetterzoo*. It was one of my favorite places when I was younger. Besides, some friends of mine might meet us there. We will have a grand time. Don't worry."

So Rachel reluctantly said good-bye to the children, wishing them *"Viel Spass"*—lots of fun, and hoping that they would survive what she was sure would be a long day.

The ride to the north passed quickly, with all of them talking about their studies, both at home and here at the University of Münster. Geoffrey was a student of economics, and he and Terry apparently knew each other well. Mrs. Lin was a doctoral student, like Rachel, older than the others, who was studying linguistics.

Professor Heinrich stopped the car at a small gravel parking lot and looked at his passengers expectantly. Geoffrey was sitting next to him in the front seat, the three women in back. "Well, here we are. Let's go take a look at the Huns' burial ground."

The surroundings were different from what Rachel would have expected of any kind of gravesite, prehistoric or modern.

A lovely restaurant with a duck pond, little island at its center, stood before a path leading into a dark forest. She followed the others to a clearing where they viewed the monoliths engraved with mysterious markings.

"This burial ground probably commemorates warriors who fell in battle, and those markings are the runes that tell of their feats," explained Kurt. "The runes are examples of the earliest form of written communication by the Germanic tribes and seem to have had some symbolic significance as well."

"Are the runes like letters of an alphabet, or are they pictographs, like the drawings of cave dwellers?" asked Terry.

"Many of them date from the post-Roman period, so I would say that the markings are a crude approximation of the Italic alphabet."

Mrs. Lin examined the markings, then looked up, addressing Kurt. "Herr Doktor Heinrich, is it not true that the word *rune* itself derives from the Indo-European root meaning *mystery* or *secret?*"

When he nodded, she continued. "It seems to me that these runes likely have more of a symbolic than a literal meaning. Many early peoples before the dawn of recorded civilization engaged in divination with magically marked pieces of wood, bone, ivory, or stone, similar to the items used for the augury of the *I Ching* from my own culture."

"Oh, I know about the *I Ching*," volunteered Terry. "My college roommate back home was always into all kinds of spiritual things and she used sticks and coins connected to Chinese symbols. She had a book that explained the symbols and she would get answers to her questions about the future. I never understood it, but it seemed to work for her."

Kurt's brow furrowed, as if he wanted to say something, but Geoffrey burst in: "Terry, that's just a bunch of New Age claptrap. Excuse me, Mrs. Lin, I don't mean disrespect to your traditions, but it bothers me when people appropriate practices from other cultures and use them as psychic parlor games."

Nodding in apparent agreement, Kurt continued the line of thought. "Prehistoric spiritual practices are a matter of speculation, of course. We cannot prove that these runes had any deeper meaning in addition to that accorded by alphabetic correspondence; it remains a matter of conjecture and individual interpretation."

"But isn't that what life is all about anyway—individually constructed meaning?" Rachel asked, remembering Michael's emphasis on the value of subjective interpretation. "We may study the analyses of historians, scholars, and critics, but who is to say that any of them hold the key to our *own* understanding of the world?"

"My dear, that sounds a bit naïve, although hermeneutics, the study of meaning, is always a fascinating topic. Perhaps we can continue this discussion in the car as we continue toward Bremen. Time is getting short and we have many more things to see."

Rachel couldn't tell if Kurt was bothered by her interruption or simply in a hurry as he shepherded his little group away from the gravesite.

The others followed his lead, but Rachel lingered a moment, enjoying the primeval setting. The breeze made a whooshing sound as it blew through the needles of the stately firs, carrying their scent to her. The mystical marks, though eroded with time, had been carved deep into the stone, carrying the weight of significance of the one who had carved them so long ago.

There had to be a kind of magic even in the intention, she decided. An invocation and release of power in the symbols, whether pictures, runes, or words. And true artists know of this power. They feel it and transfer it into their works as a means of self-expression, as well as communication. Like Annette, she thought suddenly. The poet poured her heart into her writing, placing the power of her love into her words, infusing those marks with personal, yet transcendent meaning.

"I understand," she whispered to the poet, to the unknown rune marker, and to the spirit of the forest. Then she turned to follow the others on the path back to the car.

The ride to Bremen was pleasant, and they were fortunate to find a parking place near the train station, not far from the town square. They saw the famous Roland statue commemorating a medieval hero, and close to it, a statue depicting the animals from the Grimm Brothers' fairy tale, "The Bremen Town Musicians." Beside the statue stood two street musicians, modern descendants of their fairy-tale predecessors, playing the violin and ukulele, instrument cases open to catch the coins thrown by passersby.

"Well, here we are. I have two choices for you. You might visit the Overseas Museum, which is known for its exhibits of natural history and trade. Or, if you prefer, you could stroll through the Old Town, the former fishing village."

Geoffrey, Terry, and Mrs. Lin left to tour the museum, but Kurt said he would be happy to accompany Rachel, who chose to walk through the narrow alleys of the Old Town. As they explored the shops and inns, Kurt explained the history of the area.

"This section is called the *Schnoorviertel*, which took its name from the word for *string*, an indication of the way these cottages are lined or strung along the main street. Once inhabited by fishers and tradesmen, they are now, as you can see, home to artisans and retailers."

Rachel was especially captivated by a toy store that displayed dozens of realistic-looking dolls whose faces peered at her, as if waiting for her to take them home.

"Just look at those beautiful faces," she said to Kurt. "I don't suppose you're too interested in dolls, but these are real works of art. Such exquisitely carved faces, handmade clothing, and that even looks like real hair on some of them."

"I can appreciate the craftsmanship, of course. They are quite expensive, you know. Some of them cost almost a thousand U.S. dollars. My wife was fond of collecting dolls and bought many of them for Elke when she was small, even some of the special ones like these. Of course she wasn't allowed to play with them."

"Please tell me if I'm prying, but I have noticed the photos of your wife in your home. She was so beautiful. In many ways, Elke seems to resemble her. Are they very much alike?"

Kurt paused for so long that Rachel wondered if she had offended him. But then he turned to her, and she could see the emotion in his eyes.

"Erika was indeed a beautiful woman, inside as well as out. She adored our daughter and was ecstatic when she was born. Who could have known that they would be separated when the child was so young? Elke was only four when her mother became ill, and five when she died. How do you explain death to a child that age? Your mother is now an angel, we all told her, and every time she saw blond angels at Christmas, Elke was happy to see so many images of her mother everywhere. But she missed her touch and her guidance." Kurt cleared his throat before continuing.

"At one time I would have said that Elke was exactly like her mother, but as she grew older, she became rather withdrawn. She has always done everything that was expected of her and has done most of it perfectly, but she has seemed in such a hurry to grow up. She rarely takes the time to simply enjoy herself the way her mother did: gardening, crafting beautiful things for the household, or spending time with others. Please do not misunderstand, I am very proud of my daughter, but I would like to see her enjoy life more. This is one of the reasons I was so pleased that she has taken an interest in your children."

"Has she had no one to take her mother's place, no relative or older friend to take an interest in her?" asked Rachel, feeling some sympathy for the motherless girl.

"My own mother has always spoiled her, of course, and when Erika's mother was alive, she spent a great deal of time with her, but she has been gone now for three years. And then of course there's Katharina, Erika's girlhood friend. Katharina Obregón, Michael's mother."

"Did Erika and Katharina grow up near one another?"

"No, Erika and I are both from the north—not too far from here, actually. We moved to Münster when I secured my professorship at the University. Katharina comes from many generations of Westphalians. The girls met when they were eleven or twelve, at the convent boarding school they both attended about an hour from Münster, and after graduation, they corresponded until we came to live here. Then they saw one another more frequently."

"But I thought you were Protestants, Lutherans. Why did Erika attend a Catholic school?"

"That is a rather complicated story. Her mother was Catholic, and Erika was baptized into the faith and made her confirmation in the Catholic church as well. But the town where we lived was predominantly Lutheran, without a single Catholic church. The family had to travel to another town to hear Mass and go to confession. It was difficult for her to practice her own religion after her school years, so she began to attend services with me. It was easier that way. Elke was baptized into the Lutheran faith, but we don't attend church very often."

"I don't either. It didn't bother me until recently, when Lisbeth started to ask questions about what I believe, about what we are. I strayed away from church during my college years, and stopped going entirely after my mother died. Then I married a Jewish man, but he wasn't religious, either—I don't know if he ever saw the inside of a synagogue. Lately I've wondered if I'm being unfair to my children by not giving them a belief system."

"Ah, but Rachel, you are such a conscientious mother. Your children develop their beliefs and values from watching and listening to you, just as my daughter learned by her mother's example."

Rachel shook her head. Although she was flattered by Kurt's praise, she was also uncomfortable with it. She did the best she could, but she knew an important element, spiritual guidance, was missing in the life of her family.

"It's true, Rachel, and you are also a good role model for *my* daughter. I don't know if you realize this, but Elke already admires you very much."

Now she was really uncomfortable. Kurt might understand his daughter in many ways, but here he was dead wrong. Rachel had the feeling that Elke, like Frau Schmidt, was sneering at her beneath her polite exterior. Sneering at her inability to keep her husband, her determination to study, her less-than-perfect housekeeping, her casual appearance, and at her whole lifestyle, so different from that of the proper German mothers in her family's social circle.

Walking slowly down the street, peering into shop windows during their conversation, they almost collided with a breathless Geoffrey.

"Here you are!" he exclaimed. "The others just stepped inside that shop, but they'll be right out. It's almost one o'clock, isn't it? That was the time you told us to meet you at the restaurant, but I have to admit we couldn't find it."

Kurt pointed down the street. "Sorry you had difficulty. It's hidden in the garden behind the hotel." Seeing the women emerge from the shop, he said, "Come, I'll take you there."

They followed him into a flower-bedecked garden for a sumptuous meal of local specialties. Rachel was quiet during their meal, still suffering some of the aftereffects of her evening of excess, yet not wanting to acknowledge what had caused it. Still, she couldn't help thinking about Michael and their recent meeting, like a foolish schoolgirl after her first kiss. She simply had to stop this. She concentrated on listening to the others as they talked about what they had learned in the museum about the history of this seaport city. Several times she thought she felt Kurt's gaze on her, but she avoided looking at him.

The sun was still shining brightly when they rose from the table. Rachel knew from experience that the daylight lasted longer here in Germany than at home, but Kurt said they should hurry so that they could catch the light at their next stop, the village of Worpswede.

Driving toward their destination, Kurt told them something about the village. The once remote area at the edge of the so-called Devil's Moor, a sand dune at the center of a peat bog, had become a refuge for artists and writers at the end of the nineteenth century. Drawn there by its unusual landscape and the spirit of the time with its Rousseau-inspired "back-to-nature" movement, they formed a colony that lasted for almost fifteen years.

"Isn't that where the poet Rilke once lived?" asked Terry.

"There, you do remember something from our seminar," said Kurt with a smile. "Yes, you are right. During his marriage to the sculptor Klara Westhoff, the poet lived here on a piece of property called Birkenhoff. The two were good friends of the artists Otto Becker and Paula Modersohn-Becker. I'm sorry we didn't have time in Bremen to visit the museum displaying a large collection of her works."

"I am familiar with her paintings, Herr Doktor," said Mrs. Lin, who had been quiet during the drive. "Some of her depictions of peasant women and children remind me of the village women of my own country."

"Those paintings do have a universal appeal, I think, Mrs. Lin. They anticipated the Expressionist movement, and remind one of the work of Käthe Kollwitz, without the political overtones, of course," he added. "Do you know Modersohn's work, Rachel? I would think she might appeal to your taste."

When Rachel shook her head, he said they would stop briefly at a gallery to introduce her to some of her works.

Within a few minutes, they had arrived at the edge of the Devil's Moor, that area of wide moors and swampy meadows that had inspired so many artists, and the reasons were readily apparent. The landscape was indescribably evocative, dark green meadows punctuated by solid old oaks and slender white birches and dotted with aged cottages covered by mossy weathered straw roofs.

Surveying the paintings in the gallery, Rachel could easily see how the surroundings worked through the artists' hands to create such expressive works. Each painter had his or her own style, of course, but their palettes were similar—deep greens, browns, and many blues to encompass all the shades of heaven.

Gazing at the mothers and children who populated the

Modersohn-Becker landscapes, Rachel sensed a melancholy akin to that of Westphalia's Annette von Droste-Hülshoff. She wondered about the effect of a land on its inhabitants. *Was* there such a thing as a magic of place, as Michael claimed?

Suddenly she heard Kurt's voice behind her. "You know," he said sadly, "she died after giving birth to her daughter, at age thirty-one. Such a loss to German culture. And to her family as well." He sighed deeply.

Rachel wondered what to say. It was clear to her that he was thinking of his own wife, after so many years, still so much in love with her, still grieving his loss.

Kurt turned and led them outside to walk through the fields. Rachel had never seen such an expansiveness, such vivid greens, such intense blues. She imagined stretching out her arms to encompass and contain it all, wishing that she could just compress it into a little memory sphere to keep it in a box with other treasures from the past.

On the return trip, she fell asleep. She woke only when the car stopped as Kurt dropped the others off at the dormitory where they all lived. Simultaneously apologizing and bidding them farewell, she accepted Kurt's offer to take the front seat.

"I'm sorry I fell asleep. I hope it wasn't too rude of me," she said.

"Not to worry, Rachel. I think everyone was tired. There was very little conversation on the way home. It was a long day, but I hope it was one you enjoyed," he answered.

"Oh, yes, it was heavenly. Thank you so much for including me, Kurt."

"It is I who should thank you. Your presence made a pleasant outing something very special for me. I very much enjoy your companionship." Taking his eyes from the road, he glanced at her briefly but intently, as though he wanted to say something more, but kept silent, waiting for a response from her.

Rachel started to feel a nervous lump in her stomach, as she had when they had eaten dinner in the city over a month ago. She smiled back at him, but remained wondering what he expected her to say.

"Well, here we are again," said Kurt, stating the obvious as they drew up in front of the Heinrich home. "Let's hear all about your children's day at the zoo!"

Rachel half expected the children to run into her arms as they walked through the door, and she was disappointed to see an empty foyer. She heard voices in the kitchen, though, and laughter. She recognized Lisbeth's giggle, Chris's deeper chortle, as well as a high-pitched laugh and a deeper baritone.

Oh, no, she thought, not here, not now. But as she followed Kurt into the kitchen, she saw that it was so. Here and now, with Elke and her children, was Michael.

"Mommy, you're back!" said Chris, who was the first to see them. He left the table where they had all been sitting and ran to her, grabbing her around the legs. Lisbeth followed, hugging her around the waist.

The few moments of joyful reunion allowed Rachel the pause she needed before confronting the cozy scene of Michael and Elke together. She raised her head and looked at the two of them, still seated at the table, piles of modeling clay and various lumpy figures in front of them. "It looks like you've all been busy making interesting . . . creations," she said diplomatically in their direction, trying to keep her voice even.

"Yes, we decided to make a collection of all of the animals we saw at the zoo today," Elke answered. "But then Chris decided to invent some animals that no one has seen and we gave them silly names in English and German, and it made us all laugh."

"Mommy, look—Michael is here! We met him and his brother at the zoo and we went on a boat ride with them," Lisbeth added.

"How nice," Rachel answered. Her eyes met Michael's for a moment, but she couldn't read his expression. Did he feel at all guilty about that kiss, she wondered. Guilty about leading her on or about being unfaithful to his girlfriend?

But he addressed her quite normally, without a trace of anything but polite interest. "And what did your group see today?" he asked. "Elke said you went to Bremen. I hope you also went to Worpswede, one of my favorite areas. It has its own character but in some ways reminds me of the more remote part of Westphalia where my parents live."

Rachel couldn't very well avoid his direct question.

"Yes, Worpswede was so beautiful. I'll always remember those intense colors and the vastness of the sky and fields. No wonder so many artists have lived there."

"I also thought it would be interesting for our foreign students to see the Huns' graves," added Kurt. "We had a lively discussion there about the nature of the runes. But I'm afraid Rachel may be falling victim to some superstitious beliefs," he said with a smiling attempt at good-natured teasing.

But Rachel challenged the superior scholarly attitude that assumed there was but one correct way of looking at things, a unilateral interpretation. "Well, Kurt, you said yourself that there the markings might have symbolic meanings. Why is it so difficult to believe that they could have an impact, a significance even now, beyond what modern science can interpret?"

"You're really in for some trouble with that topic," said Elke. "You know, Michael loves to engage in occult and supernatural speculation. Who knows what kind of interpretation he'll think of?" She had stood up from the table while he remained seated, and she tousled his hair affectionately.

Rachel pretended not to notice the familiar gesture and tried to concentrate on Michael's words as he launched into what he knew about runic markings.

"I believe it is highly possible that the runes had and still have supernatural powers. Individual runes can represent not only letters but also qualities, events, and even deities. The markings always carry an underlying spiritual significance, whether they are etched onto jewelry, weapons, tools, altars, or gravestones."

"But Michael," Kurt protested, "we know that runes were grouped together into a primitive alphabet to form language, used, for example, for legal contracts. Now surely you would not claim that you ascribe metaphysical powers to such documents?" asked Kurt.

"Well, why not? Language carries great power. It is not too much to believe that the language that gives force to spells, charms, and prayers also gives life to other forms of communication."

"So the magic of the runes is really the magic of all language, wouldn't you agree?" Rachel asked, feeling more confident about her own recent deductions.

"Yes, Rachel, because there is always the possibility of deeper meaning just beyond the obvious. With each rune, there is a mystery that is not immediately apparent, and this mystery forces one to turn inward to understand it. Let me think how best to explain it," Michael paused, his expression intense.

"All right, it's like this. Every rune has three parts or three dimensions: the stave, or shape—that's the visible marking; then the sound—that's the vibration, and finally the rune itself, which is hidden from our physical senses and can be comprehended only on a spiritual plane."

"Michael, this is really too esoteric. I'm sure Rachel isn't interested in this metaphysical hobby of yours," said Elke, trying to keep a light tone.

"Actually, Elke, I'm fascinated," Rachel responded. "Michael has a different way of looking at the world, different from that of anyone else I've ever met," she added, surprised at her own honesty.

"This way of looking at the world, as you call it, can be dangerous, as history shows," Kurt interjected forcefully. "The late nineteenth century saw a revival of interest in the occult and all sorts of magic: automatic writing, séances, fortune-telling, and runic symbolism. And a runic society founded in the early 1900s sold rune rings to soldiers in the First World War to protect them in battle."

Kurt seemed to find it difficult to control his outrage, and his voice rose as he finished his statement. "Most of the members of the society were Teutonic purists, and one of the best-known runes was the swastika, used in the Second World War as the sign of the Nazis!"

"Papa, you know that Michael likes to talk about this kind of thing. Why do you let it bother you so?" As always, Elke tried to avoid conflict.

"It doesn't bother me. I just don't care to see such a fine young scholar waste his intellectual gifts on such foolish topics," he explained. But then he relented, smiling in Michael's direction. "Of course, what can we expect? His father is the foremost authority on ancient European culture. You may not know this, Rachel, but Professor Obregón has written a reference work that is the standard source of pagan practices for students of Western civilization."

"No, I didn't know that. I will have to go to the library to find it. I would very much like to become acquainted with

Professor Obregón's work," she answered.

"I have an even better idea," said Michael. "How would you like to meet my father in person? I am certain you two would have quite a bit to talk about."

"Well, that would be nice, but I thought you said your parents lived in a remote part of Westphalia. Could I get there by bicycle?"

"You could, but it is quite far if you are not accustomed to the distance. Perhaps I could borrow their car . . ." His voice trailed off as he thought of the possibilities.

Suddenly his eyes lit up. "In two weeks, we will celebrate Mother's Day and Elke comes to visit my mother then. Elke, you wouldn't mind bringing Rachel and the children, would you?" he asked.

It was a good thing Elke had her back to Michael, hiding her expression, thought Rachel.

Elke recovered quickly, however, her beautiful social mask covering her displeasure. She smiled sweetly at Rachel. "What a lovely idea. But I'm afraid I must visit my dear *Oma*, my father's mother. She has been ill, and we have planned on visiting her that weekend."

"*Liebchen*, I didn't know you were coming with me. How wonderful! We have too few family weekends." Kurt put an arm around his daughter and they smiled at each other.

"Well, then, my children and I will plan a family weekend of our own," Rachel said politely.

"Yeah, Mommy," Chris piped up. "Mother's Day—that's when we bring you breakfast in bed and flowers and—"

"Shut up, Chris. It's supposed to be a surprise!" Lisbeth admonished her brother, giving him a little shove.

Rachel could see that the fun was over for the children. They only started that kind of fighting when they were tired.

"I'm sorry, Kurt, but it's time for us to get home. I'm

afraid some of us are forgetting our manners. Would you mind dropping us off?" she asked.

But Michael responded before Kurt could. "I'll take you, Rachel. I borrowed my parents' car today so Paul and I could accompany Elke and the children to the zoo. I'll take you home, then and go on to return the car."

It seemed like a good idea to everyone but Rachel. She had enjoyed the intellectual conversation with Michael, once she got over the surprise of seeing him there, but she didn't want to be alone with him now.

Seeing him here again at the Heinrichs' with Elke, she realized that his kiss had probably been a momentary dalliance for him. Best to pretend nothing had happened and maintain a pleasant, friendly demeanor, she decided.

During the short ride home, Michael encouraged the children to tell their mother more about the events of their day, so she heard all about the elephant, the exotic birds, and the baby lamb that had fascinated them. When they arrived at the apartment, Michael insisted on walking them to the door. He laughed when he saw the chalk mark. "I see someone was helping you keep safe," he remarked.

"It was me! I can protect my mom," said Chris proudly.

Rachel opened the door and Chris and Lisbeth raced inside. "Okay, hang up your jackets and go straight into the bedroom," she said to them, "I'll be right in."

She didn't want to be rude, but she couldn't bring herself to ask Michael in. She thanked him without looking in his eyes and turned, but he touched her arm, making her pause. She looked up at him, then remembered her mirror-gazing from the previous night. *Mirror, mirror, on the wall, who's the fairest of them all?* Michael. But pretty is as pretty does, her mother would have said. And after seeing him with Elke today, Rachel knew his affections couldn't be trusted.

But she didn't look away when he looked down at her. His fingers tipped up her chin, and he gave her the gentlest of kisses, his lips barely brushing hers. *"Schlaf schön, Mütterchen,"* he said, then turned and hurried down the steps, leaving Rachel to ponder his words once again. *Sleep well, little mother.* She straightened her shoulders, reminding herself that she was first and foremost a mother. That was something she was proud of, something she would never change.

Still, yesterday's meeting with Michael had awakened something in her that had nothing to do with motherhood and everything to do with womanhood. That kiss inscribed her being in a way that the mystical runes marked their object, with a multi-dimensional significance that existed in a realm she could not yet define, and one that she was not sure she wanted to enter.

Chapter Seven

"Mama!" cried the child in terror. She felt herself becoming entangled in obstreperous roots and loamy earth, making every step more difficult. The branches and brambles scratching her face and needling her body made her flail her arms frantically. The darkness threatened to swallow her, and she cried out again, but she heard only the mournful hoot of an owl. Finally feeling a smooth, flat rock under her feet, she paused to catch her breath, still trembling from the cold and her fear.

Through the dense fog she thought she spied a flicker of light. Now here, now there, it played hide-and-seek with her emotions like a fickle will-o'-the-wisp. But then it seemed to become stronger, surer, and appeared to be coming closer. So she stretched her arms toward the light and cried out for the third time, "Mama!"

Light then infused the labyrinth of terror, rendering the vines, branches, and roots into a network of gossamer filaments through which she could see a golden glow. And she was lifted up, borne aloft as if on wings, drawn into a warm embrace, safe, secure, and loved.

Rachel awoke with a smile on her face, her arms around her pillow. She felt warm and content and wanted to burrow back into her covers and into the dream. Attempting to turn over, she found her movements restricted, her feet trapped, the bottom sheet and comforter in a twisted mess around her legs. Her nightgown was wrinkled and clammy and she felt the residue of tears on her face.

Then she remembered the nightmare. A child who had embarked on a path into the deep woods and had lost her way. Obstacles everywhere, no signposts, and no one to help. Darkness, pain, fear—and then the refuge of her mother's arms.

Of course, she thought. It was Mother's Day. But who was the child? Herself? Her daughter? Or someone else?

As she lay there, her eyes still closed, she heard sounds of laughter from another room. She opened her eyes realizing the children must be in the kitchen, preparing breakfast in bed for her. Following the tradition Rachel had established to honor her own mother, Brent had helped the tiny Lisbeth, then Chris, to make breakfast on Mother's Day.

But now the children were on their own, and Rachel was curious to see how they would do. They had asked for their allowances early in the week, and insisted she stand outside the corner store while they went in to buy something that had to remain a secret until today.

Rachel didn't want to worry the children by greeting them with a tear-stained face, so she jumped out of bed, washed her face, brushed her hair, and donned her robe, returning in time for them to deliver her breakfast surprise.

When they entered the room, they were greeted by their mother seated up against the headboard, bolstered by pillows, surrounded by a puffy, smooth coverlet. "Happy Mother's Day!" they exclaimed together. Lisbeth gently set down a tray with the morning's repast, while Chris handed her what looked like a stack of papers.

"What's this?" Rachel asked, taking the papers from him. She saw now that there were several sheets of lined paper, attached with copious amounts of tape. She took the corner of the top sheet, unfolding what she could now see was a long banner created with markers and crayons, the message reading *Happy Mother's Day, Mommy,* decorated with drawings of balloons, stars, some animals, a cake with candles, and lots of red hearts.

"This is absolutely beautiful," she said. "I love it!"

"If you love it so much, then why are you crying?" asked Chris, puzzled.

"You know Mommy always cries when she's happy," Lisbeth answered with the voice of authority. "Remember the concert at my school when she said she was so proud of me?"

The traces of her nightmare tears wiped away, Rachel now had to contend with the tears of joy. How very lucky she was to be a mother, and especially to these wonderful children. And today was especially meaningful, because it had been a very trying week. Nothing had gone right, from rainy weather, to complications with her research, and little contact with other people. With no one to talk to, she had experienced the intense frustration of being a single parent.

But at moments like this, she felt deeply satisfied, confident that the children were thriving. Each day, it seemed, Chris and Lisbeth were becoming more independent, more self-reliant and adaptable here in Germany. They had become acquainted with a wide variety of people, young and old, and they were maneuvering themselves through new experiences in two languages. Now they showed off their German as they presented Rachel with her breakfast tray.

"Hier ist dein Frühstück: ein Ei, ein Vollkornbrötchen mit Butter, etwas Schinken und Orangensaft," announced Lisbeth, enumerating the contents: a scrambled egg, her mother's favorite kind of multi-grain hard roll with butter, a couple of slices of ham, and orange juice. A second juice glass in a corner of the tray held a bouquet of pink roses, and beside it

was a little ceramic duck holding foil-wrapped Belgian chocolates.

"*Und Schokolade!*" added Chris proudly, the chocolate-laden duck apparently his favorite contribution.

"*Danke, meine Lieben,*" said Rachel, then switched to English. "You know what? I'm really glad you two are learning German so well. Even though a lot of people here know English, it's polite to speak to them in their own language first."

"But, Mommy, Michael and his brother, Paul, told us that they talk another language at home. I forget what it's called," said Chris.

"It's Spanish, like Manuel and his sister from upstairs," Lisbeth informed him. "But they come from Costa Rica. When we went to the zoo, Paul told us that their dad comes from Spain, and their mom is from here, so that's why they speak both Spanish and German at home. Did you know that, Mom?"

"Yes, Michael told me about his parents when he came to visit us on Green Thursday. He also told me that he has an older sister named Anna who is living in Spain. She married a man from there, and they have three children."

"Do you think their kids speak German?" Lisbeth asked.

"That's a good question. I would think so, since their mother is from Germany and the rest of her family still lives here, just as Anna and her brothers learned Spanish growing up because one of their parents was from Spain."

"Like if you married a man from Germany and had some more kids, they would learn English and German, right?" Lisbeth asked.

"Yes, Lisbeth, but we've been through this before. I'm not getting married again, and we'll only be in Germany until the end of the summer."

"But I like it here, and I want to stay in my school with my new friends!" Lisbeth insisted.

"Me, too!" Chris chimed in.

"But what about your friends at home? What about your cat, Chris? And what about your dad?" Rachel pointed out, even though the truth was that she wanted to stay here as well. For all its challenges, the lifestyle agreed with her. She loved the ways and customs of the people, loved riding her bicycle along cobblestone streets and along the many bike paths, loved the atmosphere of the city and surrounding countryside, the sense of history and culture. And the intriguing feeling that adventure and enchantment lay just around the corner.

But every time she indulged herself in the dream of a continued life here, reality intervened. And that reality was encroaching more and more every day. She was supported by her university stipend during her stay here, but she needed to find a job on her return. The alimony that had sustained her during her studies had run out, and the amount of child support that she received would not be enough to pay the rent when they got back.

She was hoping to have a job as an instructor at her home university, but she had sent several letters of application to other local colleges as well. Yet just this week she had received two rejection letters—one from her own school—claiming that all available language classes had to be offered to the graduate teaching assistants, and all the positions had been filled.

And then there was the matter of the children's father. Now happily married, Brent was communicating more and more frequently with them, calling and sending them cards and letters signed *Dad and Stacey,* or even worse, *Dad, Stacey, and Mittens,* including the name of Chris's cat. Sometimes his new bride would get on the phone or add a short note, seducing them with details about the new house and the rooms they had designated for each child. She would talk with Lisbeth about styles of bedroom furniture and colors for the wallpaper and bedspreads, and she would tell Chris about the playhouse they were having built in the backyard for him. When the children shared their excitement about her ex-husband's plans, it took every bit of self-control that Rachel possessed to smile and pretend to be enthusiastic.

"Mommy, I hope you don't mind but I took some of the flowers from that big bunch on the table, the one you said we were going to take to Michael's mother today."

"You mean Frau Obregón. No, I don't mind, and I don't think she would either. There are so many flowers in that bouquet, I doubt that anyone would notice a few were missing. It was very sweet of you to bring me some of the roses to decorate my breakfast tray. Now, are you going to help me eat some of this yummy food you prepared?"

Rachel hoped that the large bouquet she had bought at yesterday's market would please Katharina Obregón. She was a bit nervous about meeting Michael's parents, even though she was looking forward to the opportunity to speak with Michael's father. After Michael's initial invitation at the Heinrich home a couple of weeks ago, she had thought the matter had been dropped when Elke had said she and her father would be going away for Mother's Day. But earlier that week Michael had stopped her after their seminar, confirming the invitation, saying that he would be happy to pick her and the children up. Not knowing how to decline gracefully, she had reluctantly accepted the invitation.

Geoffrey Hunter, one of the students in Professor Heinrich's group on the May Day trip, on his way to an appointment with Kurt, had overheard Michael and Rachel, and readily offered his own car for her to use that day. He had no plans for the weekend, he explained, and so she was welcome to take his car that Sunday—and, yes, it had an automatic transmission.

After Rachel and the children finished breakfast, they hung the exuberant poster above the bed and began to get ready for their trip into the country. Michael had said they didn't have to be there until after noon, since his parents always attended Mass and didn't arrive home until sometime after eleven. Then his mother would prepare their *Mittagessen,* and the family would sit down to eat somewhere between one and two.

Rachel glanced at the clock. Right on time, at 10:30, armed with Michael's carefully drawn map, she and the children got into their borrowed car for their ride into the Westphalian countryside.

As they drove away from Münster and its suburbs, Rachel noticed that the trees became more sparse, the distances between inhabited areas increased, and even the colors of the landscape began to change. The dark green of the evergreens, the more vibrant emerald of the fields, and the rich, black earth gave way to gray-greens and lighter, sandier browns. Eventually even the herds of cattle became fewer, replaced by grazing sheep. She saw clothing hanging on clotheslines and evidence of carefully tended gardens, but she saw no one performing any chores. By edict or tradition, Sunday's peace had descended upon the land.

Realizing that they had plenty of time to reach their destination, Rachel decided on a whim to take a side road that led into an appealing village set off from the main highway.

"Is this where Michael's family lives, Mom?" called Lisbeth from the back seat.

"No, I just thought it would be interesting to drive

through this little town. Isn't it pretty? Look at all these old buildings."

"Can we get out and walk around?"

"I guess so. We have some time to spare before we're expected."

She parked the car, and they got out and began to walk down the street. Undoubtedly busy during the week, all of the shops and businesses were closed today. Grocery store, travel office, toy store—not a sign of life anywhere. Holding hands with Chris, Lisbeth skipping ahead of them, Rachel felt almost as though they were visitors on a movie set, waiting for the stars to hear their call to action.

As they approached an intersection, she saw some people scurrying ahead. Then they heard the tolling of bells, and Rachel realized that a church on that corner was drawing its parishioners inside. By the time she and the children reached the church, the latecomers were within and the doors were closed. A few minutes later they heard the congregation singing a hymn, led by the rich tones of an organ.

They paused for a moment outside, next to the church's small cemetery; its weathered, wrought-iron gate stood open, as if offering an invitation to enter. Rachel held a finger to her lips to warn the children to be quiet, but they seemed to know that this was a place of silence. They walked on a path between the old headstones to a bench beneath a willow tree and sat without making a sound. The breeze stirred through the tree behind them, causing the long branches to sway and rustle gently. The congregation was still singing one of the verses of the hymn, and from somewhere beyond the hedge wafted the unmistakable aroma of a pork roast, doubtless Sunday dinner awaiting a family on their return from worship.

The cemetery was well cared for, grass carefully clipped

around the headstones, which ranged from simple crosses to larger stones with carved figures. Flowers bloomed around many of them, and fresh bouquets had been placed in front of several.

Rachel's eye was caught by a headstone with an unusual shape. While most of the others were curved, this one culminated in a point, like a Gothic arch, or hands in prayer. Carved into the stone was the head of an angel, its wings extended. Not all of the letters were legible, but from where she sat, Rachel could make out the words that marked the resting place for a woman named Margrethe, beloved wife and mother. Her own mother's name, Margaret.

From inside the church, she heard the hymn draw to a close, and at the "Amen," Rachel rose from the bench. She walked over to the headstone, touched it lightly and whispered *"Ruhe sanfte"*—rest in peace.

Rachel herself felt a sense of peace as she and the children left the cemetery. Walking back to the car, they encountered an older woman elegantly dressed in a spring coat and matching hat, walking her dog, an overweight dachshund. She nodded at Rachel and the children, and they could hear her muttered endearments to the dog as she passed. Her baby, Rachel supposed, smiling to herself. Happy Mother's Day.

It seemed more than a coincidence that they had ventured into this village, to this church, to this cemetery, and to the grave of a woman named Margaret. She had been drawn to this place. In those few moments of repose, she felt she had been with her mother in spirit.

And now they were going to meet someone else's mother. Michael's mother.

Their foray into the village had taken little more than half an hour, so they would probably arrive at the Obregón home not too much past noon. Rachel asked Lisbeth to help her look for the landmarks Michael had indicated on the map. A barn with green trim, a cluster of old oak trees, a wooden signpost to mark the lane where they lived.

A short time later they reached the lane, situated between two pastures and lined on either side by a row of birch trees that formed a vaulted entryway into the clearing beyond. As they drove to the end of the lane, they saw two buildings ahead, both in the old Westphalian style of stucco with wood trim. The building to the side was obviously for implements and animals; it even had a small *Misthaufen*—manure pile— beside it. At some distance was the house. Dark green window boxes spilled a profusion of pink and white flowers and trailing ivy. The front door, too, was painted dark green and had a shiny brass handle.

As they drove up to the house, gravel crunched under the car's tires. Apparently the inhabitants of the house heard the sound of their approach, for the door opened, and Michael and his brother came out to greet them, a dog joining them from the side yard, barking happily.

"Look, a dog! He's so cute. Hurry, let's get out!" Chris exclaimed. The children could barely wait for the car to stop.

Michael came around to Rachel's side, followed by his younger brother. Rachel had heard about Paul from the children after their day at the zoo, and wondered if he was much like Michael. As the two approached, Rachel could see that he was similar in appearance—dark-haired, tall, but thinner —and when he came closer, she saw that his eyes were brown and his chin was smooth, not marked with his brother's cleft. She smiled at him, then turned to gather the bouquet of flowers from the seat and open her car door. The children were already out frolicking with the dog when she emerged and extended her hand to the younger of her hosts.

"Grüss dich, Rachel, *es ist eine Freude,"* said Paul, using the familiar form of address.

"Paul, I am happy to meet you as well. I've heard so much about you from the children. They certainly enjoyed themselves at the zoo."

Rachel turned then to Michael, briefly shaking his hand, trying not to look at him. "Thank you for inviting us here today. What a beautiful setting."

"My parents are looking forward to meeting all of you," he responded.

Rachel moved just out of his reach, when it seemed that he might take her arm.

"Shall we go inside then?"

Promising their canine friend that they would come back outside soon, the children followed the adults into the house. After the bright sunshine, the interior seemed dark at first, and Rachel was impressed by the intermingling scents before she could make out any visual details. The smoky smell of an old fireplace, the lemony aroma of polished wood surfaces, the dark fragrance of a variety of herbs and spices with just a hint of incense, and, coming from the kitchen as from the home in the village where they had stopped, the smell of a roast in the oven.

"Mama, hier sind wir!" called Michael, out came a small woman clad in a flower-patterned dress and a ruffled apron. Though she was slight of build, her brisk stride and arm movements nevertheless revealed a strong, muscular carriage as she entered the living room. Her variegated brown-blond hair was streaked with strands of gray and was pulled back into a smooth knot. She brushed some escaping strands from her flushed face as she walked toward them, the corners of her clear blue eyes crinkling as she gave them a wide smile of welcome.

Rebecca Gault

From the hallway at the other side of the room came her husband, tall, like his sons, and very distinguished looking, despite his age. From what Michael had told her, Rachel determined he must be in his seventies. Dark-skinned, with a full head of almost completely white hair and a mustache to match, he looked more like a movie actor than a scholar. No wonder the young German girl had fallen in love with this dashing older man from Spain so many years ago. He bowed slightly as he extended his right hand, on which he wore a diamond ring.

Rachel had rewrapped the floral bouquet in cellophane and tied it with a fresh ribbon, so that she could present it in the proper manner to her hostess. Frau Obregón seemed pleased with the offering, and after making all the small talk of introductions, she disappeared into the kitchen to find a vase.

Herr Obregón invited his guests to be seated, indicating the leather sofa and overstuffed chairs grouped in front of the immense fireplace.

"Papa, if it's all right, I will take the children outside again to play with the dog and show them around the grounds," volunteered Paul.

"*Ja, natürlich,* Pablito, but take them into the kitchen with your mother first and see if they would like something to drink after their ride from the city," answered his father. "Frau Simmons, can we offer you something? Some mineral water or perhaps a cup of tea?"

"No, thank you. I'm fine for now. Herr Doktor Obregón, this is such a beautiful place. Have you lived here long?"

"This property has been in my wife's family for generations. We lived in Münster when we were first married, in my bachelor apartment, but when our daughter, Anna, was born and my schedule at the university became more predictable, we moved out to the country. We have been very happy here for close to thirty years."

"Yes, we certainly have," added his wife. She had come back into the room with the flowers and now placed them on a low table before the sofa, where they stood in bright contrast to the dark coziness of the room's décor. Antiques and newer pieces of furniture, along with the many books on shelves and tables and the pictures on the wall, combined to give the room the soft patina of a well-lived-in, well-loved space.

"That is something I really appreciate about Germany, and perhaps it is so in the rest of Europe as well—the sense of history and continuity," said Rachel wistfully.

"Is it so different, then, in America? None of us have ever been there, although much of the American culture has been absorbed by our modern society, especially among the young. I'm afraid we might have a distorted view of how people in your country actually live," replied Frau Obregón.

"Everything always feels so hectic at home. Time never stands still as it sometimes seems to here. Everyone is always hurrying in cars to get somewhere, and we have access to anything right when we want it, no matter what season of the year it happens to be. Many stores never close, and most areas no longer have a quiet tradition on Sundays." Today especially Rachel felt strongly the contrast between the home she was used to and the calming atmosphere of this countryside.

"So much of modern technology and consumerism tends to encroach on the world we once knew, even here. There is not much you can do to stop that trend, Frau Simmons," interjected Herr Obregón. "But I hope you will allow me to say that you can control to some extent what you let enter your own life. It is up to the parents to create and preserve a nurturing environment for their children, and from what Michael has told us, that is precisely what you are doing for your own little ones," he continued, his voice reassuring.

"Thank you. I do try, but it can be difficult at times . . ." Rachel's voice trailed off, not wanting to talk about the troubles of single parenting in this domain of the intact family.

"Yes, and here we are on this beautiful day honoring you and my mother for everything you do on behalf of your children, no matter what their ages." Michael put an arm around his mother as he addressed Rachel.

"I am so pleased that Michael asked you to spend some time with us today. This day honoring mothers is one tradition we have taken from your country, and I must admit that I have always enjoyed the celebration. As you know, Elke Heinrich has been in the habit of coming to visit us on Mother's Day for the past few years, the poor motherless child, but this is the first time I have been able to share the day with someone who is also a mother."

"Professor Heinrich told me that you were close friends with his wife, Erika, that you attended school together?" Rachel asked.

"Oh yes, our friendship dates back to when we were in the first year at the *Internat,* the boarding school at the Convent of Our Lady. Erika and I were inseparable, although we were unalike in many ways. The other girls used to call us the Sun Maiden and the Moon Maiden, as different as day and night."

Looking at the woman's ivory skin and tranquil blue eyes, compared to the sunny radiance emanating from the photographs in the Heinrich home, it was easy for Rachel to see how Katharina Obregón could personify the quieter, more intuitive side of nature ruled by the moon.

"Come here, Rachel," Michael said. "Here's a photograph of them from the time they were in high school, and here's another one of them when my sister, Anna, was a baby. Erika was the *Patin*—the Godmother." Michael gestured for Rachel to approach the wall covered with framed pictures.

"I hope you enjoy our little gallery, Rachel," Frau Obregón said. "Please excuse me for a short time while we make some preparations in the kitchen. Here, darling," she said to her husband, "let me help you up." Frau Obregón gave her arm to the professor to assist him in rising from the sofa and they left the room.

Michael continued his explanation of the pictures on the wall. He showed her photos of his parents' wedding day, of himself as a child in short pants, and of his siblings at various ages. Then he pointed to an oil portrait of a sweet-looking woman whose dark ringlets capped a heart-shaped face, from the mode of her dress clearly painted over a century ago.

"Do you know who this is?" he asked expectantly.

Rachel was sure she had never seen another representation of this woman, but she looked familiar. The shape of the face, her mouth . . . She had seen someone who looked like that, but who? Then she recalled a face she'd seen in the mirror on May Eve, its softness, almost feminine features but for the wispy mustache—Levin.

"Is that Levin Schücking's mother? Didn't you tell me your mother was named for her? So it's Katharina Schücking?"

"Yes, you're right. Did you know that she was a writer too? She was known as Katinka Busch before her marriage, and she published her works mainly in newspapers and in anthologies. She visited Annette at Hülshoff Castle when they were young ladies and probably influenced her writing career."

"Were they good friends?"

"As a matter of fact, they were friends long before Levin entered the literary scene. They had many interests in common, from literature to music. And from what I have heard and read, Annette wasn't even particularly impressed by Levin when they first met. She became his mentor and friend as a favor to his mother, whose talent and friendship she revered."

"From the way she expresses herself in her poetry, I thought she felt a connection to him right away, in spite of their age difference," Rachel said softly.

"That would have been difficult, considering their early acquaintance. He was but a pupil of fifteen, preparing to enter the *Gymnasium* in Münster, while she was a writer of some renown and thirty-two years old. The difference in their ages might not have been a barrier to her later feelings but at that time she treated him with a combination of motherly affection, mentorship, and friendship, and he called her *Mütterchen*—little Mother," Michael explained.

Rachel started on hearing Levin's nickname for Annette, the same word Michael had called her several times. But Michael continued talking, seemingly unaware of her shock. "Look at this sketch. It's a copy of one originally done by Adele Schopenhauer, the philosopher's sister, meant to portray the relationship between Annette and Levin."

Rachel examined the pen-and-ink drawing of two children framed by a stylized bower of vines, leaves, and flowers on the right and gazing to the left toward a star twinkling just within reach. The boy rested a hand on the shoulder of the girl, who appeared to be older than he, and she extended a hand toward the star that hovered as if on wings before them.

"This is dear, Michael. Where did you find this copy?"

He seemed a little embarrassed as he answered her. "I saw the sketch in a book about Schücking during some of my research, and it stayed on my mind, so I borrowed the book from the library and copied it myself. I gave it to my mother and she liked it so much that she had it framed, but she said she would save it back to me until the time was right."

"I didn't know you were so multi-talented, Michael. You are a scholar, a singer, and an artist. Is there anything you can't do?"

Frau Obregón had entered the room again and answered for him. "You are right, Rachel. Michael has always been talented in so many different areas. Everything has come easily to him. Too easily, perhaps." She looked at her son lovingly, then continued.

"His father and I have tried to tell him that he must focus on particular goals, that there will come a time when he will have to work hard to achieve what he desires."

Michael looked as if he was about to retort, but thought better of it. He shrugged and walked to the door, saying that he would fetch Paul and the children for dinner.

Apparently, this was a topic the family had discussed many times, and from her own acquaintance with Michael, Rachel thought she could understand why. Yes, he was charming and talented, but she sometimes wondered about his sincerity.

As if she could read Rachel's thoughts, Frau Obregón spoke to her. "Please do not misunderstand. Michael is a well-meaning, sincere person, but he has many lessons to learn in this lifetime. His is an old soul, full of ancient wisdom, but he also has a childlike quality that limits the full expression of his gifts." She gave Rachel a meaningful yet enigmatic look. "But he will find the key to the purpose and direction of his life, and it will not be long now."

The children bounded into the room, bubbling with excitement about the animals they had seen outside. They had taken their shoes off at the door, following Paul's example, and had stopped at the bathroom to wash their hands, now displaying them proudly to their mother.

"Please come in and be seated for dinner," said Frau Obregón, leading the way into the dining room where her husband was already sitting at the large oval table. He rose slowly as they entered the room, his courtly nature overcoming his obvious difficulty with movement.

Michael helped them to their seats, placing Rachel between the two children on one side of the table, while he and his brother sat opposite them, their father and mother at the head and foot. Then the boys and their mother looked expectantly toward the head of the table, and they all made the sign of the cross as Professor Obregón prepared to speak. He entreated all of them around the table to join hands in a circle of love as he blessed the meal they were about to enjoy.

Rachel was moved by the family ritual, obviously one practiced over many years. The simple, shared reflection of gratitude lent a special flavor to the meal which was as important as its preparation.

And the meal was prepared beautifully. A perfectly seasoned roast, its outside crusted with garlic, crushed pepper, lemon zest, and sprigs of fresh rosemary and sage. A rich gravy of thickened pan juices with an aromatic variety of mushroom that was new to Rachel. Salad made of baby garden lettuce with colorful bits of pared and sliced fresh vegetables, tossed in an herbed vinaigrette dressing. Boiled new potatoes covered with butter and garnished with fresh green chives, and side dishes of tiny green beans and carrots.

Heavy crystal goblets stood at each place. Frau Obregón offered each of them their choice of mineral water, homemade elderberry or apple juice, or white wine. Seeing the familiar green wine bottle, just like the one standing on her coffee table on May Eve, Rachel was quick to request mineral water.

If they only knew how she had acted that night, she thought with a slight shudder—and Frau Obregón's eyes met hers from the end of the table. She smiled conspiratorially, as though she did indeed know her secret. Her eyes, paler than her son's but nevertheless Michael's blue, were deep pools of knowledge and mystery.

Chapter Eight

"Frau Obregón, this is a wonderful meal. Everything is delicious," Rachel remarked.

"I am so happy you are enjoying it. My son says you like to cook, too. Are you finding our German cooking much different from America?"

"Not so very different. We eat a variety of foods, and I've tried recipes from many countries. But unless you have a garden, it is difficult to find really good, fresh produce. I must compliment you on your vegetables—and unique herbs!"

"*Sí,* my Katharina is a very talented cook and gardener," her husband said, beaming at his wife.

"Mutti's specialty, her gardening," Paul added. "Just don't ask her for the names of her herbs—it's all a deep secret. She makes her own special concoctions, and not just for cooking. She's a healer as well—our very own witch," he added with a laugh.

"And in the deep of night," Michael added, grinning at his mother, "she goes out beyond our garden into the heath and marshes, where the wild plants grow, and by the light of the moon she selects these special morels, these wonderful mushrooms. It's magic, you know."

"*Ach,* Michael, don't exaggerate. It is nothing but learning about growing things. It is not so uncommon."

"Excuse me, Frau Obregón, but do witches really live around here?" asked Lisbeth in a soft little voice.

"Not really, child. But there are women, and men, too,

147

who are known for their ability to work with natural elements to help others. Some do seem to have special powers. It is said that they can communicate with animals and receive messages from trees, plants, water, and wind. And some even claim to have friends among the little people, the spirits that live in marshes, caves, and dunes."

"You mean like fairies and elves, or monsters?" Chris asked.

"Chris, you know all that's just pretend, right?" Rachel asked the boy.

"No, it's not! Michael told us about that invisible hunter and the White Lady ghost. And there must be witches around. Otherwise, why do people make those chalk marks on the door?" he protested.

It was difficult for Rachel to make a firm declaration of reason to her son, to stress the difference between fantasy and reality, especially here in the land that had given rise to all the fairy tales she loved. And how could she assure him with conviction that spirits weren't real, when lately she wasn't sure herself?

This time Michael answered. "Chris, there is much that happens in the world that we don't understand very well. Sometimes people like to explain unusual happenings with stories about magical things. But there's nothing you need to be afraid of here. Our Westphalian magic is good magic," he said, smiling reassuringly.

"Do we have magic in America, then, too, Mommy?" Lisbeth asked.

"Maybe, honey. I don't know. When I was a little girl, I used to think if I believed in something hard enough, it would happen by magic—and sometimes it seemed like it did. But then I grew up and realized that was a silly way to think."

"Then I'm not going to grow up. I like playing pretend,

and I like magic!" declared the girl.

Once again, Rachel had to admire her daughter's spirit. When had she stopped believing in magic—at ten, twelve . . . or not until after her marriage?

"Okay then, you know what?" Rachel's mind was racing for an explanation, and it came to her almost without thinking. "Let's just say that magic is when good things happen to us. And of course, that can happen even when you grow up. So go ahead and believe in magic, because then maybe good things will happen!" Rachel responded.

"That is a very good way to think, Lisbeth. So, *Kinder,* listen to your mother—she knows," said Frau Obregón with a smile.

"It's really hard to avoid magic around here," Paul mused. "There's Papa, who tells us stories from his childhood in Spain—you know, Gypsy tales and things the maids told him. Then there's our mother, with all of her country stories. It's like they just grow here, like weeds."

"Perhaps they are created here, of the heath, moor, and mountain, carried by the wind and in the current of the river . . ." his mother said expressively.

"Mama, please. This countryside is really quite boring," Paul objected. Nothing ever happens here and it's always the same. Flat, flat, flat. The sand below, the sky above. The mountains are too far away to make a difference, and the river is a pathetic trickle. Sorry, I know you love it here, but I can't wait to go to the university, in a real city where something— anything — happens!" Paul's voice was impassioned.

"Perhaps Rachel would like to see for herself something of our boring country land. Would you like to take a walk along the river after dinner, Rachel?" Frau Obregón inquired.

"Yes, I would, very much. But I'm afraid I didn't dress appropriately for hiking," Rachel responded, looking down at her white blouse, long, gathered skirt, and flimsy strapped sandals.

"That won't be too much of a problem, if you don't mind wearing borrowed clothing. We seem to be about the same size, and I still have some of Anna's things if mine don't fit."

"Okay then, sure. That would be nice. What do you think, guys?" she asked, addressing the children. "Want to go on a walk after we eat?"

Lisbeth answered for both of them. "No, Mommy, I want to play with the dog, and Paul said there's a goat and a cat and some chickens, too. We want to stay here, right, Chris?"

Chris nodded, his mouth full of potatoes.

"*Gut.* Let me clear away these things, then we'll find you something to wear. Is everyone finished? *Hat's gut geschmeckt* —did it taste good?"

Frau Obregón smiled as everyone expressed their appreciation, then stood and started to collect the serving dishes. Rachel rose as well, reaching for the children's plates.

"No, dear, don't worry about the dishes," Katharina said. We will just be a few minutes. Paul, you can help me, if you will. Michael, will you please help Papa out to the garden?"

Rachel collected the children and they went back into the living room again, chatting amid the sounds of clattering dishes and laughter from the kitchen. But spying Professor Obregón through the window as he sat alone in the garden, Rachel decided to join him. As she walked through the patio door, followed by the children, she saw Michael approach them, soccer ball in hand. Within a few minutes, Lisbeth and Chris were happily playing ball, while Rachel became involved in a discussion of ancient Germanic and Celtic practices with the professor.

Before long Paul and his mother came outside. "Here we are again. Are you ready, Rachel?" Katharina asked.

Paul took the children to the barn, and Rachel followed her hostess into the house and down the corridor to the master bedroom. It was spacious and beautifully appointed, with massive mahogany furniture. Frau Obregón went over to a *Schrank,* a large clothing cupboard, and opened the door. "Let's see. You'll need a sweater and a pair of trousers—try these, though they may be too big. Ah—Here's a pair of Anna's old jeans. They'll probably be better for you. What else? Here are some sweaters and socks. I'll look for some shoes in the other room. Why don't you try these clothes on and see if something will fit you? I'll be back in a few minutes."

Rachel tried on the trousers—a khaki pair, and then darker brown corduroys, and she was right, they were much too big. So she unfolded the jeans, shook them out to rid them of their creases, and pulled them on. Wow, these were tight, she thought. Anna must have been really tiny. She zipped and buttoned them with difficulty, then turned toward the full-length mirror. She had taken off her dressy white blouse, and in her lacy camisole, Rachel was almost embarrassed at her reflection.

She looked like a promiscuous teenager in tight, tight jeans that hugged her round bottom and accentuated her still-small waist. Her breasts appeared larger than usual above the tight pants, barely covered by the lacy top, making her feel shameless. Mothers shouldn't dress this way. She quickly grabbed one of the sweaters, a pink one, that Frau Obregón had laid out on the bed and pulled it over her head.

Frau Obregón came back into the room with a pair of sturdy hiking boots in one hand, a pair of sneakers in the other. "And you could try that pair over there," she said, gesturing to a pair of no-nonsense oxfords next to the cupboard. Rachel tried all of them on, feeling like Goldilocks. The first pair was much too big, the next pair too small, but the sneakers were just right.

"I guess that's it, then. Oh, but you're not ready!" Rachel noticed.

"Oh no, dear, I'm not going. I'm helping my husband with one of his gardening projects. Michael will take you. He knows all the pathways around here and will be a good guide," she said guilelessly.

Rachel suspected that the woman had arranged this little outing for the two of them. But Katharina couldn't have known about the complicated emotions Rachel had for her son, and she surely wouldn't want anything to come between him and Elke, that young woman who was like a second daughter to her. But still, there was something in her eyes and the way she had looked at her over dinner.

Michael bounded into the room. He had changed his clothes, too, putting on a pair of faded jeans and replacing his loafers with sneakers. And instead of his long-sleeved striped dress shirt, he now wore a navy T-shirt under a plaid flannel shirt, its sleeves rolled up almost to the elbow.

"*Na, los geht's*—let's go!" His eager attitude and fresh good looks almost made Rachel forget her resolve to keep her distance. He was just so *cute,* as the kids would say, and it was really difficult not to like him. Maybe here, in his parents' domain, he could be trusted, even if they were going on their walk alone.

They headed outside and said good-bye to the children, who were having a grand time feeding the chickens with Paul. They waved to Michael's father, who was still sitting in the sunshine, and promised his mother that, yes, they would return in time for coffee and cake.

They set out from the back of the house, crossing a field of wild flowers, and as they walked toward the trees, Michael pointed out the river bank.

"Aren't these flowers beautiful?" she exclaimed, her arm sweeping the scene of poppies, daisies, and Queen Anne's Lace. "What's this?" She paused before a cluster of unfamiliar blooms.

"I think you call them cowslips in English. But the more poetic name for them is 'keys of heaven.' You know how much we like our stories here. Once in this area lived a woman who was reputed to be quite mad, driven to despair mostly by her deceased husband's bankruptcy. She was only happy during the spring, when these flowers bloom, because she was convinced that she could unlock the gates of heaven with them. So she gathered huge bouquets and carried them around until they wilted—then afterward, took to her bed and ranted wildly."

"So then did she die and become magically transformed into one of your White Ladies who rattles the keys at her side?" Rachel guessed.

"No, this was a confused, pitiful woman who tried to redeem herself and gain a way into paradise, despite her earthly misery. It's a true, sad story. But such a woman would not become a White Lady. They are different. Most of them die while waiting for love, believing in it all the while, and they appear only to those who can understand their message."

Rachel was again struck by how seriously Michael took supernatural—or spiritual—matters. It seemed to be much more than a scholarly interest in folklore. It was almost as though he had a personal stake in the myths and legends of this land. Strange . . .

They came to the edge of the river, and Michael parted the foliage between two poplar trees, clambered down the steep embankment to the path alongside the water, then turned and held out his hand to her. "Come on, I'll help you," he said.

It was dark at first, among the trees, as Rachel stepped to the edge of the rise, and her eyes needed to adjust to the dimness. As Michael spoke, a ray of sunlight shone through the foliage, bathing him in radiance. Standing there, his hand outstretched—there was something about that pose . . .

Suddenly Rachel felt dizzy. She had wanted to descend the bank on her own, without touching him, but she stumbled and skidded into his arms.

"I . . . sorry, I lost my footing," she said weakly.

He held her firmly, steadying her. "Are you all right now?" he asked solicitously.

With the warmth and strength of his arms around her, Rachel felt strangely at home. Reluctantly she stepped back. No way, this wasn't going to happen again, no matter how good it felt, she told herself.

"Rachel, what's wrong? Why do you always pull away from me? Am I such a dreadful person?"

She couldn't believe he could be so direct, almost like a little boy. How could he ask such a question, as if he really cared, when he was probably just leading her on? Did he need her to fawn over him, like all the others? And what about Elke?

"Of course you're not a dreadful person. It's just not right for us to be . . . too close. We're friends, nothing more."

His face flushed, and his manner almost made her think that her statement had hurt him. But he recovered quickly and turned toward the stream, pointing to a large boulder in the middle. The current splashed against it, sparkling droplets creating a jet spray that resembled an iridescent veil. The surface of the water, which reflected the green-dappled trees along its banks, shattered on impact of the spray, causing the images to flutter away like little chartreuse butterflies.

"Oh, how beautiful that is," Rachel exclaimed. "And look over there—the water is so clear, you can even see the fish!"

They began walking upriver along the narrow path, Rachel asking questions or making comments, and Michael describing flora and fauna. Gradually, she became more relaxed, and their conversation jumped from one topic to another. They even burst into song a couple of times, singing a medley of European and American folk and show tunes. Michael told her a silly joke in German and she countered with one in English, both of them !aughing even more when they realized that their humor wasn't quite translatable. Rachel realized she was seeing a new side of Michael, neither the intense scholar of literature and folklore, nor the ladies' man whose motives she distrusted, but simply an appealing and endearing man.

They must have walked for about an hour, when they reached a spot where underbrush had overgrown the path.

"It's difficult walking through here, Rachel. Let me lead you through this part of the trail," Michael said, extending his hand.

"No, it's all right. I'm fine." She wouldn't admit that she could use his help. Truth was, her borrowed sneakers weren't such a good fit after all. A bit loose, they had started to chafe her feet, making her steps feel clumsy.

Michael walked ahead of her, trying to pull brush and twigs out of the way. The mid-afternoon sun had become hot, so he stopped and took off his flannel shirt and tied it around a walking stick he'd found, and it looked like he was a flag-bearer in their procession of two.

Rachel felt increasingly heated and stifled in her movements, and immodest or not, she just had to take off the pink sweater. She stopped for a moment to do so, and tied it around her waist. Then she bent over to pull up the socks that had scrunched down into the heels of her shoes.

Not noticing that she had paused, Michael continued his steady stride ahead, and Rachel hurried to catch up. But she tripped over a tree root that jutted out onto the path, and she cried out as she fell. Michael hurried back to her. "I'm so sorry I did not see that you had dropped behind. Are you all right?"

"I'll be okay. I think it's just a scratch," she lied.

Rachel winced. In fact, she was not all right. She had cut herself on a sharp stone when she fell, and under the jagged rip just below the knee of the jeans, she could see blood starting to flow.

"But look, you're bleeding! Let's see how serious that cut is." Michael knelt and leaned over her where she still sat as she had when she landed, legs sprawled in front of her. His fingers grazed her ankle as he tried to roll the pants leg up from the bottom, but he didn't get very far—the jeans were too tight. He reached into his back pocket and took out a Swiss Army knife.

Once he had extracted the blade, he cradled the back of her knee in one hand, while he deftly began to cut the denim.

Rachel tried not to shiver visibly as he assessed her bruised and scraped shin, fingertips pressing gently around the edges of the abrasion.

"Ow! There aren't any broken bones," she muttered. "It's just a stupid scratch."

"Perhaps, but this 'stupid scratch' wound needs to be cleaned and bandaged."

"Yeah, right, doctor. Too bad there aren't any pharmacies around here." Rachel said, and would almost have laughed at her own clever comment, if she hadn't been in pain.

"Wait, I'll be right back." Michael strode down to the

river, tore off his T-shirt, dipping it into the current, then wringing it out. But before he rejoined her, he foraged among the grasses and brush. When he came back to her, one hand gripped his sodden shirt, and the other held an assortment of weeds and wild flowers.

"What's this? Your idea of bringing a bouquet to the injured?" Rachel teased awkwardly, to hide her physical discomfort and the breathlessness she felt at the sight of his bare chest.

"Shh. Sit still." Michael tenderly applied the cold, damp cloth to her leg, causing her to gasp. He cleaned the wound, then tore the shirt into several pieces, draping them across his knee while he again took out his knife. He cut off the roots from his handful of weeds, cast them aside, and wrapped the remaining leaves and blossoms in a section of the wet cloth, making what resembled a large, primitive tea bag. He kneaded the bundle for a few minutes, and placed it on the wound, and with the remaining strips, fashioned a bandage, wrapping it around her leg several times to hold the poultice in place.

"One of my mother's remedies. Now, can you stand? Let me help you." He stood up and then bent over to help her up, using both hands.

Rachel had no choice but to hold on to him, one arm across his smooth back, the other across his naked chest. As she tried to steady herself, her face rested briefly against his muscled chest.

It was just for a few seconds, but it was long enough for her to register a foreign, prickling sensation. She felt the flat smoothness of the area under his clavicle, felt the soft tickling of the damp hairs on his chest, breathed in his musky, masculine scent. In those fleeting instants, she wanted to burrow farther into the haven of his arms.

But he broke away abruptly, putting several inches of distance between them, and she felt a cold shock, as if a blast of cold air blew across her body. She shivered, and was chagrined to feel her nipples become erect under her thin top. But Michael didn't seem to notice; in fact, he didn't even look at her. His hands supported her lightly under her elbows, but otherwise he no longer touched her.

"All right now?" he asked. Not waiting for an answer, he bent down to make sure the bandage was still in place, and when he was satisfied with his doctoring, he stepped back.

"Here. Hold on to this tree for a moment. I'll run up ahead and pick up my walking stick, if I can still find it. I must have dropped it on the path when I heard you cry out."

Standing under the silvery branches of a willow, Rachel watched him as he ran quickly up the path where he had left the stick. She took in the easy grace of his loping stride, his long legs in the faded jeans, the movement of his arms, and, as he returned, stick in hand, the sight of the gleaming chest where her head had rested a few minutes earlier.

Standing before her again, Michael stuck the stick into the earth and untied his flannel shirt from its tip. He didn't appear to be at all winded after his exertion, but after he slipped his arms into the shirtsleeves, and began buttoning it, she thought she noticed that his hands were shaking.

"Do you think you can walk, using the stick?" he asked.

"Of course I can. I might be a little slow, but I'll be fine." Rachel's pride insisted, even though she wasn't at all sure she could walk the whole way back. "Unless you could just call me a cab," she joked feebly.

When he didn't answer right away, she took it a step farther. "Or I guess you could carry me, huh?"

She suddenly imagined him lifting her up and cradling her against his chest, leaving her no choice but to put her arms

158

around his neck and hold on.

For a moment she closed her eyes against the compelling image. She felt him taking hold of her hand, and for an instant, thought he was about to sweep her off her feet and into his arms—but instead, she felt the cold, rough surface of the walking stick as he fastened her fingers around it.

"Let's head up this bank then, very slowly," he said matter-of-factly. "You go first, so I can make sure you don't fall. Once we're through this grove and across the field, we'll get to the main road and maybe we can find a ride. Even if not, it's still a much shorter way back than re-tracing the river path."

Rachel turned toward the slight incline, stuck the walking stick into the ground, and took her first step, leading with her good leg. She moved slowly, limping a bit until she cleared the rise at the edge of the grove of trees. Conscious of Michael's presence behind her, she tried to move more quickly. She wasn't sure if she was glad or sorry that she had tied that sweater around her waist, concealing the sight of her behind in those tight jeans.

When she made it past the trees and into the meadow, where the ground was firmer, she was able to walk almost normally. She hadn't heard anything from Michael, so she turned around.

"Everything all right?" he asked calmly.

"Sure. Just fine," she answered. He moved to walk beside her, keeping pace with her, but not looking at her. They walked toward the road in silence.

"Here we are, back in civilization again. I thought you were talking about the highway. This isn't the same road I took when I came out here. It looks pretty deserted. Do you really think a car might come along?" Rachel asked dubiously, eyeing the deep ruts in the dirt lane, certain that it saw little traffic but for farm vehicles.

"Maybe not a car, but look over there." He pointed and Rachel saw a horse and rider. Michael waved and called out, and as he approached, she saw that it was Paul.

Michael strode up ahead to greet him, and the brothers talked for a few minutes, Michael looking back at her a couple of times. She couldn't hear their conversation, but it was obvious they were discussing her. Then Paul rode toward her, as if the matter had been settled.

He greeted her and dismounted. "Mama was worried about you, since it was getting late. I told her I would come out to see if anything happened. I see you've had a small accident. So let's get you up on the horse, and I'll take you home."

"But what about Michael? Surely your horse can't hold three people!"

"He'll be all right. I offered to let him ride home with you, but he insisted on walking. Don't worry—it's not too far."

"Let him have his walking stick back then."

Paul got up into the saddle, then secured the stick under his arm as he reached down to help her up onto the horse. He handed it back to her when she sat securely behind him. "Hold on tight to me, all right? I don't want you to fall off."

Rachel nodded, and put her arms around his waist. They rode up the road to Michael, who had already started his walk home.

"*Hallo, du Michael!* Here's your pathfinder," Paul said.

Michael looked up at the two of them, took the stick without saying anything, then stepped back, flinging it far into the meadow.

"I know my way. I know it very well," he said, and turned away, walking along the edge of the road, with strong, determined strides.

"What's wrong?" Rachel asked into Paul's shoulder.

"I'm not sure. My brother seems angry, and that's unusual for him. He doesn't let things bother him too much—not like me. He didn't even fight with me when we were little. If something troubles him, then it's important."

As they continued their ride, Rachel thought about what Michael's problem could be. Was he upset because their walk was interrupted? He mentioned something about wanting to show her a special place. Was that why he was upset, because they hadn't reached it? Or maybe he was disappointed in her for being such an uncoordinated hiking companion. But that didn't make sense, either. They were having such a good time. Surely it wasn't anything she said—or was it?

The horse continued its steady gait, and Rachel tried to answer the questions her mind raised. Still holding on to Paul in front of her, she couldn't help wondering what it would be like if she were riding home with Michael, her arms around his lean waist. At sixteen, Paul was slender, still boyish, not as muscular as his brother. Michael's upper body had more definition. She could still see his strong biceps, tanned skin, and the dark hair that curled across his chest and tapered to a thin, wispy line before disappearing into his jeans.

She closed her eyes and imagined her hands playing across the surface of his bare chest, fingers dancing and swirling through the curly mass, fingertips lightly tracing designs from the hollow of his neck, arching across his pectoral muscles and down into the valley between them, trailing oh so delicately to the well of his navel . . .

She shook her head, as if to shake loose the errant thoughts. What had gotten into her, she wondered.

They rounded a bend in the road and Rachel saw the Obregón homestead appear before them. She expected the children to run out to greet them, but only the dog came toward the horse with its tandem riders. Paul rode right up to the front of the house so that she could dismount using the high front step. "Are you all right now?" he asked as she loosened her hands from around his waist.

"Uh-huh," she mumbled, and she slid off the horse onto the step.

"Can you get inside by yourself while I stable the horse?" Paul asked, gazing at her with concern.

Rachel nodded, then opened the door and walked inside, again struck by the ambiance of the living area, the special combination of natural and cultivated objects that characterized the space and gave her such a sense of well-being.

Hearing voices from the back of the house, she walked down toward the master bedroom, but didn't see anyone there. So she walked back, feeling foolish. As she paused to listen at the door of another room, she heard a voice—Katharina Obregón, no doubt. She started to walk by again, but then she realized the voice was reciting a story. She lightly tapped on the door and pushed it open. As she suspected, her children were in the room, listening in rapt attention to Frau Obregón.

Lisbeth looked up. "Mommy, you're back! We were wondering where you were, and Chris fell asleep while he was waiting for you."

"No, I didn't. I'm not a baby. I was just resting, that's all," the boy exclaimed. But Rachel could tell from his flushed cheeks and the way his hair was matted on one side that he'd had a little nap.

She looked around, wondering for a moment whose room it was. Clearly a masculine environment, but was it Paul's or Michael's boyhood room? The children were sitting on a daybed, covered in dark green corduroy, while Katharina sat in a leather chair, her back to the desk to which it belonged, a floor-to-ceiling bookcase and a stereo set beside it. Rachel saw framed pictures, one of Michael with a small, dark-haired woman. His sister, or another girlfriend? Then she spotted a silver framed photo of a pretty blonde standing at the top of a hill, her long hair blowing in the wind. Elke Heinrich.

Katharina turned toward Rachel with a smile, but it was quickly replaced by a look of concern. "Oh my goodness, what has happened to you? You have injured yourself!"

"Mommy, what happened? Ooh, there's blood on that bandage thing!" Lisbeth cried.

"Oh, it's nothing much. I'm quite all right now. I was just very clumsy and fell down, but Michael was a good doctor and fixed me all up. It doesn't even hurt any more." As she spoke, Rachel realized it was true. She couldn't even feel the scratch.

"Please, Rachel, sit down here on the bed and let me look at it." Katharina quickly slipped Rachel's shoe and sock from her foot and lifted the leg onto her lap, then unwrapped the makeshift bandage and gently removed the poultice. She briefly checked its contents visually, and nodded to herself.

"Good. He found the right combination of herbs there near the water to help stop the bleeding and minimize the pain. But I have an ointment that will help you to heal faster. Just a moment, and I will get it. I will be right back."

When she got up from the bed and left the room, the children climbed up next to their mother, wanting all the details on her adventure. Rachel described the incident vaguely, her mind on Michael.

She still didn't know what she had done to make him so angry. And here she was, sitting in his room—and it was obviously his domain, not Paul's. It was clear, now that she could see some of the book titles and CD covers. And of course, there was that framed photo. As she looked around, her eye was caught by a small grouping of objects on the end of the desk, near the window. Something that looked like a fossil or rough rock, cut away to reveal a shiny interior—a geode; and a feather, a candle, and an iridescent bluish marble—almost like a miniature crystal ball. How strange, and how beautiful. She wondered . . .

Katharina returned, carrying a small jar containing a fragrant substance. "Here, let me rub a little of this on the wound. Don't worry, it shouldn't be painful."

Rachel was surprised to find that it was true. She didn't feel the slightest discomfort, only a soothing sensation as Katharina rubbed the cream onto the wound, using the lightest of touches, applying it in a circular motion.

"Well, now do you think you are ready to have some coffee and dessert with us? The children must be very hungry by now."

"I hope they weren't too rude about it." Rachel turned to them, "Did you guys remember your manners?"

"*Ach,* of course they did," answered Frau Obregón. "They are lovely children!"

"Yes, actually, I would love a cup of coffee, and maybe some dessert as well. The walk was good exercise, so I did develop an appetite after that wonderful big dinner we had. But don't you want to wait for Michael? He insisted on walking home, and I don't know when he will get back."

Katharina assured her that Michael would make it back just fine, and invited Rachel to wash up and change into her own clothing, which she had left in the bathroom. She offered to let the children help her whip the cream, so they left the room and went into the kitchen with her.

Rachel rose from the bed and walked toward the door, finding it difficult to leave the room. On the back of the door hung a dark brown velour robe—Michael's. She couldn't help herself; she pulled it off the hook and held it close to her, remembering the moment when he picked her up after her fall. She buried her face in its folds, so redolent of him—that musky, herbed dark warmth. Michael, oh Michael . . .

Good Lord, what was happening to her? She must be going crazy. She quickly hung the robe back on the hook and went to the bathroom to wash up.

As she took off her borrowed clothing, she hoped that removing them would help her shed all traces of the besotted teenager she seemed to have become during that walk. She washed quickly, in a hurry to return to the safety of her own clothes. After drying herself, she ran a brush through her hair and donned the long, loose skirt and blouse she had worn when she arrived earlier. And when she walked into the dining room a few minutes later, she felt much more herself.

The family was sitting at the table again, which had been set for the *Kaffeestunde,* china cups and saucers at each place, silver coffeepot on a warming plate, and a ceramic teapot atop a footed stand with a votive candle. A cake, a torte, and a huge bowl of whipped cream sat nearby.

Rachel smiled at her children as she slid into the empty seat between them. But then she noticed that there was another empty chair. Michael was still missing.

"Has Michael decided not to join us?" she asked.

"He hasn't yet returned," Professor Obregón answered. "I apologize on his behalf. It's unmannerly for him to take so long when we have vistors. He should have been here by now."

"Maybe he fell down and got hurt, too!" chirped Chris. "Do you think he's okay?"

"Oh, yes," laughed Katharina. "If anyone would be all right wandering the heath and marshes, it would be Michael.

We need not wait for him. Who knows how long he will be?" As she spoke, she began to slice the torte. "Rachel, will you please help yourself to coffee or tea? I've already given the children some *Schokolade*."

Instead of their usual juice or milk, Chris and Lisbeth were sipping the cocoa from the same china cups the adults used, both trying to be very careful and grown-up. Rachel poured herself a steaming cup of coffee and inhaled its strong aroma, hoping that the caffeinated brew would jolt some sense into her. Something had happened to her during that walk along the river—something far more serious than her injury, which she could no longer even feel. It was almost as if . . . She soberly set her coffee cup back in its saucer. As if she were falling in love. But that was ridiculous.

"So you did not visit the Hidden Lake then, Rachel?" asked Katharina, her eyes again expressive.

"No, what lake is that?"

Paul jumped in. "It's Michael's favorite place. He goes there to meditate. One day he took me, and I wanted to go for a swim, but he wouldn't let me."

"Why not? Is the water polluted?" asked Lisbeth, who was just learning about environmental protection in school.

"I bet there's a monster in the lake! That's why Paul couldn't go swimming," theorized Chris.

"Those are good ideas," Paul agreed, "but I think it's something else, probably quite mysterious, that makes Michael's lake so special. I don't really care, though. There are plenty of lakes and ponds around here that are good for swimming in on a hot day—and others, well, some people think they are enchanted, and no one swims there."

"Enchanted lakes?" Lisbeth echoed.

"There's a story about one of them near here, in Osnabruck, that's called a Holy Lake," Paul continued.

"They say a monastery once stood there but that the monks were leading a wild, Godless life. They wouldn't change their ways, so God separated them and their cloister from the earth, and then He made water to flow all around the buildings, covering everything, so that no one could ever build there again. People say they can still see the balconies and towers and can hear bells ringing and the monks' chanting, even from under the water."

"Ooh, that sounds scary," said Chris.

"It's all rubbish, of course, but that's the story of the Holy Lake? Did I tell it correctly, Mutti?" Paul asked impishly.

"Yes, Paul, that is the legend of the Holy Lake, one of many legends about lakes in this region. But let's hope that Rachel and her children won't be too overwhelmed by all our country tales."

"Oh, Frau Obregón, please don't worry about us. I have told my children many stories, and they can usually tell what is real and what is pretend," Rachel reassured her. "Besides, it doesn't hurt to have *some* magic in our lives, does it?" She gave Lisbeth a wink. "But it is getting late, and we must be going soon. Chris, Lisbeth, finish your cake."

Encouraged by Frau Obregón, the children chatted a little while longer, telling her about school and their friends and quizzing her on one of their favorite subjects—the Obregón's animals. After Katharina promised them they could come back to visit the goats and the dog any time, Rachel persuaded them to get up from the table and make their way to the door.

The family, minus Michael, walked them to the car, and they said their farewells.

Despite her intentions and her caffeine-imposed dose of reason, Rachel found herself feeling tense as she drove away. The Obregón family could not have been more gracious, and no one seemed to blame her for Michael's absence, but she felt guilty nonetheless. Something she had done or said had caused him to delay coming home. He was not lost, they had assured her. But he was missing, and Rachel felt it keenly. She looked around all the way down to the end of the drive and beyond, but saw no one. Where was Michael?

Chapter Nine

The phone rang early on a warm Sunday morning in June, catching Rachel off guard. Could it be Michael, she instantly wondered. No, she knew it wouldn't be. She answered the phone's summons automatically, with her other hand holding the book of poetry she had been reading.

"Rachel, how are you doing?" Brent's voice sounded unusually cheerful.

"Fine," she answered tersely. Of course it wasn't Michael. Ever since Mother's Day, a month ago, when she had telephoned to see if he had returned home safely, he had been polite, nothing more.

And now she had to contend with Brent. Besides her natural antipathy toward her ex-husband, she was angry because the support check had come late this month.

"Hey, I wanted to—" Brent's voice faded as Rachel held the phone out toward the children, who had just come into the living room. "It's your dad," she announced.

Lisbeth grabbed the receiver eagerly, welcoming the chance to tell her father all about her recent activities. But instead of prattling as usual, she was quiet for a time, listening to the voice on the other end. Rachel wondered what her father was talking about to cause the flushed excitement in his daughter's face.

"Really, Daddy? Do you mean it?" The little girl squeaked her pleasure.

"Chris—here! Daddy wants to tell you something. It's so

awesome!" She handed the phone to her brother and ran to Rachel, her eyes shining.

"Mommy, know what? Daddy said that when school ends, he's going to take us on a trip to Disneyland! Stacey and he are going to get a big camper, and we'll see all the national parks and everything on the way. Isn't that great?"

"Yeah, and he says we can even take Mittens with us," added Chris, holding the phone away from his ear for a moment.

Rachel clenched her jaw. How dare her ex-husband plan something like this without asking her first? She tried to control herself for the sake of the children, but didn't trust herself to speak just yet.

She took a deep breath and wordlessly motioned Chris to give her the phone.

"What's all this about?" she asked Brent in what she hoped was a neutral tone.

"Rach, I tried to tell you first thing, but you didn't let me finish, and then Lizzy got on the phone, so I told her. She sure seems excited, huh?" He talked about the planned month-long trip across the country, through national parks and on to California and back to the Midwest.

Rachel listened to his narrative, nodding her head as he described the itinerary. Yes, it sounded like a great opportunity, she had to admit. But it was so sudden, and it wasn't according to the schedule they had agreed on.

"And just how are you able to get so much time off from work?" she asked.

It seemed he had a lot of accumulated vacation time, and he and Stacey had taken only a weekend for their honeymoon.

"And what about the fact that the court granted you only two weeks' visitation in the summer? And you agreed you would take that time after we got back! You know my semester isn't over until the end of July, and we hadn't planned on coming home until August!" Rachel could hear her voice getting louder, and she noticed the children's rapt attention.

"Mommy, please let us go, please!" wailed Lisbeth.

Rachel felt backed into a corner. How dare Brent do this to her, making her the mean mother, when he was the one changing their arrangement? And using the kids as a lever!

"Brent, we'll have to discuss this later. Yes, I know I'm always gone during the week, but I'll be home Wednesday afternoon, and we'll talk about it then." Rachel hung up the phone without saying good-bye.

"I didn't get to tell Daddy about Heide's birthday party. Why did you hang up so soon?" complained Lisbeth.

"Yeah, and I didn't get to say hi to my kitty or talk to Daddy more about our trip," whined Chris.

"Well, who said you're even going on that trip?" Rachel retorted, regretting her words the minute she uttered them, especially when she saw how they were received.

"I wanna go to Disneyland!" Chris cried. "You're just being mean!"

"Yeah, Mommy! Mean!" echoed Lisbeth with a glare, and she turned and trounced out of the living room toward the door. "Come on, Chris, let's go outside!"

As they thundered down the stairs, Rachel burst into tears. It just wasn't fair, she thought. It was hard enough to be in a foreign country on her own with no Julie to confide in, no Sharon to help with the kids, without Brent making things more difficult. Sometimes she felt so alone . . .

The phone rang again, and she grabbed it angrily, almost shouting into the receiver, "What now?" But it wasn't Brent, as she had thought. It was Kurt.

"Rachel, what is wrong? Have I called at a bad time?" asked the friendly voice.

"Oh, Kurt, I'm so sorry. I—I thought you were someone else." She sighed and admitted, "I just got off the phone with my ex-husband, and I guess I was a little upset."

"Can I be of any help?" he asked solicitously.

"No, I don't think anyone can help. He wants the kids to come home early, so he can take them on a trip. He even promised them Disneyland without asking me first, and when I didn't agree right away, the kids got mad and ran outside. Now they both really hate me, of course."

"My dear, it sounds like you could use a friend. Might I come over to see you? Actually, I called to ask you if you were interested in going to a concert tonight—I have an extra ticket. But we could talk about that later if you wish."

Caught in a weak moment, Rachel readily accepted Kurt's offer to visit. She didn't want to use him as a shoulder to cry on, but he was right that she could use someone to talk to. Conversation with another adult sounded pretty appealing right now.

She went into the bathroom and washed her face. What a mess you are, she said to her reflection. Who are you trying to kid anyway? Just when she thought she had it all together, that she was managing her family and her life well, something like this would happen, suggesting that she wasn't as capable as she thought.

She went back into the living room and picked up the book she had discarded when the phone rang, a volume of Annette von Droste-Hülshoff's poetry, opened to the poem *"Carpe diem."* She smiled at the irony of the Latin dictum, "seize the day." Well, today certainly didn't seem to be a great one to hold on to, but most of her days here in Münster were truly times to be treasured.

She thought about the lifesyle she and the kids had established. Everyone had a comfortable schedule, and they were all enjoying their studies and their daily experiences. Rachel was very conscious of the fact that their overseas adventure would soon come to an end, and she wanted to "seize the day" and appreciate every fleeting minute of it.

The children liked their school, their teachers and classmates, and they now had friends in the apartment building, and at their playground. Since their outing to the country on Mother's Day in May, they had all been content to stay close to home, even on the weekends.

Rachel's mainstay, that clunky, old-fashioned bicycle, had become not only a dependable way to get around, but also a vehicle that transported her through a world that had long existed only in her imagination. At first, it seemed a mere convenience—cheaper than taking the bus to the university, a good way to stay in shape, speedier than walking, and, with bags in its basket and hung over the handlebars, a way to carry more than one bag of groceries. But it also took her to historic buildings, occasional concerts, and into nature. Münster was a paradise for cyclists, with paths everywhere —alongside streets, through parks, and even into the countryside.

By herself, with that bike, Rachel was happier than she had ever been during her marriage. Alone but not lonely—except, of course, for times like this, when she wished she had someone to share the trials of single parenting as well as the moments of joy. For the most part, though, she felt self-confident, keeping a balance between being a mom and an individual in her own right. It was such a relief not to have to face her ex-husband's overt and tacit criticisms and negativity.

Not wanting that part of her past to intrude on her new

life, Rachel generally avoided talking to Brent during his phone calls to the kids. Since he usually called on Sunday mornings, she tried to make sure the children answered the phone. But this time she'd forgotten, lost in Annette's poetry, and she hated the insecurity and emotionalism Brent's call had dredged up in her.

She shuddered slightly at the thought of that phone call, and willed herself to think of something else. She turned again to her book, losing herself in Annette's words about love and friendship, nature, and self-reflection until she heard a knock on the door. She closed her volume, returned it to the bookcase, and hurried to the door. When she saw Kurt standing there, she was so relieved that she gave him a big hug.

"Kurt, I'm so glad you called! Come in, come in!" she said, drawing him into the room.

He seemed a bit taken aback by her enthusiasm.

"Well, well," he chuckled. "That's certainly a nice greeting!"

"I'm just so glad to see someone my own age!" Rachel remarked fervently.

"Thank you for the compliment, but I would hardly call us the same age, my dear," he replied jovially. Then his tone changed, sounding almost wistful, "You are still quite young . . ." and his voice trailed off.

As they went over to the sofa and sat down, Rachel looked at him, for perhaps the first time really seeing him as a person, an equal, not only as her generous professor and mentor. He was older than she, true—probably about fifty—but he stayed fit with tennis and jogging, and today he was dressed casually, appearing younger than his years in an open-necked cotton shirt, khaki pants, and tennis shoes.

When he took her hand, she felt a fleeting moment of confusion, but it was replaced almost immediately by a feeling of comfort.

"Now, Rachel, tell me all about it," he said encouragingly. So she did. She spoke of her anger at Brent, about their unfortunate conversation, and about her worries for the future. She poured out everything to her patient, understanding listener, barely pausing for breath.

"I can understand your concern, Rachel. I didn't realize the university had not funded a teaching position for you next year—I know you were counting on that. And your other applications have been turned down as well?"

She nodded. Altogether she had written to six colleges in the area and had received rejections from all of them. No one seemed interested in a Master's-level instructor. Either they had full-time faculty with doctorates or they employed part-timers to teach a course or two. Rachel needed a full-time position, with benefits and health insurance.

"Have you thought about staying here in Germany with your children?" he asked.

Rachel was surprised at his suggestion. Of course she had thought about how wonderful it would be to live in this land of her dreams, but she knew it wasn't possible. She was having enough trouble finding a teaching job in the States. What good was a German teacher in Germany?

She looked at Kurt, shaking her head, wondering what he could be thinking of.

His expression changed, and he dropped her hand, nervously twisting his fingers together. And, avoiding her eyes, he started to speak in a low voice.

"Rachel, I have something to say to you, something I hope you will not misunderstand. I had wanted to wait for a while to say this, but perhaps now is the right time after all." He swallowed nervously and then continued.

"As you know, I have been a widower for a long time. I have had some women friends—have spent time with some of them, what you Americans would call dating. But for some reason, no new relationship resulted with any of them, and that did not bother me too much, since I was busy with my research, my students, and of course, my little daughter.

"But now the situation is different. My daughter is older and doesn't need as much attention from her father. She has missed having a mother, though, and still needs a woman's influence in her life. In short, Rachel, she needs you. And what is more, I need you as well."

Rachel stared at him, her eyes wide. She couldn't believe what she was hearing. "But, Kurt—" she began.

"My dear, let me continue," he said, looking up at her, his warm eyes almost pleading.

"Rachel, I am very attracted to you, and I have been for a long time, though I didn't think I would ever find the courage to tell you. But I have been dreading the day that you leave my country and I would no longer see your lovely face.

"I cannot expect that you would feel the same way about me," he added, "at least at first. But you might get used to the idea in time. And now that I know you do want to stay here, and there is nothing waiting for you at home, well, perhaps you might consider allowing yourself to know me as more than a friend?"

He paused, looking at her beseechingly, waiting for a response to his confession, but Rachel was struck mute and could only stare back at him.

"Oh, don't think I mean to suggest anything improper. To the contrary, I would like to be very proper indeed. I would like you to be my wife, Rachel. Would you consider marrying me?"

Rachel found her voice and answered, albeit weakly.

"Kurt, I don't know what to say. I am just so surprised! You are a dear man and a good friend, but *marriage?*"

"I know it is sudden. I don't expect you to answer right away. Just think about it for a while. I won't pressure you. But I believe it would be a good arrangement for all of us—for me of course, but also for you and Elke. You would not have to replace her mother but be more like an older sister or friend to her. You and your children would be well cared for, and you could have everything you want. And you could have a real family again."

Kurt moved next to her, placing his arm around her shoulders and moving his face closer to hers. "I do care so very much for you," he said huskily.

And then she felt his prickly beard and moist lips graze her cheek in an attempt to find her mouth and kiss her.

She turned her face away quickly, improvising, "I think I hear the children calling me." She rose and hurried to the balcony. Of course there was no emergency, just the usual group of kids playing an animated soccer game, complete with shrieks and yells.

"I guess they're okay," she said lamely, "just playing."

Ever the gentleman, Kurt acted as though nothing untoward had happened. He came over to stand on the balcony with her, looking down at the children. "So, Rachel, do you think you might be interested in attending that concert tonight? One of my colleagues had planned to go with his wife, but he was called out of town. It's to be a concert of chamber and choral music, performed by members of the summer institute here at the university."

Rachel moved back into the living room. "Thank you so much, Kurt, but I promised the children that we would spend time together tonight before the school week starts again. It's our habit to watch television and have popcorn on Sunday

177

nights. Well, that is we usually do—when they're not so angry with me," she said wryly.

"Rachel, you need some time for yourself too, you know. And your children will soon get over their anger, no harm done."

Did she detect a note of impatience in his voice? Was he concerned about her well-being, or about his hoped-for companion for the evening, she wondered.

Just then the door flew open, and Lisbeth and Chris came bounding in, along with two of their friends. "Mommy, guess what? Francisco invited us to his house for dinner tonight. They're having a party. His mom and dad said it was okay, so can we go?" her daughter asked breathlessly.

Kurt smiled at her, with a shrug and a "well?" expression.

"First of all, children, where are your manners? You didn't even say hello to Professor Heinrich," she remonstrated.

They greeted him effusively, and while they chatted, she thought about what she should do. Still a bit upset about the way she had snapped at them earlier, she decided to acquiesce to their request—and to Kurt's.

So Rachel found herself, later that day, getting ready for a date. She had to call it that, given the circumstances of that morning, but was unsure how she felt about it. Accepting the help of her professor friend had been one thing. Having him show her around the city, going on outings with him and other students, doing errands, even visiting his home—all that had seemed normal and comfortable. But dating? For a student to date a professor was unthinkable at home. But here in Germany, where she was taking postgraduate classes for enrichment, not grades or even credits, maybe dating was acceptable. Surely the ever-proper Kurt would not otherwise have suggested it.

Still, he'd made it clear that he intended to court her. Of

course, she had no intention of marrying him, or anyone else, for that matter. The idea was ludicrous. And he knew she wasn't in love with him. But then, he'd said he didn't expect that, at least at first. To be able to stay here, though, to have everything taken care of . . . she had to admit it was tempting.

Maybe, with his help, she could find a job, perhaps giving private English lessons, or even helping him with his research. She remembered how enthusiastically he had spoken about literary couples during some of their discussions. Maybe they could be like Rilke and his wife, Klara Westhoff, or the artist Modersohn-Becker and her husband, Otto. As a professor's wife, Rachel mused, she would be part of a modern-day, scholarly, intellectual couple, part of the stimulating university community here . . . part of a family.

Envisioning herself as a proper *Hausfrau* made Rachel smile. Still, the possibility of staying on here, studying and learning to her heart's content, intrigued her, and she couldn't help but become a little excited as she got ready to attend the concert.

She stood in front of the wardrobe, gazing at her choices. Not pants—too student-like for the occasion, she decided. Have to be a little more proper tonight. So she chose a multi-colored floral dress with lace trim. Perfect—ladylike and decorous, befitting the companion of a professor.

Kurt's knock on the door came at exactly seven, just as he had said. Unlike Brent, he was always punctual, courteous, and considerate of her. Since the children had been invited out for the evening, he had suggested dining after the concert.

"My dear, you look perfectly charming!" he exclaimed with pleasure as she opened the door. "I am so happy you decided to join me this evening." His tone was upbeat, confident, without a trace of the nervousness he had displayed earlier that afternoon.

They drove toward the university, making small talk about the weather and local events. Rachel chatted animatedly, not looking at him, although she could feel Kurt looking at her whenever he could safely take his eyes off the road. He parked the Mercedes in front of some of the buildings near the marketplace.

"Which building is the concert being held in?" Rachel asked, glancing toward the grouping of classrooms and lecture halls that were now familiar to her.

"I am happy to say that the concert tonight will be held in our cathedral. You have been inside it, have you not?"

"Oh, yes, but only as a tourist, looking at that fantastic astronomical clock and the incredible sculpture and the Gothic architecture. I didn't know they had concerts here!"

They had walked across the broad brick plaza and joined the throng of people who were lining up to present their tickets at the church's entrance. This was apparently quite an event, Rachel realized.

"Come, my dear, this way," Kurt said as he took her elbow and guided her through the crowd. He nodded to some familiar faces, and Rachel thought she felt people assessing her as they made their way down the aisle toward the front of the sanctuary.

"Here we are," he said, allowing her to precede him into the pew. Rachel sat down quickly, eager to take in everything around here—the concertgoers still finding their seats, the stage attendants readying the chairs and stands for the musicians, the technicians monitoring sound and recording equipment—all the commotion and excitement promising a memorable musical offering.

Kurt handed her a program, and she saw that the string quartet would perform several selections, interspersed with pieces by a small choral ensemble, then after the intermission, the university choir would present a longer choral work.

Kurt pointed at the program, indicating the longer piece, *Missa Pange Lingua* by Josquin Deprez. "Do you know this piece?" he asked.

Rachel shook her head.

"It's a late medieval work, important in musical history because of its unusual setting of the Mass. We'll talk about it during the intermission," he whispered hastily, as the musicians began to take their places, signaling the beginning of the performance.

Hushed expectation—then the music began. Seated close enough to the performers—completely unlike hearing a recording, or even from listening anonymously from the back of a large concert hall—to see their movements clearly, Rachel was soon caught up in their movements, expressions, and energy, as though she were a part of the music itself. She recognized the individual voices of the instruments—the lively, high tones of the violin as well as the mellower tones of the viola and cello, and completely under their spell, Rachel was surprised when the intermission came, the audience applauding and beginning to stir.

"By the look on your face, I would say you enjoyed the music," said a voice into her right ear.

"Kurt—oh yes, very much," she said. "It's simply wonderful to sit so close to the musicians—and in these surroundings. I almost forgot where I was!"

"Yes, the acoustics are exemplary in our cathedral, are they not? I think you will especially like the second half of the concert, with the Josquin piece, since the choral idiom is quite enhanced in this space. Shall we go outside for a moment?" Kurt asked, extending his arm.

As they wended their way down the aisle, Rachel self-consciously felt several pairs of eyes follow her. She decided she was being silly—it was unlikely, even as Kurt Heinrich's companion, to draw so much attention.

But when they stood outside in the cool evening air, she wasn't so sure. It seemed as though everyone in town knew Kurt, and they all greeted him tonight. Face after face appeared in front of her, Kurt making introductions, followed by smiles and handshakes. It all became a blur, until she recognized Kurt's friends, the Schmidts.

"Good evening, Mrs. Simmons—Rachel, isn't it?" said the elegant Caroline, extending her hand. "We haven't seen you since that pleasant afternoon we spent at Kurt's home. I hope you and your children are still enjoying your stay in our city?"

Before Rachel had a chance to reply, Kurt jumped in, having finished his conversation with the man at his side. "Yes, Caroline, as you can see, Germany quite agrees with our American visitor. And I am hoping she will consider making this her home," he added, smiling broadly, moving closer to Rachel and placing an arm briefly around her shoulders.

His proprietary movement clearly registered with Caroline, whose expression changed as she realized the implications behind Kurt's words. Her eyes narrowed as she took in the scene, assessing them as a couple.

"Oh, really? How nice for you. You know, I have known several English women—what would you call them, expatriates?—who thought they would like to settle here but soon became discouraged with the complexities of our language and our way of life."

Her husband, Stephen, joined the conversation. "Now Caroline, that would hardly be the case with Rachel. She has studied German extensively, and remember, she is even researching our Frau Droste!" He smiled at Rachel.

"Well, of course I didn't mean to imply that she could not speak the language. But you know those women I am speaking of—from the English military base that was located here. The young women, children of those military families, married German men and even had children, but never really seemed to become part of the community. Remember, one lived on the next street. She went back to Britain, taking the children from their father!"

"Yes, *Schatz*, I do remember that family. But it was also rumored that the husband was a heavy drinker and that he perhaps mistreated his wife," Stephen added dryly.

"*Ach*, Caroline, always with so many stories!" Kurt interjected good-naturedly. "You must come visit us again and share some of your less sordid tales with Rachel. I'm sure she will appreciate your knowledge as she prepares to live among us."

Rachel was less than enthusiastic about spending more time with Frau Schmidt and also felt she should say something to clarify her situation. "Well, that would be very nice, but you know, I'm not really sure that I—"

"Hi, Rachel!" A familiar voice called her name, interrupting. It was Geoffrey Hunter, the English student who had been on the outing to Bremen with the group, and from whom she had borrowed the car for Mother's Day at the Obregóns.

As she turned toward him, the Schmidts moved away, much to her relief. Good, now she can look elsewhere for her stories, Rachel thought fleetingly as she smiled at Geoffrey.

"Hi, yourself, Geoffrey. How are you?" she asked.

"Fine. Delightful concert, isn't it? Oh, good evening, Professor Heinrich. I didn't see you right away. I'm sure you're both looking forward to the second half—especially since we have a mutual friend who is in the choir."

"What do you mean?" Rachel asked, puzzled.

Geoffrey unfolded his program and held it out to her. "Look at the list of chorus members. See? Here it is—Obregón. Didn't you know Michael was in the choir?"

"I knew that he was a good singer, but no, I wasn't aware that he would be part of the group tonight," she replied. She would have had little chance to hear about any of his activities, since he had not talked to her, not in weeks, aside from a few general comments during class, or courteous greetings in passing. He was definitely avoiding her, though she could not say why.

"I knew that Michael would be singing with the group tonight, but I forgot to mention it to Rachel," Kurt said. "Elke told me last week, I believe. By the way, she is supposed to be here tonight as well. Have you seen her, Geoffrey?" he asked.

"I saw her before the concert. She and Michael were just coming from a café and they seemed to be in high spirits, but I haven't seen her here yet," he answered. "But they said they were going out to a disco with some other friends after the performance, and they asked me to go along. Would you like to come with us?" Geoffrey asked Rachel.

"It's very kind of you to ask," answered Kurt for both of them, "but we have dinner plans of our own."

If Geoffrey was surprised by their companionship, he didn't show it. He simply smiled and shrugged. "Looks like we'd better get back inside. Intermission is just about over."

As they walked into the cathedral, Kurt tried, as promised, to explain to Rachel something about how this composer's setting for the Catholic Mass was different from others of the period.

Rachel heard him speak about the melody, the text, and the holy sacrament for the feast of Corpus Christi, but her attention wandered. For once she found herself uninterested in historical facts about the music—she was looking forward simply to hearing the music. And Michael would be singing . . .

When they were seated again, she pulled out her program and looked at the list of the performers. Yes, there was Michael's name. She used to be listed in programs too, when she sang in college choirs, but those days were long gone, recalled only when she sang with the children. Or, she remembered, in spontaneous moments such as the one she had shared with Michael at the House in the Rushes, and during their walk in the country near his parents' home. And look where that singing had led—to a kiss that never should have happened, but one that she could not forget. And that unforgettable kiss had led to all kinds of inexplicable feelings for a man with whom she no longer had any significant contact.

So she tried to forget the unforgettable by force of will. As if to prove her resolve, she turned toward Kurt with a smile, but just then, the lights dimmed, and the audience grew hushed in anticipation of the music to follow.

The choristers processed quietly to the front of the cathedral and stood before the altar. Michael was unmistakable among the others, distinguished by his height and his black hair, which glistened in the candlelight. The director entered from the side, bowed to the audience, and then motioned to the choir, who bowed in turn to the applause.

Within minutes Rachel was affected by the music in a way even more intimate than during the earlier part of the concert. The four voices joined and separated, weaving of the sections of the Mass a smooth tapestry of sound. And as she heard Michael's rich baritone, Rachel felt as though she were being carried away by the music, back to the Middle Ages, to a time when the strength of the human spirit and religious faith gave rise to cathedrals such as this and the music that graced the space within.

Even after the "amen," when the last notes of the music had faded away, she remained in a realm far from the modern world, removed from the crowd that applauded the singers and from the man by her side.

And a few moments later, without being aware of any specific intention, she found herself standing in front of the altar, in front of Michael, oblivious of the others congratulating friends and family members on their performance. She gazed at him, all ambivalence forgotten, breathed rapturously, "Oh, Michael, you have truly created something holy."

Michael was clearly moved by her response, and he took both her hands in his, looking down at her. "Thank you, Rachel. It means much to me that the music spoke to you." He moved closer to her, as he continued. "But you must know that neither I nor this group has made this music holy. The composer, this sanctuary, and the singers are each part of something that touched you—as together we have all paid homage to the Holy Spirit."

Rachel looked back at him, feeling as though they were the only two people in the world, knowing that what he said to her was of importance, that she was on the edge of comprehending an essential truth.

But a hearty voice abruptly broke the connection between them and Rachel returned to her surroundings, Kurt standing beside her.

"Look, Rachel, I found Elke," he said proudly, stepping aside to let them greet each other. But his daughter sprang from his side, flinging her arms around Michael's neck, seemingly uninterested in acknowledging her father's companion.

When she turned to Rachel a few minutes later, Rachel had to strain to hear her over all the other conversations going on around them. She caught only the last few words.

"... then I hope you and Papa have a nice time at dinner. *Tschüss!*"

Bye-bye yourself, thought Rachel as she and Kurt turned to go down the aisle to leave the cathedral. It might have been fun to go out with Michael and his friends, to laugh, to dance, and to talk with Geoffrey and the others.

But Kurt had other plans.

Chapter Ten

White, white, white. Sun-bleached, moonlit, snow-blossom paleness accentuated by a headdress and long train of ivory netting. Rachel looked at her reflection in the colorless river. The landscape around her was eerie, sparse, as though in the deepest winter but without a touch of chill air. Everything was still, as if nature were holding her breath. . . .

And it was her wedding day. She was clad in silk, lace, and delicate netting, in her arms a huge bouquet of snow-white blossoms. Cowslips—keys of heaven—more than enough to open celestial doors. She was the moon goddess awaiting her consort, the sun god, who would arrive in a chariot of fire to take her to their shared domain in the heavens. Surely a cause for celebration—but where were the heralds with their brass fanfare? Where were the maidens of spring, summer, and fall, who were to strew their path with petals and leaves? Why were the nighttime stars denying them their illumination? And where was her bridegroom?

A shiny walking stick suddenly appeared before her, hovering in the air, glistening, inviting. She reached out and took it and followed it where it led, away from the riverside path, across a meadow, and into a deserted churchyard. The frame church had lost most of its whitewashed finish, and its empty front windows and doorway resembled a face gaping mockingly at her entrance. The stick made a swift turn in front of the building, and Rachel held on, tugged toward the cemetery to the left. Rows of curved white tombstones interspersed symmetrically with black mounds of earth gave the impression of an oversized chessboard.

She would have found the fantastic scene amusing, were it not for its underlying sense of the macabre and the feeling that a message awaited her here. She tried to read the inscriptions on the tombstones, but all were blurred. The stick jerked her ahead, and Rachel lurched forward to see two headstones chiseled from one piece of alabaster, their double curve creating a heart shape. Could she read the words? Almost. She leaned over, fingers tracing the letters on the left headstone: A-N-N-E-T-T-E. No last name, no dates. And on the second stone, even without touching, she could see the letters deeply engraved into the surface: L-E-V-I-N.

Again led by the stick, she walked to the far end of the cemetery, where a new grave had just been dug. A fragrant mound of fresh dirt lay under a willow tree, blades of grass and colorful blossoms still clinging to the upturned earth. She stood on the pine boards covering the cavity and tried to read the inscription on the headstone already in place. She gasped as she made out the words: RACHEL ELIZABETH SIMMONS.

She jumped back, but felt the boards splinter beneath her and she fell, down, down into blackness, landing on a cushion of white satin. Black changed to white as she lay cradled in the fluffy, soft coverings. All around her hovered a white, undulating fog and she felt ever so comfortable.

Yes, I am to be married. This is my marriage bed, and I will be comfortable here, cared for, safe. She turned slightly, seeking her beloved, and clasped a bony white hand. She tried to look into his eyes but saw only hollow sockets set in a grinning skull. And as the fog lifted slightly, she glimpsed the willow tree above, which had taken on the shape of a woman kneeling at the grave.

Bent over in abject grief, keening a requiem without words, the willow woman's long leafy tresses brushed the edges of Rachel's conscious mind and she awoke, finding herself alone in a moonlit room in a bed that was not her own. Wearing a long white cotton gown, covered by a downy comforter, Rachel felt a moment of calm and peace before she was fully awake. Where was he, her beloved? She lazily stretched out her arm toward the other side of the bed but felt nothing. Slowly she opened her eyes wide and stared at the empty pillow next to her.

Oh, Lord, what had she done? Was he really here with her? And where was she anyway? She wished she could think clearly, but the fog that had hovered around her in her dream lingered. She felt dizzy, confused, and lethargic. All she wanted to do was go back to sleep, but she couldn't return to that dream scene. She had been in her grave.

But she wasn't dead, she knew. She felt a breeze from the window, and saw light from the full moon. With an effort, she threw off the cover and sat up, still feeling dizzy and unable to rise from the bed. So she squinted and tried to peer through the window, but all she could see was a bit of swirling mist as it lifted a corner of the curtain.

"I'm so tired," she mumbled to whatever presence might be in the room. "I'll just go back to sleep for a while, and I'll figure it all out in the morning." She felt strangely light and airy, like the mist, despite a compelling power that forced her back into the warmth of the bedclothes.

As she lay down again, burying her head into the pillow, she wondered if she was, in fact, married. With difficulty she moved the fingers of her left hand, but couldn't feel a ring. And surely if she were really married, she would know it. But she felt no change in her own body, no memory of the heaviness of another body atop hers, and as the shadow of a cloud fell across the moon, Rachel again closed her eyes and fell into a dreamless sleep.

Long after sunrise, she awakened to a knock on her door. A strong, determined knock, unlike the hesitant announcement of a maid or innkeeper. It was a familiar sound, but whose? It must be—

"Good morning, are you ready for a visitor?" called a male voice through the wooden panel.

And suddenly she remembered. She sat up quickly, despite her aching head, and reached for the shawl that rested on the end of the bed. Decently covered, she invited him into the room.

Carrying a huge breakfast tray, a cheery Kurt walked into the room. "How have you slept, my dear?" he asked as he carefully set the tray on the bed. When she didn't answer immediately, he looked at her more closely. "You look pale this morning. Are you all right?"

"Yes, or I will be. I'm afraid I was careless last night when we ordered that bottle of wine with dinner. I should have known better than to drink more than one glass. That seems to be all I can drink without suffering consequences."

Solicitous as ever, Kurt had taken her out to a lavish restaurant last night, wanting to find a way to cheer her up after she put Lisbeth and Chris on the plane that would take them to their father and their Disneyland vacation. Letting them go had been a difficult decision to make, but it didn't seem fair to deprive them of that trip to California, especially since their school term ended several weeks before her semester did.

Kurt had driven them all to Frankfurt for the international flight early the previous day, leaving Münster before dawn. The children had been too excited to sleep, chattering and giggling in the back seat, eager to see their old friends, their new rooms at their father's house, and, of course, wondering about their trip out West.

Chris and Lisbeth didn't notice how nervous their mother was, how she paced and even started biting her nails while they waited at the gate. She had thoroughly grilled the ground staff, making sure the airline personnel would protect her precious ones on their transatlantic flight.

And when a flight attendant came to escort them aboard the plane, both of the children went without a backward glance, confident and mature.

It was their mother who fell apart, even before the jet departed. Kurt held her, assuring her that the children would be all right, that their father and stepmother would take good care of them, and that they would certainly not forget her during their month-long separation.

And then Kurt drove south to Munich, where he had promised her a weekend of sightseeing and fun. They visited museums and churches, enjoyed the antics of the figures on the famous town clock, and found a charming inn just outside the city in a wooded area from which the Alps were visible.

Everything she saw reminded Rachel of her children, though, and several times she had to bite her lip to keep tears from falling. A hand-carved cherub with outstretched wings she spotted in a shop reminded her of Lisbeth. A little boy exclaiming over the hidden prize in a chocolate egg reminded her of Chris. And everywhere here, in folksy, traditional Bavaria, she spied the outfits she had envisioned for her children before she arrived in Germany—a puffed-sleeve white blouse and patterned green-striped *dirndl* decorated with heart-shaped silver buttons and an edelweiss applique across the front straps of a pair of small gray *lederhosen*.

Here she was in *The Sound of Music* land, or close to it, and all she could think about was how much she missed her children. How many times had they seen that movie? How many times had she envisioned herself like Maria, standing on a mountaintop, arms outstretched to take in all the magnificent scenery? But now she couldn't sing, dance, or yodel despite the beauty surrounding her, because, without her children, she could hear no music.

Poor Kurt. He had done his best, but she wasn't a very cheerful companion for him, especially during last night's dinner. They had entered the quaint dining room late that night, at a time when few others were dining. Rachel barely touched her dinner, although it was one of her favorites: veal cutlet in cream sauce, red cabbage, and *spaetzle*—curly homemade noodles. Kurt ordered a bottle of wine and ate voraciously, almost as though he were celebrating. He was animated, full of ideas and plans, alluding to a shared future for the two of them. But the more he talked, the less Rachel felt like replying, and when he ordered a second bottle of wine, she drank with him.

And here she was, on a lovely sunny morning, with a pounding headache. Once again, after his perfunctory questioning, Kurt seemed to be undisturbed by her demeanor. Full of energy, he buttered their *Brötchen,* ate several slices of cheese and cold meat, and chatted happily, not noticing that Rachel was merely picking at her roll.

He was saying something about a picnic and hiking into the mountains, or perhaps to the Starnberger Lake, when Rachel interrupted him.

"But, Kurt, we can't travel so far. We have to get back to town today. We have our seminar tomorrow. And in case you don't remember, I'm due to present my report to the class."

"Of course I remember. But I knew it would be important for you to have a pleasant diversion—a vacation of sorts, too —so I changed your report date to Thursday. And the class will be fine. I asked Michael to lead the discussion tomorrow."

At the mention of his assistant's name, Rachel's stomach lurched. One way or another Michael was always there—in class, in concerts, riding by on his bicycle in the streets of Münster, popping up in someone's conversation. Or springing up suddenly from the well of her memories.

"Kurt, no, really. I need to be back in Münster tomorrow. It's important to me."

"Why? Surely you have no more worries about your children. We called, and you talked to them. They arrived safely and they are happy with their other parents."

Rachel bristled at the term. Other parents, indeed. She grudgingly allowed their father to exercise his parental rights, but that woman—no, Stacey was no parent to *her* children! She stifled her retort and forced herself to smile at Kurt.

"No, it's not the children. But I would feel better if we returned. I've written my paper, and it's ready to present. I'd like to have closure on it."

"But you haven't even shared it with me. Do you have exciting new research on our Frau Droste? Whatever have you discovered that is so important?"

"You'll have to hear for yourself. All I will say is that it is not so much new information as it is a different view of her works and her life."

"Now I am curious. All right, then, Rachel, if it is so important to you, we will return in time for our class tomorrow. But let me show you this lake first."

A lake. Wasn't that what Michael had wanted to show her more than a month earlier? A hidden lake. Thinking of that day brought a flush to her face, reminding her of a complex of emotions she still didn't know how to sort.

"Ah, *meine Liebe,* so the idea of a bit more sightseeing is appealing to you after all—as long as I get you back in time for your presentation!"

Kurt's eyes glittered as he smiled at her, encouraged by whatever emotion he thought he had recognized in her face. "All right, then, you get dressed, and I'll meet you in the front hallway in half an hour." He moved the tray to the floor, then touched her lightly on the shoulder, which caused her shawl to fall from her shoulders onto the coverlet.

She leaned over to recover it, unwittingly revealing her breasts through the unbuttoned bodice of her thin night-gown. Now it was Kurt's turn to betray his emotions. He flushed and picked up the tray and hurried out the door.

Rachel fought an odd urge to laugh. Married? How could she have dreamed such a thing? Despite what Kurt said he wanted, he had made no overtures of intimacy. He had, without comment, reserved separate rooms for them, and except for that attempted kiss during his proposal, he scarcely touched her, save for occasionally taking her arm. He never crossed the boundary of what he considered proper behavior in a suitor.

And if we were to get married, what then, Rachel wondered. Throughout her German spring, she had begun to feel the stirrings of life within her, an awareness of her capacity for passion, which she had long hidden from herself. Here in this mystical land, she was beginning to know herself in a different way—as a person in her own right, not as just a graduate student or mother. But as a wife? She wasn't sure what that meant to Kurt. Partnership? Parenthood? He implied that he loved her, but could they become lovers?

Not that she and Brent had been very accomplished in that department. She had been a virgin when they married, whereas he considered himself experienced, the veteran of many fraternity party liaisons. She was shy and afraid to ask questions, and he wasn't very communicative to begin with, so her ignorance continued through most of their marriage.

Rachel laughed to herself as she washed up in front of the little sink in the corner of the room. Brent might as well have been this piece of soap, for all the good he did, she thought wryly as she scrubbed her nude body—at least in terms of any pleasure he gave her. But the marriage had brought two pregnancies, which had filled her with wonder, so she had convinced herself she was satisfied.

Then there was that awful period when Brent's behavior began to change. He had been having job trouble, and spent a lot of time away from the house, working out for hours at the gym, coming home with liquor on his breath. One time he brought her a book on sexual techniques and insisted on trying all of the positions suggested in its pages. Once he brought her an unexpected gift—a bright red, skimpy, almost transparent nightie, demanding that she put it on immediately and service him, despite the fact that the children were playing in the living room. His sexual ministrations became more intense but almost impersonal. She shuddered as she remembered. And then later, she found out he was having an affair.

Remembering that time, Rachel angrily yanked her clothing out of her suitcase and dressed quickly. She just wanted to leave this place and go back to her normal life, whatever that was now that the children had departed. Marriage indeed. She stuffed her nightgown and toiletries into her bag and left the room to join Kurt downstairs.

A glorious, sunny day presented itself, perfect for an outing into the foothills of the Alps. As they hiked, Rachel almost forgot her worries about the past and future and her usurped motherhood and enjoyed her surroundings. They had walked for hours and were in the middle of their picnic when she thought to ask Kurt the time. She was astonished to find out it was almost 4:00 P.M.

"Kurt! We'll never make it all the way home now!"

"Not to worry, my dear. It has been a good day, has it not? Well then, we will find our way back to the car, and I will drive us home, just as I promised."

"But we must be at least eight hours away from Münster!"

"That is no problem. I can drive through the night, I assure you. I prefer it, actually. Less traffic on the Autobahn, and driving at that time is actually very calming. And you can certainly sleep in the car if you need to."

Rachel sighed, hoping her sense of foreboding wasn't warranted. She hurriedly finished her apple, picked up the water bottle that was lying at her feet, and stood. *"Los geht's*—let's go!"

But it took even longer than the expected eight hours before they arrived in Münster. Halted by a flat tire, they had to wait for a tow truck to help them change it. After that incident, Rachel slept fitfully as Kurt continued driving their northwest route. They finally entered the city just after daybreak, when people were beginning their workday.

Rachel awoke as Kurt pulled up in front of her apartment building. Seeing one of her neighbors walking down the street to the bus stop, she was shocked. "Kurt, it's tomorrow already! How could we be so late?"

"True, we don't have too long until class. Why don't you go inside and pick up your research paper, and we'll go straight to the university."

Rachel ran inside as bidden and picked up her things, but she was distressed to realize that she wouldn't have time to bath or even change her clothes. This wasn't how she had planned to make her presentation.

By the time they found a parking place at the university

and walked into the classroom, most of the students were already there.

Michael looked up as Kurt entered. *"Ah, Herr Doktor Heinrich, Sie sind doch hier!"* he said with a smile. *"Aber . . ."* It seemed as though he was about to make a teasing comment about Kurt's appearance—his wrinkled clothes and tired expression—but then he saw Rachel, who had come in behind the professor, and his demeanor changed abruptly. He narrowed his eyes, taking in her mussed hair, rumpled clothing, and bags beneath her eyes. And he turned his back on both of them.

Rachel felt disconcerted, nervous. What was Michael thinking? That they had just hurried in from an overnight tryst, no doubt. She wondered what the rest of the class thought, and she grew more nervous when the first student finished reading his paper. How could she even dream of presenting her work, this personal look at the life and love of the famous poet, in this emotionally charged atmosphere?

But Kurt was already introducing her and her topic. "And now we will hear from Rachel Simmons, who will present her findings on our Westphalian poet, Annette von Droste-Hülshoff."

Rachel felt all eyes on her as she stood to read her paper. Her hands shook as she recited what she had painstakingly researched and written about the poet and her life. Using many of Annette's own words, she constructed a picture of the woman behind the pen, the woman who lived in a world of fantasy and whose work was inspired by the all-encompassing love for her soul mate, Levin Schücking, the much younger man who had left her for another.

She glanced up briefly toward the close of her paper and noticed how Kurt's expression had changed. Initially encouraging, his face now registered disappointment. She faltered for a moment, almost losing her place, but then recovered and kept reading. And as she reached her conclusion, quoting lines of poetry addressed to Annette's beloved Levin, Rachel again glanced up—and met Michael's eyes. He was staring at her, mesmerized.

A moment of silence followed as she put her paper down in front of her. Then, slowly, the others began knocking with their knuckles on the table, the German student version of applause. Kurt asked for comments from the group, and a discussion ensued about the relative importance of biographical criticism to the analysis of a literary work. Rachel barely heard what the other students were saying. She looked at Michael, who had withdrawn within himself, no longer meeting her gaze.

He left immediately after class, walking out of the room first, as if in a hurry to escape. And Rachel, oblivious to what Kurt or the others might think, ran after him. "Michael!" she called as he started to climb onto his bike. He paused and looked at her as she approached.

"What do you want, Rachel? To torment me further? Is this a game for you?" he asked, his eyes intense and pained.

"I don't know what you're talking about. How could I torment you? We don't even talk anymore. What have I done to offend you?"

"*Um Gotteswillen,* Rachel. How can you not know? The things you have said to me! You have made your feelings perfectly clear. To you, I am merely a boy, one who means nothing to you. You flaunt your liaison with Professor Heinrich, coming into class after spending the night with him, no doubt. And, as if that's not enough, you bring back Levin to torture me—my ancestor, my nemesis. Why, Rachel?"

Rachel was aghast. She could feel the pain he expressed, could feel it acutely, but she did not know where it came from. How could he be so affected by her actions unless he really cared about her? And that was impossible. She was much too old for him to be seriously interested in her, and he had a girlfriend.

"But Elke . . ." was all she managed to blurt out in her confusion.

"What about her? She has nothing to do with this."

"But you're going to marry her. You love her."

"Elke Heinrich? The daughter of my professor and of my mother's best friend? I have grown up with her, and of course I love her. She's like a younger sister to me. Where did you get the idea that I was to marry her?"

Rachel didn't know how or what to answer or how or what to ask. Everything seemed turned upside down and inside out, and she was totally bewildered.

"Michael, I really don't understand whatever is happening. Can we go somewhere to talk about it?"

He gave her a measured look. "Maybe you are telling the truth. All right, then, tonight. I will borrow my parents' car and pick you up at eight, and take you to a place of special meaning for me. Maybe then you will understand."

He swung a long leg over the bike and rode away, leaving Rachel to ponder his words.

For the rest of the day, Rachel wandered aimlessly. Not wanting to go back to her empty apartment, she strolled the streets of the city, window shopping, observing the passersby, and dropping into a shop here and there with a feigned interest in purchasing.

In the middle of the afternoon, she stopped for a cup of coffee at an outdoor café and watched the patrons around her. Mothers and children. Lovers young and old. Groups of friends chattering animatedly. A little old lady dressed in black, sitting by alone at the next table. Where do I fit in,

Rachel wondered. Children no longer here, no real friends, and not really part of a couple, no matter what Kurt thought.

Maybe she'd end up like that old woman, sipping hot chocolate, all alone, remembering who knew what. What would she remember most when she reached that age? A lonely but contented childhood, an unsuccessful marriage, raising her own children, studying and teaching? And how would she look back on her time in Germany? She did not know where this German adventure would lead, but she knew, even as it was drawing to a close, that it would change her life.

Still, she hated the uncertainty. With little more than a month left here, she had no idea what the future would bring. If she returned home, what awaited her? Her children would be waiting for her, but the house she and Brent had owned, where she and the children lived after he had left, had been sold just before they left for Germany, all their belongings put into storage. The proceeds of the sale had gone into a savings account, which she hoped was enough to make a down payment on another house. But how would she afford monthly mortgage payments without a job? Even if she got an apartment, how would she pay the rent? She sighed, put her head in her hands, and closed her eyes for a moment.

When she looked up, she saw the old woman from the next table standing in front of her, blocking the bright sun.

"Was ist los, Kind—Liebeskummer?" asked the quavering voice.

Rachel couldn't believe her ears. Proper German people didn't invade the privacy of others, and here was this stranger asking her if she was having love problems. But on closer observation, she could see that this was no "proper" old lady. No hair net or hat, no sensible shoes, and no dressmaker's or even department store's attire. This crone had wispy white hair floating free of its haphazardly pinned arrangement, a long, gauzy black dress that fell to her ankles, and high-topped black shoes. She looked like something out of a fairy tale, a kindly witch or a fairy godmother, Rachel thought. So she replied.

"No, it's not really love problems. It's more like life problems. And I'm no child—I'm in my thirties and I'm a mother of two children, though they are with their father at the moment."

"May I sit down?" the old one asked, and Rachel nodded.

"So you say you are not a child, that you have your own children. And you are not from here, as I can tell from your voice."

"No, I am from America. I have been studying here. But my studies are almost over, and I don't know what I will do next. I love it here, but I don't know if I can stay. I have no job here or at home, so . . ."

"What does your heart tell you to do?" asked the old woman.

"What do you mean, my heart? This is a matter of survival, of making a living, not making love. I don't mean to offend you, but it must have been different when you were young. Women lived with their fathers and then with their husbands, and everything was taken care of. But times have changed. Modern women are responsible and capable of living without a man in their lives."

"Why do you speak so angrily? Is there no one, then, you love or who loves you?"

"Well, yes, but . . ." Rachel still couldn't believe the audacity of the woman, well-meaning though she might be. Love. Kurt had said he loved her, and he wanted to marry her. But . . . she couldn't find the words to explain her situation to the old woman, so she fell silent.

"Look into your heart. Listen to what it says. Love is always the answer. There is one who loves you, and if you let yourself love him, you will find everything you need in your life."

Rachel looked at the old woman with wonder. What was she, some kind of fortune-teller? Or was she simply a silly old lady? Maybe she did indeed know something about love. After all, at her age, she certainly could have had her share of life experiences. But what could she know about Rachel's life? Really, this was too much.

"Thank you for your interest, but I'll be fine—with or without love. I'm sure my life will work out somehow." Rachel busied herself with her change purse and satchel, preparing to leave the café.

The woman stood up slowly and extended her hand toward Rachel, almost as if she were holding something in her palm. "Refuse not the gift, my dear. For life is short and happiness so rare . . ." She stepped back then, and disappeared around the corner of the building.

Lord, that was so strange, thought Rachel as she rose from the table and left the café. She looked around the corner, but there was no one in the alley. The old woman had spoken the words of Annette's poem. Well, maybe she, too, read poetry. Or perhaps the words had become a common saying in German, though Rachel hadn't heard the expression from others. And, why had the old woman thought Rachel was troubled by love to begin with? Because she was sitting by herself and looking sad? The woman couldn't have known about Kurt's proposal, yet she seemed to be encouraging Rachel to accept it and stay in Germany. "Refuse not the gift," she had said.

Rachel knew she should be grateful for Kurt's affection and attention, and he *was* good to her, but she often felt that he was secretly annoyed when she asserted herself, like this morning, during her presentation. He seemed happiest when she agreed with him, when she thought the way he did, basing all her opinions on rational fact. And her heavily biographical, subjective interpretation of the poet's work was an approach he deplored as unscholarly. It probably also bothered him that she hadn't stayed after class to discuss the paper with him, running out of the room after Michael.

Oddly, though, Michael's reaction to her paper had proved more distressing to her than Kurt's. His troubled reaction had seemed not academic but personal, as though her discussion of the relationship between Annette and Levin touched him. And what had he said about Levin—that he was his nemesis? And how could he think that Rachel didn't like or respect him or whatever it was he had claimed?

But he said he would explain himself tonight. She had several hours before he was to pick her up, and she was tired of staying in the city, so she looked for a bus to take her home. Running out of the class had cost her the ride she might have had if she had waited for Kurt. Empty nest or not, it would be a comfort to be home and to rest before she went out this evening. She would worry about Kurt later.

It was still quite light when Rachel woke from her nap. The early-evening sun was shining in through the half-closed curtains. That it stayed light so long here still surprised her. Kurt had explained that their northern latitude made summers here more like those in Norway, Land of the Midnight Sun. Maybe the sun would never set on wherever it was that she was going tonight.

She looked at the clock: 7:30. Just enough time to wash and dress before Michael was to pick her up. She wondered what she should wear. What was the special place—a restaurant, a theater, a church? Would they be outside? Would they have to walk to get there? Even if the sun didn't set until quite late, it would still be cooler, so she would need a wrap.

Feeling rushed, she went into the bathroom, wishing for the hundredth time that she had a normal shower, instead of this tub with its spray attachment. She had no time to linger in a bath. She ran a few inches of water, enough to wash herself off, and shampoo her hair. As she bent to rinse her hair, she was reminded of the weeping-willow woman kneeling over her grave in her dream. The dream of her marriage that had become a nightmare of her death.

The phone rang while she was still rinsing out her shampoo. Damn, she thought. She was tempted to ignore it but thought it might be the kids. Or maybe it was Michael, changing their plans. She turned off the water, grabbed a towel, ran dripping into the living room—and got to the phone just as it stopped ringing. While she waited for the answering machine to record the message, her gaze caught on a splash of red on the sofa. One of Lisbeth's hair ribbons, caught in the crease between two cushions. Her little girl—how she missed her.

She raised her eyes to the picture above the sofa, that floaty, impressionistic watercolor of a woman in a white dress, like one of the White Ladies Michael talked about.

That was what she'd do, she decided. She'd wear her white dress. Surely a woman in a soft, old-fashioned white dress would convince Michael that she wasn't capable of deliberately tormenting anyone.

That decided, Rachel hoped he hadn't been the one to call, especially not to cancel their date. Date, she thought. How odd. She was supposed to be dating Kurt.

She smiled as she pressed the Play button on the machine. It was Kurt, wondering where she had rushed off to after class and if she was all right. She should please call him back. No, she would not call him back. Not tonight. She was still upset by his apparent disapproval of her report, and angry about his delay in returning them to town. She knew that she would have to make peace with him eventually, but tonight she was going to try to make peace with someone else.

Tonight did not belong to Kurt—it belonged to Michael.

Chapter Eleven

"This may not be the Land of the Midnight Sun," said Michael with a laugh, "but here and other places this is a special evening of light—it's Midsummer."

On their ride out of the city, Rachel had commented on the lingering light, which made her think of Scandinavia. Back in the States it was always dark by nine, even in the brightest days of summer.

"Midsummer—isn't that when the day and night are equally long?" she echoed.

"It's the longest day of the year, the summer solstice, and not a particularly German celebration, although it was important to the Celts and the early Germanic tribes."

"Is this one of those pagan holidays taken over by Christians, like Ostara becoming Easter?"

"Not really, although *Pfingsten* or Pentecost, when the Holy Spirit came to Christ's disciples, falls at about the same time. After this evening, the days will become shorter until the winter solstice, the shortest day of the year, just before Christmas."

Winter. Christmas. At the height of summer, Rachel turned her thoughts toward the seasons to come. Who knew where she would be by then? Here in Germany or back in Illinois, where winters were dark and cold?

As if already feeling that chill, she wrapped her sweater more tightly around her. She hoped she had not dressed inappropriately for the evening. Her full-length green cardigan sweater coat covered her white dress, and she wore slipper flats that she thought were neither too flimsy for walking nor too sturdy-looking for the dress. Her hair was pulled back in a roll at the nape of her neck.

She looked at the scenery as they sped along the highway and realized they were proceeding in the direction of his parents' home. "Michael, aren't you going to tell me where you're taking me? Are we going to see your family?"

"No, we aren't going to my parents' house. I think it is better that you wait and see." He glanced at her. "What special place would *you* like to go?"

"What kind of a question is that? You already have a place in mind."

"*Na, und?* That doesn't mean I'm not interested in your preferences," Michael said with a grin.

Rachel sighed. "All right, I'll play your little game. Okay, if I could choose someplace to go, it would be . . . well, let's see. Not a restaurant, not to a movie. To a concert, perhaps? I always love music. Or dancing? That's something I almost never do. Or," she said, thinking back ruefully on the weekend she had not really been free to enjoy in the Alps, "maybe a picnic in the woods."

"All right, then, I will grant your three wishes, and on this evening, this Midsummer Night."

"Michael, are you teasing me? Or is this one of your magical pagan days—or nights—where everyone here in the country thinks they can have their wishes granted?"

"No, I am not teasing you. And if it *is* a magical night, why should that bother you? Remember what you told Lisbeth— that if she believed in magic, good things would happen to her?"

Rachel did remember. At the time, it had seemed to be positive response to her young daughter's need to believe in magic. But to believe in magic herself, as a grown woman, after all she had been through? Only in Michael's presence, with his unique mix of folklore and spirituality, was she tempted to believe once again in the magic of childhood.

They drove on in silence for a while. Rachel was pleased, but once again puzzled, at how her relationship with this enigmatic man had changed. She felt more comfortable with him tonight than she ever had before.

The sun was finally sinking, and long shadows fell on the countryside as Michael turned the car into a meadow between a row of trees. The vehicle bumped along slowly, clearly not meant for this kind of terrain.

"I'm sorry for the rough ride, but if I drive a little farther, we won't have so far on foot."

The car lurched and hobbled until they came to a dense grove of trees at the end of the field.

"Here we are," he said as he braked and turned off the engine. "Are you ready to take a little walk?"

She shrugged. "Sure, why not?"

"Good. I will get a few things from the back of the car, and we will set out."

After rummaging in the trunk, Michael emerged wearing a backpack over his pullover and carrying a large wicker basket. He opened the car door for Rachel and held out a hand to help her out.

"Gracious lady," he said with a bow. She flung the strap of her bag over her shoulder, and gave him her hand, but she let it drop as they walked toward the trees. He strode in front of her when they got to the grove, and as she followed, she could see little glimmers of light here and there shining through the treetops. Quiet and remote, it seemed a perfect place for them to come to make peace with each other. So this dark forest must be the special place.

But Michael kept walking, and she wondered where he was leading her.

He turned around. "Are you all right? I don't want any more accidents." He didn't offer her his hand this time, and she didn't ask for it. She would not run the risk of insulting him again.

He took a few more steps, then stopped and put down the basket. Rachel halted at his side. Surrounded by the pine-scented green-black dimness of the forest, they stood together in a moment of complete stillness, as if all of nature waited for them to move. Gradually the darkness lifted, and a beam of light illuminated the clearing in front of them. And there was a lake. A small, shimmering lake.

"The Hidden Lake, Michael. The one you wanted to show me before. This is your special place," she whispered.

He nodded.

Together they gazed at the dark blue, gently rippling water on which thousands of tiny pinpoints of the waning sunlight danced. Rachel had never seen anything so enchanting.

And then, rising almost imperceptibly from the silence surrounding them, she heard something. Like a woman's soft hum. She listened intently but could discern nothing more. She turned to Michael to ask him if he had heard it, too, when once again came a low crooning, like a lullaby, reminding her of her mother—and of her own bedtime singing to her children.

Michael looked at her. "It's late, and the sun will soon leave us. It is time for evening vespers." He put his arm around her, drew her close, and hummed phrases of Gregorian chant.

Rachel was moved. It did seem as though they were in a holy place. Tall trees arched together, forming the praying-hands shape typical of a Gothic cathedral. And in the woodland sanctuary was a holy chalice of water sparkling through the hushed dimness, as though the dark blue waters had offered a prayer to the sun, which in turn graced the lake with the gift of light.

"Oh, Michael, I hear, and I see, and I feel . . ." For perhaps the first time in her life, Rachel was touched in a deeply spiritual way, feeling a sense of holiness dictated not by a church or a clergyman or ritual but one that she experienced through her senses.

She looked at Michael gratefully, inexpressibly moved.

He smiled down at her, then drew a blanket from the wicker basket. He unfolded it and spread it on the ground, but remained standing for the moment.

"I wanted to bring you here tonight for two reasons. The first was to share this place with you. It has been special to me for as long as I remember, and later I will tell you why. I wanted to show you the lake earlier, when you were with us on Mother's Day, but after you hurt your leg in your fall, I knew it was not the right time."

"And the second reason?" Rachel asked quietly.

"I wanted to give you something." He reached into his pocket as he spoke. "It's a good-bye present, a wedding gift. . . ."

Rachel reached out and clutched his arm. "No, Michael, don't. I don't want you to give me a good-bye present. I'm not going anywhere yet. And what do you mean, a wedding gift?"

"Come now, Rachel, I may be young, as you claim, but I am not stupid. I know that you and Kurt are to be married, and I will be happy for both of you if that is truly what you want."

"To be married? Did he tell you that?"

"Elke told me first. But it has always been clear to me how much he cares for you. He talks of you all the time, and he went to great lengths to arrange your studies here for you and your family."

"But it's not true! Yes, Kurt has arranged everything for us, but I never said I would marry him. And what would Elke know about it, anyway?"

"Rachel, don't deny it, please. Elke said you went away for the weekend with him, and from your appearance this morning, I imagine that it must have been a wonderful prelude to your honeymoon."

Rachel winced at his uncharacteristic sarcasm, then glared at him angrily as he continued speaking.

"I must admit that I was angry this morning, and I'm sorry for acting the way I did. I was jealous, I admit, and, I suppose, disappointed in you for sending your children away. I guess I held higher ideals for you, and held a higher opinion of myself than was warranted."

"Whatever do you mean? Are you crazy?" Rachel was so incensed at his insult to her mothering that she overlooked the remark about his jealousy. "You know I would never send my children away willingly. They went on a vacation with their father, that's all. It's what they wanted, and I couldn't deny them."

"If you care for them so much, how can you stand such a long separation?"

"It's not easy, believe me. I'm counting the days until the end of July when I can see them again."

"July, is it? Well, you had better check with your fiancé. He has other plans."

"What the hell are you talking about?" she asked, her voice rising in her agitation.

"I was at the Heinrichs' home one evening a week or so

ago, and Kurt was discussing you and your children. He boasted about your upcoming marriage, and Elke seemed to be enthusiastic as well. But he said he was worried about your being so self-sacrificing and doing so much for your children. He said it would be better for you if they attended a boarding school, and he said he had found an excellent *Internat* for them."

"What? That's impossible!" Rachel exclaimed indignantly.

Michael continued. "When your ex-husband invited the children to join him on a vacation trip, Kurt said that made everything much easier. They could remain in the States until after you were married. Then in the fall they could go to the *Internat*—and you could see them again at Christmas, of course."

Rachel was stunned. "Michael, Kurt is imagining things that are simply not true! Please believe me. He did ask me, but I never told him I would marry him, and I could never stand that kind of separation from Chris and Lisbeth. We belong together, and that will never change, no matter where we live."

Then she laughed bitterly. "And you think Elke was happy about my marrying her father? That'll be the day. The girl can't stand me. The only reason I can think of that she would pretend such happiness is because of her feelings for you. She's in love with you, you know."

"But, Rachel, that is not possible. And I am not in love with her, as I told you this morning. How can I be? I'm, I'm . . ." Unable to complete the thought, he closed his mouth and shook his head slowly. He chewed his lip and looked down at the ground for a moment. When he looked up at her again, his eyes were filled with emotion.

"What is it, Michael?" Rachel asked. "I've never seen you

like this." Normally so self-assured, Michael's agitation was unusual.

"Rachel, it's—it's, well, it's that I'm actually in love with you!" he blurted, seeming surprised at his own admission.

Rachel couldn't believe what she was hearing. Surely he couldn't mean it. Yet his expression was deadly serious.

"I know what you are thinking," he said. "That it is impossible, that what I feel is nothing but a boyish infatuation. But that is not true. And this gift to you may help explain why I am so sensitive about the fact that you won't take me seriously."

"But I told you I don't want a good-bye gift, and a wedding gift is totally out of the question—more than ever, now that I have heard about Kurt's plans for my family."

"All right, then, it will not be a wedding gift. And whether or not it is a parting gift will be up to you."

She watched, mesmerized, as he reached into his pocket, enclosed something in his hand, and extended it to her . . . a familiar, evocative gesture. Meeting his outstretched hand with her own, she received his gift. She felt a smooth roundness and then looked down at the object in her palm closely. A small, perfect, iridescent blue sphere. It, too, seemed familiar. She remembered seeing it somewhere, thinking that it looked like a little crystal ball.

"Here, let's sit down while I tell you about this." Michael sat on the blanket and motioned for her to do the same. "I have had this piece a long time. For as long as I can remember, it has been a part of my life, just as this Hidden Lake has been. I have kept it in my boyhood room with a few other mementoes from my childhood. Does it remind you of anything?"

"Yes, now I remember seeing it in your old room when I visited that day. But what else should it remind me of?"

"Do you remember the collection of objects in the glass cases in the House in the Rushes?" he asked.

Rachel nodded, recalling the cases holding shells, fossils, pieces of coral, geodes, and gemstones, memorabilia collected by the poet.

"You may remember from your research that Annette was a true nature lover who was always gathering strange and beautiful things, assembling quite a collection."

"Yes, and I read that she would sometimes take a little hammer to stones to look inside, into their crystalline depths, to try to understand their mysteries."

"She had a passion for beautiful and odd things from nature, and because she was so passionate about her treasures, she wanted to share them with her dear friend Levin. On his visits to her, she would often fill his pockets with her treasures—little eggs, gemstones, shells. Out of respect for her, he would accept the gifts, even keeping some of them for a while, but then he would discard them without telling her. Except for this one. He kept it for a long time, though eventually he gave it, too, away—to one of his relatives, one of my ancestors, just before he married. It has been handed down in my family ever since."

"Why did he keep this gift longer than the others?"

"Perhaps because of the story behind it, and perhaps because he knew how special it was to Annette."

"And what might the story behind it be?"

"First of all, do you remember reading anything about Annette's nursemaid, Frau von Plettendorf?"

"Yes, I do. I know that they had a close relationship, that she was like a second mother to Annette. But what does she have to do with this blue crystal?"

"She told the little girl, little Nettchen, all the myths, stories, and legends of the area, including, I believe, those about the Hidden Lake and its White Lady. The legend is that this lake was once a magical spring with life-giving properties, guarded by virgin goddesses who ensured that only those who were worthy were allowed to drink from its waters. But as time passed, the guardians were no more, though magic still resided in the depths of the pool. Bubbles like this one would float up to the surface to be retrieved by those who understood the message."

"So you're saying that this was one of those bubbles? But it's a piece of glass!"

"That makes no difference. Don't you see? The little girl who heard this story from her nursemaid believed in it, believed in love. She heard about the guardians of the sacred waters, and she remembered the story I'll soon tell you about the White Lady who would not marry but for love. She kept the crystal sphere as one of her treasures, and when she fell in love herself, she gave it to her beloved, the only one who would understand its message."

"But Levin didn't understand, did he?"

"No, Rachel, he didn't understand," he said sadly.

"But why did this come to you instead of to your sister? She is the oldest."

"Tradition. It is handed down to the first male child in each generation. My mother had it only because it had come to her twin brother, who died in childhood. She waited to give it to me until I was old enough to appreciate it without playing with it or losing it."

"It's so beautiful, Michael. How can you bear to part with something so precious?" Rachel held the sphere in her hand, watching how the shiny surface reflected the light, as well as seeming to glow from within.

"It has held a special meaning for me, and has given me comfort in difficult times. And it will sustain you, too, if you look deeply into it and let it speak to you."

"I will do that, Michael, I promise. Just think—something that belonged to Annette, and then to Levin. I can hardly believe it. You must feel very close to him."

Michael's eyes narrowed and became very dark. "No, quite to the contrary. I despise him."

Rachel stared at him. Not only had she never heard Michael speak so strongly against anyone, but he also spoke of the long-departed writer as though he were still alive, a rival.

"Yes, you're right," he said as though reading her thoughts. "I've expressed my feelings very strongly. But Levin has been with me all my life, almost part of me, as a dark shadow."

She shook her head and looked questioningly at him. "But how can you believe that? You are nothing like him!"

"Perhaps I am. This may be difficult for you to understand, because I'm sure you do not believe in the concept of *Seelenwanderung*—soul travel—or reincarnation, I believe it is called in English. But I grew up believing that his soul had found a home in my body, that I was in fact Levin Schücking, in a more modern incarnation. And that has been very difficult to bear."

"But surely he was not such a terrible person. He was a famous writer with an excellent reputation."

"My feelings have nothing to do with his writing abilities. It is a personal matter, a matter of the spirit, a conflict that divides my heart." He looked at her intently, took a deep breath, and continued.

"Growing up as I have, with the Spanish Gypsy blood of my father and my mother's heritage from her line of Westphalian visionaries, I have received messages about my purpose in this lifetime. One of those messages revealed itself in the little blue ball you now hold in your hand, and another came from the lake here in front of us. But what confuses those messages is the sense that I must take responsibility for the thoughtlessness of my ancestor with respect to Annette von Droste-Hülshoff, the woman whose love he rejected."

"But why should his actions and decisions be yours to resolve? And how could you possibly do anything to change something that happened well over a hundred years ago?"

"I'm not sure about that, Rachel. Some piece of the message is still missing. But that is why I have been so disturbed by your dismissal of me as too young, too immature, too selfish, or irresponsible—young Levin's characteristics, at least in regard to Annette—to be worthy of your affection."

"But you don't understand. I have always been attracted to you, and haven't really perceived you as a boy, but as a man . . . ," she blurted. "All right, maybe you're not too young for me, but I am too old for you—almost ten years older. You should enjoy your youth, then marry and start your own family, not tie yourself to someone who already has one. Why would you even want to?"

"Rachel, you cannot know the effect you have on me. I find it difficult to explain myself, but surely you have felt our kinship, our connection, the many shared interests between us, like those between Annette and Levin."

"Yes, I feel a connection to you. I can't deny that. But we really don't know each other well, and we can't base a relationship on the feelings of two long-lost lovers."

"You know the kind of admiration we have here in Westphalia for our dear poet, Annette, but perhaps as an American, you cannot feel the interconnection of the place and the poet. Just as Nette was imbued with her homeland, feeling every nuance of the natural world around her, many of us also feel her presence around us."

"But I, too, have felt her presence, even heard her voice," Rachel admitted, "here in her homeland."

"I know you feel a bond with her. That is why I was so deeply affected by your paper. Your deep understanding of her and how her love for Levin shaped her work amazed me. Whether you realize it or not, your insights went far beyond what is found in books. You and Nettchen are truly kindred spirits."

"Yes, perhaps . . ." she said in confusion. She did feel she had received messages from the spirit of the poet, had long felt that there was something special she was meant to learn here in Germany. But Michael's talk of reincarnation and superstitious guilt—even his impulsive declaration that he loved her—was just too difficult to believe. Shouldn't love be more straightforward, based on the knowledge of who they were and on their *own* shared feelings and experiences, not on projections into the remote, romantic past?

All his philosophizing seemed to have made Michael hungry, for he was now calmly foraging in the picnic basket he had brought, spreading out its contents before her.

Rachel realized she had not eaten all day, not since Kurt's picnic the previous day. That thought alone was enough to take her appetite away, but she put aside those associations, realizing that she was actually quite hungry, and turned to the provisions Michael had brought.

To her relief, their conversation took a lighter turn as they ate, and soon they were laughing and chatting about favorite foods, childhood memories, books and music, and travel. It was so easy to talk with Michael—he had a way of looking directly at her, in rapt attention, as though the conversation mattered to him. For the first time in months, Rachel felt the warm glow of companionship that came from sharing ideas.

Michael opened a bottle of wine, and their conversation

drifted once again to more serious matters of philosophy and faith, of life itself—how precious it was, and how precarious.

"Yet you don't seem to share the pessimism of your *Kommilitonen*—your fellow students—that we live in an endangered world, and that it could all collapse soon," she suggested.

"It's a beautiful world," he said. "Do you know the story about Martin Luther and the tree? It's a perfect affirmation of faith."

"I've heard about his resistance to Catholic dogma and his founding of Protestantism, as well as his contributions to the German language, but I never heard anything about a tree."

"He once said that even if he knew the world were to come to an end the following day, he would still plant a tree that day. And you know, that's what I would do. Maybe I'd even plant a whole orchard!"

"So you are not afraid to bring new life into our desecrated world, then, like some of your peers?"

"Not at all. I would like to have children someday, for their own sake, of course, but also as an extension of myself and as a testament to my belief in humanity."

Rachel was moved by his rare optimism, hoping it was not simply the naïve idealism of youth, but a heartfelt, lifelong conviction—because it was one that she had to admit she shared.

"So you see, Rachel? We are not so different. Your goals for yourself and your family are not unlike mine. These are not matters of the material world alone, but also concerns of the spirit."

"Perhaps . . ." Her voice trailed away. She wasn't willing to commit to the possibility of shared spirituality. He was avowedly spiritual, but she still felt the need to be in control of herself and to apply reason to her life.

As they spoke of life and love, Michael talked about his first girlfriend and a few other women he had cared about, and Rachel told him about her former husband and the pain of her divorce.

"Michael, there's something I don't understand. Once before when we discussed love, you insisted that you would marry one day—that it was your destiny, I think you said. I thought you were referring to an arranged marriage between you and Elke Heinrich. But that wasn't what you meant, was it?"

"No. Ever since I was a boy, I knew I was destined to marry. It was foretold long ago and in this very place."

Rachel put down her glass of wine and looked around. The shadows had lengthened, and although it was not yet completely dark, light no longer danced on the lake.

"Do you mean the lake gave you a message?"

"In a way, yes. Let me tell you more about the legend of this lake. Long, long ago, in the time of the early Germanic tribes, there was a magical spring here, as I told you. During the Middle Ages, when it was not uncommon to erect cathedrals and monasteries on sites that were already holy to the people, a grand water castle was built here. The noble family had one child, a daughter, and when she came of age, they wanted to arrange an auspicious marriage for her. The young woman insisted on marrying for love, but her parents would not listen to her pleas, and they arranged a union with a powerful nobleman. Defying her parents, the woman refused to wed the man, and willed herself to die. She was found on her wedding day, lying in the marriage bed dressed in a simple white shift, her bridal gown in a heap on the floor.

"Her heartbroken parents abandoned the castle after that, and were never heard from again. Over time the castle fell into disrepair and ruins and sank into the water. But the daughter's spirit remained and those who listen with their hearts can hear her voice, from the depths of the lake."

"I thought I heard a woman's voice when we arrived here . . ." Rachel interjected softly.

Michael nodded. "And sometimes, on night of the full moon, she rises from the submerged castle as a White Lady, keys at her side, waiting for the one man who is strong enough to break from tradition and redeem the sacrifice of one who died for love."

"That's a beautifully romantic story, Michael, and I know how you cherish the tales of the White Ladies. But you said that your destiny to marry was somehow tied to this place. Did you mean to the White Lady of the Lake?" Though meaning no disrespect, she found it difficult to believe.

"Yes, her voice has spoken to me many times, and it has said to be patient, that my intended would reveal herself to me in time, and that I would know her by a sign."

"And what might that sign be?"

"I don't know that yet, but I will when it is given to me."

"And what are you supposed to do in the meantime? You say you were in love before—with your first girlfriend, when you were a teenager. And now you claim to love me, too. Just what does that mean to you?"

"It means what I said it means. I love you. Why should I deny the truth?"

Rachel didn't know whether to be touched or frustrated. These were not the words of the smooth Don Juan she'd once feared him to be. But they were those of a hopelessly romantic, idealistic, naïve young man. He said he loved her, but he was still waiting for a sign from his bride-to-be. It didn't make sense. Didn't people who loved each other want to get married?

Rachel stopped in mid-thought, reminding herself to be

realistic. After all, she didn't even believe in marriage.

That decided, she relaxed a bit. "Thank you for sharing your feelings with me, Michael. You're very special to me, too. But don't forget, you promised to grant three of my wishes tonight, and so far you have fulfilled only one of your promises—this lovely woodland picnic. But where are the musicians, and where's the dance floor? Are they hidden, like the lake?" She laughed.

"Listen and you will hear the music of the forest," Michael said softly. He pushed the picnic basket aside and moved closer to her, so close that she could feel his warm breath on her neck.

Rachel trembled at his nearness, at the irresistible combination of raw, masculine sensuality, and sweet idealism, the feelings he expressed for her and the sense of connection between them. But she forced herself to remain motionless.

And then she heard it, the music of nature. The wind rustled gently through the trees, creating a breathy whistling sound, like that of a distant pan flute. The frogs rumbled their percussive bass tones. The song of the cicadas rose and fell as if in response to the heartbeat of an invisible but sentient being inhabiting the forest. From the depths of the lake, the dark, mournful tones of the cello, and the higher-pitched sound of violin strings, sounding so much like the entreaty of a human voice. Together they created a symphony of pain and joy, of beauty, and of hope, and it was the most incredible music Rachel could imagine.

A feeling of transcendent bliss rose within her, in a wave so powerful that she could not contain the emotion, and a tear droplet escaped from the corner of her eye. Michael leaned closer and ever so gently caught the tear and held it on the tip of his finger, as though it were a precious crystal. Then, looking into her eyes, he drew his finger to his lips and kissed the tear away before reaching out to stroke her cheek.

Through a watery veil, she gazed back at him. It was happening again, that magnetic attraction, that uncontrollable desire to be closer to him. She wanted to melt into his arms, to be with him in body as well as spirit. But he moved back and in one graceful, fluid movement, rose and stood before her.

"Milady, may I have this dance?" He held out his hand to her, the gesture evoking his proffering of the blue ball.

Rachel felt a tingling sensation. The gesture was so familiar. . . . And suddenly, the veil lifted. She looked back into her memories and recognized him. The man from her vision of the marketplace—it was Michael.

As though enchanted, she almost floated up from the ground to stand before him. Her hair loosened from its roll at her nape and flowed down over her shoulders. Her long cardigan, draped on her back, slipped down her arms and dropped to the blanket.

She saw Michael's look turn to one of wonder as he gazed at her in the white dress.

"Die weisse Frau," he whispered reverently, and he reached out and took her into his arms.

His feet led them into the gliding steps of a waltz, his arms swirling her in a tender, elegant dance in their lakeside ballroom. Suddenly, though, the tempo sped up, and she laughed with delight as he twirled her around, her skirt flaring, her feet seemingly of their volition following his lively choreography. They spun faster and faster, around and around, until, dizzy and exhausted, they collapsed, laughing, onto the blanket.

As they lay there trying to catch their breath, and once again, she looked into his eyes. Their indigo depths beckoned, this time smoldering with a dark intensity that reflected her own newly awakened inner fire. He grabbed her into his embrace, kissing her furiously, as if to devour her. She gasped and pulled back, stunned at his strength and fervor, put her fingers to her lips.

Slowly, tenderly, Michael took her hand into his own and brought it toward his lips. He brushed her fingertips with the lightest of kisses, then drew them, one by one, into his mouth in turn, gently suckling their tips.

Rachel gasped at the sensation of warmth and moistness. What was he doing to her? She felt a yearning she had never known, a hot tightness at her center, as he lowered her hand to his chest and drew her closer to him.

"My love, I did not mean to hurt you. Here, let me . . ." And he touched the tip of his tongue to her mouth, tracing the contours and crevices of her lips, which became soft and pliant, parting to join his in mutual exploration.

She found her hand moving across his chest, much as she had imagined doing when she had ridden on horseback with his brother. Her fingers played across the fabric of his sweater, dancing and swirling, lightly tracing a design from the hollow of his throat, arching across his pectoral muscles and down into the valley between them.

Rachel felt the warmth of his hands on her then, one supporting her back, the other matching the movements of her hands. Gently proceeding from the hollow at the base of her neck, his fingers stroked a pattern of his own, moving lightly across the top of her breasts, then over the soft mounds, dipping into the valley between. The tips had become pointed, crying their need through the thin fabric of her dress, but he did not touch them, not yet.

Instead he slid his hand to her back, next to the other one, and pulled her up against him. She nestled into the warmth of his chest as she felt his fingers begin unbuttoning the back of her dress. One by one, the buttons escaped their looped closures, and she felt the fabric gradually loosen, baring her back. His hands then moved across her skin, working in counterpoint, creating intricate designs from the nape of her neck and down her spine to the small of her back.

Rachel arched, pushing up against him in supplication, her body whispering what she could not say, begging his hands to continue their search, to explore all her terrain as no one else ever had.

She moaned and shook her shoulders, letting her dress fall to her waist, and she felt no shame as her breasts welcomed him, entreating him to appreciate their round fullness.

"Rachel, beautiful Rachel," he murmured.

He reached for her, but she moved back, just beyond his grasp, and slowly, rose to her feet, letting the dress slide down her hips and legs to fall in folds at her ankles. She stepped over the soft mound, then with her fingertips tugged at the last wisp of lacy fabric covering her. Without a trace of embarrassment, she stood nude before him.

Naked at Midsummer's twilight, Rachel's body shone in an alabaster glow, outlined by the faint gold line of the last rays of the sun against the rosy background of the sky. She felt timeless, ageless, not bound to her earthly form, though she was conscious of her body and, for the first time in her life, felt oh so beautiful. She felt as weightless as a water sprite, a fairy being, a night butterfly with glistening wings that fluttered, inviting capture. Her eyes caught his, daring him to approach her, to catch her, to pin her down, impale her, and make her the queen of his collection.

But she underestimated Michael's inner strength. His eyes never leaving hers, he rose and began to strip himself of his own clothing. He removed his sweater, baring his firm, hard chest, gleaming in the twilight. He kicked off his sandals, and finally his pants. Then he stood before her proudly like a creature of the forest, although unmistakably a man. And his eyes seemed to challenge her, daring her to come to him, offering the promise of a passion beyond her experience.

Rays of heat and light seemed to emanate from Michael's body as he extended his arms toward her, inviting her into his embrace. The beauty of his body was an incandescent candle, its light and power drawing her winged being into its flame. So Rachel flew to him, joining him in fiery celebration of the pentecostal fire of their passion.

Chapter Twelve

The first rays of the new morning shone in gentle beatitude on the slumbering couple. Rachel felt the sun's touch, but scarcely dared to breathe, unwilling to disturb the warm perfection of the moment. Half-remembered sensations suffused her, and she wondered if she had been dreaming. But then she stirred slightly and immediately felt strong arms tighten around her, bespeaking the reality of her situation.

Prickles of delight welled up from inside, causing a legion of tiny goosebumps to march across her arms.

"Michael," she breathed into the morning hush.

He responded without words, murmuring sleepily, erotically, into the nape of her neck. She felt the warmth of his breath with the rising and falling of his chest, which supported her as they lay together in an intimate swirl. Her head was pillowed on his left arm, while his right one encircled her waist, and his legs followed the bend of her own.

Spooning—that's what they called this, she thought. But she didn't feel hard or metallic. She felt warm, pliant, malleable. And the curve she and Michael formed was not like flatware, but more like a fluid, living letter of the alphabet. An *S*. *S* for *sensual, sexual*. And *sinful?* She quickly banished the unwelcome idea. No. *S* for *sweet, sleepy, safe*.

The other half of the living letter behind Rachel began to awaken, and the shape formed by their bodies began to undulate and change. Legs moved and straightened, shoulders shifted, and arms slid away as the couple reluctantly prepared to meet the day. Then Rachel felt his hand move up from her waist to encircle her breast, and she felt the heat of his rising hardness against her bottom. Suddenly she stiffened. No, not like this. Not a nameless and faceless coupling.

"No!" she cried out, and in an instant, Michael sat up and looked down at her.

"Rachel, what is it? What's wrong?" He tenderly wrapped the blanket and then his arms around her, lifting her up to his chest, trying to reassure her. With her head resting against his strong chest, she managed to quell her fears. She smelled him, felt him—this was Michael, no one else. She took a deep breath and let the past go.

She had squeezed her eyes shut, but now raised her head and opened them to see his earnest gaze. His hair tousled, a tinge of uncertainty in his eyes, he looked for a moment like a troubled child. How could she explain to that sweet, innocent-looking face the dark moments, the fear, the disgust and loathing she had known?

"I'm sorry, Michael. You must think I'm crazy. Last night was so magical—I didn't want to wake up this morning, because I was afraid it hadn't really happened."

"Then why were you so shocked when I touched you again? Did I do something wrong? Did I hurt you?" Once again, the voice sounded boyish, confused.

"No, it's just—it just reminded me of another time, that's all. A nightmarish time when I was used as a woman with a body, with no name and no face."

"What! When was that? Not while you were married!"

She didn't want to admit it, knowing that Michael still held lofty ideals about marriage.

"Yes, there was a time when my husband couldn't see me as anything but a receptacle for his anger and frustration. He had finished business school but was having trouble finding a

Rebecca Gault

job. I was always busy with the babies, and he became more and more desperate. He started drinking and staying out until late. Then he would come home drunk and demand sex, and it wasn't always very pretty."

"But why couldn't you just refuse him, Rachel? No one should be forced to have physical relations."

"I was afraid," she admitted. "Afraid of what would happen to me and the babies if I didn't do what he wanted. Remember, I didn't have a father when I was growing up—he died in an accident when I was still an infant—I didn't know how to accept men as real people with faults as well as good qualities. I thought when I got married, it would be to a prince who would always take care of me and our children. When things went wrong, I took the blame. I thought if I were a better wife, everything would be all right."

"And did everything turn out all right?"

"No, of course not. I did everything Brent wanted me to, or at least I tried. I kept the apartment clean, I tried to make sure the kids were nice and quiet, and I let him do whatever he wanted with me. And things did seem to get better for a while. He got a good job, and we bought a house. He even left me alone for a while, and I thought we were going to be happy. He went to work every day, and the heavy drinking stopped. I had enough money to decorate the house and buy nice clothes for myself and the kids. And when Lisbeth started school, I enrolled Chris in day care and went back to graduate school."

"It sounds as if that was a more peaceful time, at least."

"I think I pretended it was peaceful. I mean, because Brent wasn't bothering me. He wasn't even home very often. We lived side by side, talking about the kids when we did have conversations. Then there was a time . . ." Rachel shuddered, and forced herself to continue. "There was a time when he

230

seemed to be interested in me again . . . in that way. Sexually, I mean. But . . ." Visions and ugly emotions returned—images of bright red rayon, leather, twisted contortions, pain, and embarrassment.

"Rachel, you don't have to say any more. I think I understand."

"Well, you know the rest. I already told you that Brent met someone else. Anyway, it didn't take very long until his little games with me ended and he went running to her. And now look: they're married and living happily ever after." She laughed cynically.

"*Meine Liebe,* of course that experience hurt you, but must you be so bitter? Can you not believe in love?"

"I don't know. Last night I almost believed. . . . But maybe I was just enchanted by the surroundings. Everything was so perfect, so beautiful."

"And our lovemaking? Was that beautiful to you as well?"

"Oh, Michael, it was. I've never experienced anything like it. So tender, yet so powerful. It was—it was something I don't even know how to describe. It was magic. Midsummer's magic."

"And don't you think this magic came from love, true love?"

"I don't know. Why are you so insistent about it? Why do you have to classify it anyway? It just happened, that's all. And I'm not sorry, not at all, because I know . . . something now. I'm very glad we were together, but I don't know what it's supposed to mean," she said in her fear and confusion.

"It means love, Rachel. Real, magical, love, the kind that happens only once in a lifetime. The kind of love that makes a *real* marriage."

"Now you're being absurd. You're contradicting yourself. You yourself said you were waiting for some kind of sign to help you find your bride. Now, after we spend one night together, you're talking of marriage?"

"But I did receive a sign. She came to me, as I knew she would one day. The White Lady. It's you, Rachel. You're the *one,* and I want to be with you forever. *You're* the one I'm meant to marry."

"Michael, you can't be serious. How can you expect me to believe you, anyway? Your obsession with the White Lady—believing I'm the *one* on the basis of some kind of vision? That's not why people marry!"

She felt irritated and exposed, despite the fact that she was still covered by the blanket. "Can you hand me my clothes, please?" she asked, gesturing to the heap a foot or so away.

Michael did as he was asked, exposing his firm backside as he turned to collect her dress, and she tried to stifle the urge to laugh. It all suddenly seemed so absurd. She grabbed her clothes from him and turned to slip on her underwear and pull her dress over her head. She had just received a marriage proposal, her second within months, and now couldn't imagine a less romantic setting. Here they were, two naked people out in the middle of nowhere, in the light of day, arguing about a ghost—one that manifested itself into a marriage directive. It was too much. She could no longer control her laughter, but tried to stifle the sound, her shoulders shaking with her effort.

She felt an arm wrap around her shoulders.

"Rachel, what's wrong?"

Michael's voice was full of sympathy. Dear Lord, he thought she was crying again.

"Nothing's wrong, Michael. It's just—" She turned around, facing him, and then laughed aloud at the sight of him. In his haste to comfort what he thought was a tearful woman, he had rushed to her side only partially dressed.

Rachel tried to control herself, afraid he'd think she was making fun of him. But much to her surprise, he started to laugh as well, after glancing down at himself.

"*Raquelita, mi amor,* you're right. This is a silly spectacle." He took his arm from her shoulders and used both hands to pull his pants up to his waist and zip them. "Here, turn around, and let me help you button your dress." She lifted her hair so he could fasten the top buttons, then turned to face him, having regained her composure.

How easy it was to be with him. Brent would have been furious if she had laughed that way, thinking she was insulting his masculinity. He would have stormed off or pouted for days. But Michael didn't blow things out of proportion. Despite his youth, he was more mature and self-assured than Brent had ever been.

Grateful for the ease between them, Rachel threw her arms around him, "Michael, you're just sooo adorable!" she gushed, and gave him a quick, affectionate kiss.

"Hmmm, I thought we were arguing a few minutes ago."

"Well, yes, as a matter of fact, we were. You were telling me that a ghost made you propose marriage to me. . . ." She almost started to laugh again, but controlled herself.

"Yes, and what was it you said? Something about that's not the reason people get married. All right, then, why do you think people get married, Rachel?"

Rachel looked at him, speechless. What could she say? The obvious platitude that people got married when they loved each other wouldn't work. Because people got married all the time and then divorced, just as she and Brent had. And were they ever really in love? No.

"Tell me, Rachel," he persisted. "What does marriage mean to you? You say you married your husband because you thought he would take care of you, and you see how that turned out. And Kurt? Admit it: you've thought about marrying him—and if you don't love him, then that sounds like the same kind of motivation you had for your first marriage."

She wanted to deny it, but she couldn't. Michael was right. She had been briefly tempted to accept Kurt's offer for the chance to stay in this country, for the comfort of becoming part of an established couple, to have the children's material needs taken care of—all social and economic reasons that had nothing to do with emotion.

"All right, you have a point. But people can't live on love alone, can they? Real life demands certain things—jobs, a roof over your head, and, when children are part of the picture, their needs take precedence over everything else."

"Still, love is the foundation, Rachel. Everything else can build upon it."

"And in our case? I can't find a job, here or at home. And here you are, finished with your studies, earning a small stipend with your assistantship for Kurt, but still dependent on your parents. What about your future? What do you know about earning a living?"

The minute she said the words, she regretted them. Michael lowered his eyes, wounded, and said nothing.

"I'm sorry, Sweetie." The endearment came surprisingly naturally to her, as did the urge to comfort him. "I didn't mean to hurt your feelings. I just think you're being unrealistic."

"And young and irresponsible, right?" His eyes met hers accusingly.

Her silence seemed to affirm his accusation, but he regained some of his earlier brash self-confidence, and he spoke firmly.

"Rachel, I want to prove to you that you're wrong about me, and that you're wrong about love and marriage. Will you give me the chance?"

"And how will you do that?"

"First of all, tell me once again that you are not interested in marrying Kurt."

She nodded.

"Will you go back to town and tell him that you will not marry him?"

Again she nodded. After last night, that would be impossible anyway. "Yes, I will tell him. But then what? What can you do that will make it possible for us to be together? And how? Where? Here, or in the States? Don't you see, Michael? It's just too difficult. We're too different."

"No, we're not too different. We're alike. We are *seelenverwandt,*—soul connected, Rachel. You know it's true, although you attempt to deny it."

"But that's not . . . not *real!* In real life, there's almost ten years of difference between us. I'm raising two kids, while you don't even know what you're going to be when you grow up!"

Good Lord, she had done it again—insulted him and his youth.

This time his face didn't register a reaction. His stance was self-confident, as though his request alone had given him strength of purpose.

"I love you, Rachel. If you will have faith in me, we will work it out. You'll see. Trust me."

Michael held out his arms to her, and she let herself become enfolded in his strong, warm embrace. It always felt so right to be near him like this, her head resting on his chest, near his heart. So she allowed herself to believe, despite her doubts.

"We'd better be getting back," he said at last. "Don't you have classes today?" He pulled away, gathering up their things. He found his sweater and pulled it over his head, put on his watch and looked at it briefly, eyes narrowing as he looked at the time.

"How late is it?" Rachel asked. "Do I have time to go home and bathe and change?"

"It's eight. When do you have to be at the university?"

"Not until noon. Can you drop me off at home?"

"Yes, of course," he said. He suddenly became all business as he bent over, picking up the remains of their picnic. That accomplished, he put on his shoes and was finished packing everything up before Rachel had even found her shoes.

"Let's go then," he said, holding out his hand.

"Wait. Aren't you going to say good-bye to the White Lady of the Lake?" She glanced over her shoulder at the water, where a light morning mist floated in thin wisps above its surface.

"You said yourself that we have to live in the real world, Rachel. So let's go. We have work to do. And I hope I never again have to say good-bye to the White Lady, *my* White Lady."

He smiled down at her, a precious smile of confidence and love. She put her hand in his, and they walked away from the lake and into the dawn of new possibilities.

Rachel found herself caught up in those possibilities, believing in Michael and his dreams for the two of them, in spite of her initial reluctance. During her Danish class, when the rest of the group worked on translating an especially challenging paragraph, her mind was at work analyzing and replaying the conversations at the Hidden Lake. And after class, riding down the street on her bicycle, she felt like waving to all the couples she saw walking hand in hand. Me, too, she wanted to say. She wanted to announce it to the world. I have someone who loves me too!

Wheeling her bike toward the building where Kurt had his office, Rachel felt her excitement change to nervousness. She dreaded the confrontation, but her promise to Michael gave her the confidence she needed to enter the building and go up the stairs.

She knocked on the door.

"Herein!" said the voice from inside. Rachel turned the knob and pushed open the door, and was greeted by Kurt's wide smile as he rose from behind his desk to greet her.

"Rachel, there you are! I have been concerned about you. Did you not get my message?"

"Yes, I did. I'm sorry I didn't call you back, but I needed to talk to you in person."

He looked at her inquiringly. "What is it? Is something wrong?"

"No, I mean, yes. Kurt, I don't know how to say this except straight out. I can't stay in Germany, and I can't marry you. It's just not possible."

"Is it because of the children?"

"No, it's because of me. I can't tell you how much I appreciate everything you have done for me, for us. And it was very tempting to continue to let you take care of everything, to stay here as your wife, but that wouldn't have been fair to you. I know I could not love you the way you should be loved."

"Is it because of Michael?"

His words struck Rachel as though he had thrown water into her face. How could he know?

"What . . . what do you mean?"

"I have tried to ignore it, but I have seen the way he looks at you, and the way you look at him. There is something between you, almost like an electrical current. I saw how bothered he was when we returned from our trip to Bavaria, and he seemed quite agitated when Elke and I were discussing the prospect of your marrying me and remaining in Germany."

"Was that the same conversation when you talked about sending my children away to boarding school?"

He frowned. "Perhaps," he admitted. "I thought that would be for the best. You would have more time for yourself and far fewer worries. Lisbeth and Chris are fine children, but I'm afraid at my age I lack the patience for everyday family life. If they attended a boarding school, you and I would have more time to attend cultural events and take trips, and I thought we would become closer."

Rachel shook her head. "That never would have worked, Kurt. Until my children are grown, they belong with me. They are my responsibility and my joy. And as far as having time together to become closer—don't you see that if we aren't emotionally close before marriage, it's not likely to happen afterward either?"

Kurt sighed. "I thought it would be a way for both of us to be content. We would have a productive partnership, and I was hoping that we could make our mutual affection grow."

"Yes, Kurt, I believe affection and even love can grow—but not when forced. Let me ask you something. Did you wait for love to grow when you married Erika? Or were you already in love with her when you asked her to be your wife?"

Kurt lowered his head as she spoke, and when he raised it again, Rachel thought she saw the beginnings of tears in his eyes behind their glassy frames.

"My beautiful Erika. Yes, I was very much in love with her, and that love grew stronger every day of our marriage," he answered.

"You see, Kurt? That's love—real, magical, love, the kind that happens only once in a lifetime. The kind of love that makes a real marriage." Rachel realized with a start that she was repeating the same words Michael had said to her.

"You may be right, my dear. I was indeed fortunate to have had that kind of love with my wife. Perhaps I was just deluding myself about having it again." He sighed. "I hope you will forgive me if I misled you."

"There's nothing to forgive, Kurt. I'm flattered that you were interested in me and, as always, grateful for all your help. And I should not have encouraged you when I was also uncertain about my feelings."

"And Michael?"

"I don't know," Rachel answered honestly—or so she thought. The flush on her face betrayed her emotions, but she very much wanted to be rational and objective. "Michael . . . is, he's just very special. I don't know what will happen."

"You know I wish you the best of everything, Rachel. I hope we can still be friends, and I hope you will continue to rely on me."

Kurt extended his hand, and when Rachel gave hers in return, he clasped it in both of his for a moment. They looked at one another with affectionate understanding that needed no words, and Rachel left his office with a feeling of bitter-sweet contentment.

Her words to Kurt, Michael's words, echoed in her mind as she got back on her bike. *Real, magical love, the kind that happens only once in a lifetime . . .* Could it be that she really believed what she had just said?

Wheeling down the street toward home, she passed a florist's shop and was impressed by the colorful array of the flowers in the window. The joyful exuberance of the bright blossoms matched her tumultuous emotions, and she impulsively stopped to buy a bouquet, as if to commemorate the day. Deep blue, romantic forget-me-nots were the flowers she chose to take home.

After she got there, she puttered around, cleaning a little, reading a bit, and beginning to relax. For the first time since she had taken her children to the airport, she didn't feel their absence so poignantly.

Michael had kissed her ardently when they parted that morning, promising to call her later in the afternoon to make plans for dinner. Rachel tried not to watch the clock, but she could hardly wait for the time to pass before she heard from him again.

By 4:30, when he still hadn't called, she decided she had better take hold of herself. She was mooning around like a schoolgirl with a crush, and that wouldn't get her anywhere. She went into the bedroom to collect her laundry and headed for the washing machine in the basement. On her way back up the stairs, she remembered that she hadn't checked for mail since she had taken the trip to Munich, so she stopped at the bank of mailboxes near the entrance to the building.

The little compartment was filled to the brim, envelopes stuffed so tightly that she could barely extricate them. She looked through them briefly as she climbed the stairs to the apartment. Some catalogues and flyers—junk mail, even here in Germany. A letter from Julie, a thin envelope from one of the colleges to which she had applied for a teaching job— another rejection, no doubt, and an official-looking letter from an unfamiliar sender, Mansfield, Cohen and Howard. What in the world could that be, she wondered. She shuffled it back into the pile as she unlocked her apartment door and went inside.

She couldn't help herself. She went straight to the answering machine to see if Michael had left a message while she was downstairs. But the machine was blank.

She sat on the sofa and began opening the mail. Right, another rejection letter from the college. "We have found a candidate whose qualifications better match our needs, but we will keep your application on file . . . blah, blah, blah." Even when you expected it, it still hurt, she thought.

Rachel sighed and turned to Julie's letter. Hers were usually entertaining and always confirmed the fact that someone from home still cared about her. She skimmed through the gossip about the other students' lives, read about Julie's progress on her dissertation, and stopped when she came to a newspaper clipping that Julie had taped to the letter. It was an employment ad from their local paper, describing an opening for a teacher at the prestigious Waldorf School, a private institution that served students from kindergarten all the way through high school. Beneath the clipping Julie's script flowed in animated pen strokes, as though it were her voice.

Rach, this would be a super job for you! German for middle and high school kids—language and literature. You'd be perfect for it. I know the elementary-school German teacher, and I gave her your name. She's waiting for your application. So send off a résumé already!

Waldorf. Rachel knew of the school, knew that it had started in Germany and that it provided a nurturing and creative atmosphere for children. She had even thought about sending her own children there, but Brent wouldn't hear of it. He had gone through public school, and if it was good enough for him, it was fine for his kids, too. But the ad stated that tuition was free for children of teachers, and this had promise. Okay, Julie, she said silently to her friend, you've got it. I'll send a résumé right away. You never know.

But first she pulled out the strange, thick envelope from Mansfield and colleagues. She opened it slowly, wondering if it was just a rarefied form of junk mail. But this was no solicitation, no mass-produced correspondence. In official, no-nonsense language, the letter addressed Ms. Rachel Simmons, demanding her immediate attention to the black letters across the top of the page: PETITION FOR SOLE CUSTODY OF THE MINOR CHILDREN, LISBETH ANNE AND CHRISTOPHER JON SIMMONS.

Rachel's hands shook as she made her way through the legal document. My God, how could Brent do this? How could he make these accusations, state that he and Stacey would provide a more stable environment for *her* children? And they were with him now, somewhere out West, where she couldn't reach them. Brent had once threatened to do this if she stayed in Germany, but she hadn't taken it seriously, not planning to remain. But Brent had probably had this in mind all along and had deliberately planned the Disneyland trip to separate the children from her. How desperately did Brent and Stacey want the children? And what was she going to do about it?

She felt shaken, terrified, and alone. She had to talk to someone—but who? She didn't even know a lawyer, except for her divorce attorney, whom she had never really liked or trusted, and here she was, overseas. She was so upset, she couldn't think logically. She knew only that she couldn't face this alone. She ran to the phone to call someone . . . Michael, where are you? She had depended on Kurt, but she couldn't call him, not now. Julie, she'd call Julie. Her fingers recalled the phone number, even though her mind was racing too fast to remember it—but she reached only an answering machine.

Michael, she thought again. He had said they would be together, that she wouldn't be alone anymore. She wouldn't wait any longer; she'd just call him. She tried his dormitory but there got no answer. All right then, his parents' house.

She managed to find the Obregón's number, and unsteadily dialed it. It rang and rang. No answer. Maybe Geoffrey had some idea of where Michael was. But his roommate said Geoffrey was at the library. She was becoming increasingly desperate. Where was Michael?

She could feel her heart racing as panic set in. Her hands began to perspire, and she dropped the phone. It crashed against the answering machine, sending it to the floor, popping the cassette from its slot.

She forced herself to calm down and took a shaky breath, then another and another, until her breathing was steadier. Emma. She'd call Emma. She and Rob would know what to do. She dialed the number, and was relieved when someone picked up the phone.

"Janie, hi. It's Aunt Rachel. Is your mom there? May I talk to her please?"

It seemed to take forever for Emma to come to the phone.

"Rachel, what a surprise! How's it going? Everything okay with the kids?"

"Emma, they're gone. You know Brent persuaded me to let them go on that vacation they wanted, and I took them to the airport last week. But I just got a letter from some hotshot American attorneys—Brent's going to keep them, Em! They're not coming back!" She felt her voice becoming shrill and again tried to force herself to calm down.

"That's crazy, Rachel. He can't take them from you just like that. You were granted custody in the divorce, and for him to reverse that decision, he'd have to prove you unfit. And that's not going to happen. Read the letter to me. Let's hear what it has to say. Wait, let me call Rob to the phone . . ."

Comforted by her cousin's take-charge attitude, Rachel was able to make her way through the papers, reading aloud the statements and interrogatories. Rob said he had a contact in a Chicago law firm who might be able to help her, or at least advise her as to her rights and refer her to an appropriate attorney. They promised to get back to her the following day. When she replaced the receiver, Rachel felt a little better. She knew she could trust Rob and Emma to get back to her. There was nothing she could do at the moment, so she resolved to try to stop worrying.

Of course, she thought she could trust Michael, especially now, after everything that had happened between them. But where was he? And why hadn't he called? Maybe something dire had happened to him . . . but she shrugged that thought aside. No. She pushed the thought aside. Women always thought that when a man didn't call, it was because he was lying in a ditch somewhere, gravely injured, but that was never the case. When a man said he was going to call and he didn't, it was because he just didn't want to, that was all.

But Michael had promised. And he was so sincere. She had to believe in him. He had implored her to trust him. So she would faithfully wait until she heard something.

Rachel went back to the sofa and sat down. The bouquet of blue flowers stood in silent, cheery greeting and she acknowledged them with a weak smile. She grabbed a pillow from the other end of the sofa, placed it against the arm, and lay down. No wonder she was tired, she thought. So little sleep last night—the shortest night of the year—then this terrible news. Remembering her Midsummer Night, she felt her face flush, enjoyed a secret moment of delight, and closed her eyes, immediately falling into a dream. A dream of a blue flower . . .

The world was deep asleep. She could hear the steady ticking of the clock and the occasional rustling of the breeze as it wafted through the windows, the curtains parting and illuminating the room with the glow of the moon.

Restless, she thought about stories she had heard, feeling an inexpressible longing for something she could not define. She thought about times long ago, when it was said that animals and plants and rocks could speak to humans. It seemed to her as if that could happen again even now, if only she knew their language. What were the words, she wondered. But perhaps there was a language beyond words, like dance or music. And she motionlessly pirouetted and chanted a silent song into the night air.

Losing herself in her fantasies, she saw herself entering an enchanted landscape into a forest in which only a rare beam of sunlight penetrated the dense green net of foliage. The path soon became rocky and rough, and she saw that it rose steeply, leading up to a mountain.

She climbed the rocky path upward and into a mountainside cavern that seemed to be illuminated by light from within. She became aware of a powerful fountain of water shooting up as from a magic spring, reaching the top of the vaulted ceiling and descending in countless sparkles to collect in a pool of water below. The stream of pulsing water glowed like molten gold, but not the slightest sound could be heard. A holy stillness filled the cavern.

Its walls were damp, mist rising from their surface and from within them shone a soft bluish light. She approached the pool, which shimmered with an endless display of iridescent color.

All around her bloomed flowers of every color, and the most exquisite fragrance imaginable filled the air. But the vision that attracted her with overwhelming power was a tall, pale blue flower that stood at the far edge of the spring. She gazed at it with ineffable tenderness, and drew closer to it.

At her approach, the blue flower began to move, to transform itself. Its leaves became shinier and wound themselves around the lengthening stem. Then the flower inclined its head toward her, its petals parting to reveal its center, an iridescent crystal sphere. Looking through the blue depths into its core, she saw a series of images that revealed the mysteries of creation, the essence of beauty, joy, and perfect love. She reached out to touch it, and she felt herself on the very brink of realization . . .

But suddenly she heard a voice from outside, and she was awakened into the light of day.

Rachel opened her eyes and sat up, shook her head quickly to loosen the strands of hair that had stuck to her face during the night, and stretched. She massaged the crick in her neck caused by the awkward angle in which she'd slept, and she wondered how she could have spent the whole night there on the sofa in the living room. And how she could have slept so soundly, given her worries.

Her worries. Lisbeth and Chris. And Michael. Where were they? Where was he? What was she going to do? What *could* she do but wait?

It was getting lighter, and she had no choice but to attend to business as usual. As if on automatic pilot, she went into the bathroom to get ready for the day of classes ahead.

The last lecture was so boring that Rachel had trouble paying attention to the professor. She could hardly wait to get home to see if there was a message from her cousin or from Michael. She took a quick detour on her way home to stop by the post office to mail her résumé and letter of application for the teaching job at the Waldorf School, then jumped back on her bike and sped home.

When she walked into the apartment, the phone was ringing. She dropped her satchel and ran to pick up the receiver. "Michael?" she asked, breathlessly.

Her cousin's voice answered her. "Rach, it's me, Emma. You were expecting your friend Michael to call?"

"Yes. He promised he'd call yesterday, but so far, I've heard nothing."

"Did you have plans to study with him or something?"

"No . . . things have changed. We kind of became a little closer recently."

"Hmm, this sounds intriguing. I don't suppose you'd like to explain what you mean by 'a little closer,' huh?" She laughed.

"Emma, don't make me spell it out. I'll tell you about it later. Anyway, did Rob find out about a lawyer?"

Rachel rummaged through the bookcase to find a pencil so she could write down the name and address of the attorney Rob had contacted. Martin Harmon, Esquire, with an office on Monroe Street in Chicago.

"Okay, I'll contact him right away. I'll make a copy of this petition and write a letter with details of the original decree. Yes, Emma, I'll send him the names of both of our divorce attorneys. Okay then, I'll talk to you tomorrow. Thanks so much to both you and Rob!"

Getting the papers together let Rachel feel she was making some progress, not waiting passively for Brent's next sneaky move. And what could she do but wait for Michael? After spending less than half an hour in the apartment, Rachel left the building and set out on her bike for the post office to mail the package to the attorney. Standing in line behind other customers, she saw a familiar figure up ahead.

The young woman chatted animatedly with a group of friends, tossing her golden mane with a shake of her head for emphasis. One of her companions dropped a book, and the girl bent to pick it up. As she straightened up, she looked toward the back of the line, and her eyes met Rachel's. It was Elke Heinrich, and the look she gave Rachel before quickly turning away was glassy and cold.

Rachel wondered what she had done to offend her this time. Undoubtedly the girl's anger had something to do with Rachel's involvement with one of the two men in her life—her father or Michael. Had her father told her that his planned marriage had been called off? Contrary to what Kurt had maintained, Rachel was quite sure Elke would be relieved if she did not join their family. And Michael? Maybe Elke had some idea of where he had gone.

Rachel hated to lose her place in line, but she needed to know what was going on. She walked up to the group of young women. "Hello, Elke. How are you?"

The girl turned to her, affecting a friendly demeanor, though her eyes shot daggers. "Oh, Rachel, hello."

"I'm sorry to interrupt you and your friends, but do you think we could talk privately for a moment?" Rachel motioned to the other side of the room.

Elke nodded and reluctantly followed her to the quieter area. There she simply stared at Rachel, as if daring her to ask.

"Elke, do you by chance know where Michael is? I had an appointment with him, and I haven't been able to reach him for a couple of days."

"Michael? Of course you couldn't find him. He's out of town." She smiled slightly but said no more, as if to make Rachel beg for information.

"Where is he, then?" Rachel was unwilling to play Elke's cat-and-mouse game, but she had to get to the bottom of this.

"Oh, I'm surprised he didn't tell you. He has gone to Spain. But then, maybe you don't know Michael as well as you think you do." She smirked. "This is a pattern of his, you know—running away when someone tries to get too close to him. Last time he did it the other way around. He had a love affair with a Spanish girl and ran back here. To me, actually. He always comes back to me."

Rachel couldn't believe her ears. What was the girl saying? Was it possible? Had Michael really gone to Spain? And if so, why? Why would he have said nothing to her? It didn't make sense.

Elke laughed. "Perhaps it is only fair this way, Frau Simmons. You Americans think you can have anything you want." Her tone became more strident. "Do you think it's right to trifle with people's affections? You have broken my father's heart, and if you fancy Michael has broken yours, then perhaps that is as it should be. That's the way he is, after all." As if finally becoming aware of her loss of composure, she modulated her voice and said more sweetly, "Sorry, but it's better that you just go back home to the States and leave us alone. I'll take care of my father and Michael."

She turned away and trounced back to join her friends, who had completed their transaction at the window and were heading toward the door.

Rachel leaned against the wall for support, aghast at the girl's words and the coldness with which she had delivered them. She wanted to run away herself—go somewhere, anywhere—but she forced herself to move from the wall and back to the customer line. She needed to send this package to the attorney, Harmon; her children's welfare depended on it.

The wait seemed interminable, and Rachel's mind was spinning with the ramifications of Elke's words. Could the girl be telling the truth? She'd have to find out. She once had thought Michael was a flirt, but he had seemed so sincere when they were together at the Hidden Lake. Why did he implore her to believe in him? And, worse, why did she?

After she reached the window and paid for shipping the package by international express mail, Rachel felt calmer. She would call the Obregóns again and make some calls to Michael's friends. Maybe she would reach someone who knew where he was.

Home once again, Rachel immediately went to the phone, preparing to place her calls. Maybe there's a message, she thought, remembering the answering machine. But it wasn't in its place near the phone. Good heavens, she had forgotten to pick it up after she'd dropped it. No wonder she hadn't received any messages. She pushed the cassette tape back into place, then dialed the number for Michael's parents, but again, no answer. What about Beate, Michael's friend from the seminar? She hated to call the woman; it would just rub more salt in the wound if she learned that Elke's accusations were true. Oh well, then, she'd try Geoffrey again.

This time she was successful. "Hello, Geoffrey, how's it going? It's Rachel Simmons. Listen, I hate to bother you, but have you heard anything from Michael Obregón lately?"

"Well, I didn't talk to him directly," he answered, "but Erich told me that he had gone to Spain. Such a shame . . ."

Rachel couldn't bear to hear the rest of whatever Geoffrey might say. She made a quick excuse and apology, and got off the phone.

So it was true, then. Michael had left the country. He had run away from her, from commitment, stability, and responsibility, and he hadn't even had the decency to tell her. Maybe Elke was right. Maybe this was a pattern, and Michael would return to his family friend again and again. But how was that possible? Had he really meant to deceive her? Had he just wanted to conquer her resistance, gain another trophy? Rachel couldn't bring herself to believe that of him. More likely it was as his own mother had suggested, that he was still a bit immature.

She broke down in tears. How had everything changed so drastically? This place of enchantment, the land of the blue flower of her dreams, had suddenly become a dark, confusing wasteland. Perhaps she had never belonged here to begin with, she said to herself as she wept. All she knew was that she needed to get away.

Reaching for the phone again, she dialed Emma's number.

"Emma, I have to get out of here. I've made such a mess of everything," she wailed into the receiver.

"Leave Münster now? But what about your classes?"

"They're almost over. I gave my seminar report, and I can come back for final exams in the other classes, as if it matters. I've already earned my degree at home anyway. Maybe I was as stupid as Brent said to come here for the semester just to pursue some silly dream."

"You, Rachel, 'stupid'? Impossible. It sounds as if we really need to talk. Do you want to come here, or should we meet somewhere in between?"

"I don't know. I thought I'd come to you in Geneva, but maybe it would be good to go somewhere else, where we can spend time together by ourselves. Can you get away for a few days? And where should we go? You know Europe better than I do."

"Remember when we came to see you for Easter, how we both wanted to visit that castle on Lake Constance where your favorite poet spent the last years of her life? What was the name? Oh, yes, Meersburg. I could meet you there."

"Oh, Emma, that's perfect. A chance for us to spend time together before I go home again, and a chance for me to gain closure on the story of Annette's life. I'd like that. I'll see about renting a car."

After a few more minutes of discussing the logistics, the matter was settled. And for the first time in days, Rachel felt some of her optimism return. They would meet in Meersburg, final resting place of "her" poet. Maybe Annette will even speak to me there, Rachel thought. Maybe she will somehow let me know why all of this is happening.

The bouquet she had bought to celebrate the love she thought she had found now seemed to mock her with bright blue effrontery, and the volume of poetry lay face down on the table where she had left it days earlier. "Your love abandoned you in Meersburg, Annette," she said softly to the spirit of the poet. "How did you endure the pain? How can I endure mine?"

Her mind's eye brought her to a vision of a turreted castle far above raging waters. A lone figure watched on the balcony of a tower, and as she stood there, the tower began to tremble and quake. Cracks formed, stones crumbled, and pieces of brick and mortar shattered and fell, dashing the tower and its inhabitant into the sea . . .

Chapter Thirteen

"Oh, Emma, I'm so glad you suggested this trip. I really needed to get away." Rachel gazed around in fascination as they strolled down the narrow alleyway, taking in the gabled, half-timbered old buildings with their carved wooden trim, and their window boxes overflowing with colorful blooms. "It's so different here from Westphalia—more what I considered typically German before I came to the country."

"I love these southern German surroundings, too—the lake, the Alps in the background, the magnificent colors. Do you know the slogan for Lake Constance?"

Rachel shook her head. "One lake, three countries, and a thousand possibilities!" Emma said.

"I believe it. Remember all those brochures at the tourist office? There's Mainau, the flower island, the prehistoric village of Unteruhldingen, Konstanz, of course—I just wish we had more time!"

"It's not so very far from Geneva. You'll just have to come back here with the kids. Maybe we can all rent a cottage on the lake next summer."

"Maybe . . ." Rachel's voice trailed off dubiously. How could she even think about next summer, or any time in the future, when everything in her present was so uncertain?

They followed a group of tourists up the slight incline to the old castle, where Annette had lived with her sister and brother-in-law during the last years of her life.

"Here we are, Em. Look up above. I've seen pictures of

this tower. It's where Annette spent most of her time when she left Westphalia."

"She must have had a stunning view of the lake. I would guess that provided a lot of inspiration for her work."

"Yes. She was certainly prolific when she was here. And so eloquent. In one poem she's standing on the tower, her hair fluttering in the wind while she looks down at the sea below and considers her situation as a woman—and how different her life would have been if she were a man. And she wrote some truly heartrending poems that serve as a final farewell to her lost love, Levin Schücking."

"Didn't she also live in that little house in the vineyard —what was it called, the prince's house, where they have that Droste museum?"

"Yes, but I think that was just her summer place—it was sunnier there and better for her health. Maybe it was easier for her to be there than in the tower—on account of the memories. Come on, let's see what they have in this museum."

They walked through the rooms of the old castle, which dated from the seventh century, and its displays of armor and memorabilia from the days of the bishops of Konstanz, as well as the collections of Josef von Lassberg, Annette's brother-in-law.

Finally they came to the private tower rooms that Annette inhabited during her tenure in Meersburg. They contained a narrow mahogany bed, a writing desk, a small, ornate settee, and a smattering of framed pictures on the walls. And, as in the *Rüschhaus*, a large framed portrait of the poet.

This one portrayed a woman in a lighter-colored dress, holding a book. One of her own manuscripts? Rachel gazed at the woman in the portrait, and the blue eyes seemed to shimmer briefly, as if they held a secret for her. What is it, what do you want of me, she asked silently. But the moment passed, and the painted eyes stared back at her lifelessly. But for that single instance, Rachel felt no presence of the poet in the tower rooms, much to her disappointment.

And, try as she might, she was unable to feel her presence in the Droste Museum in the small summer house in the vineyard, which she and Emma visited on their second day. It was a pleasant little museum with a collection of items that had belonged to the poet, but Rachel did not feel that her spirit inhabited the place. Annette, where are you, she asked, but again, no answer.

She tried to explain her frustration to Emma as they sat together at dinner. Their waitress, a buxom young woman in a *dirndl*, had just taken their order for the famous local dish, *Blaufelchen*, fish from Lake Constance. Emma enjoyed her wine as Rachel sipped mineral water.

"I know it sounds crazy, but sometimes Annette speaks to me, even without words. There's a connection, an understanding, or at least there was at home—I mean in Westphalia. But I just don't feel it here."

"Well, it does sound a bit odd to me, but, then, I never did understand your relationship to fairy tales and fantasy. I remember when you were little, how you always bugged Aunt Margaret—I mean, your mom—to read you one more story from the Brothers Grimm before bedtime. And then your tantrum when she said your twelfth birthday was going to be your last to get a doll for a present! Did all those dolls talk to you too?"

"Gosh, Emma, I don't know. I guess I made them talk. But I knew that was pretend—it's not the same thing as this bond with Annette. She spoke to me even before I came to Germany, and her voice is not coming from me. It's coming from her. For all I know she called me to come here."

"You know what, the more of this wine I drink, the more I

believe you. I don't know why you're not having any. It's from one of the local vineyards. You should have a glass."

"I don't think so, Emma. German wine always gets me into trouble. I see things, visions, and I get strange feelings."

"All the more reason to have some, then. Look, you've been bemoaning the fact that this woman isn't speaking to you here. Well, maybe drinking wine is a way for you to allow her to cross over from her world to ours." Emma giggled as she emptied her glass and poured herself another.

Rachel stared at her. Her cousin was getting pleasantly tipsy and a bit silly, but maybe there was some truth in her assertion. As the Romans said, *in vino veritas.* She thought back to the times she had heard the voice of the poet. The first time had been when she was totally exhausted, sitting in her library carrel back in the States. When she had visited the House in the Rushes, she felt her there. And then there was that May Eve, when she saw the faces in the mirror. That night, she had seen herself become Annette, and Levin had become Michael—the fairest of them all.

She winced at the memory. Michael. She had fought her attraction to him for so long, and when she finally succumbed, believing his words, he left her. Just as Levin had left Annette.

Rachel impulsively grabbed the wine bottle and filled her empty water glass. Maybe this will force the truth, she thought to herself. If Annette appears to me, it will prove that Emma is right. If not, I'll just enjoy the wine and maybe it won't hurt so much to think of Michael.

By the time the two women had finished their meal, they had depleted not only the first wine bottle, but also a second, brought by a disapproving waitress who had replaced Rachel's water tumbler with an appropriate wine glass. They left the restaurant in good humor, walking arm in arm through the narrow alley to their hotel.

Back in their room, Rachel slipped on a long white cotton nightgown and crawled under the down comforter but didn't let herself fall asleep until she had entreated the spirit of the poet to come to her. "Tell me, Annette, tell me, . . ." she whispered as she closed her eyes.

It was dark in the castle. Everyone slept but for the two who had arranged their tryst. Annette ran through the corridor in her sleeping gown, hair fluttering down her back. It had been a glorious day, filled with the sights and sounds of the people and creatures they'd met during their walk along the lake. Lassberg was pleased with Levin, and she was gratified. It was important for Levin's career, as well as for the two of them, that he not fail in his position as Josef's librarian. For here they had uninterrupted time together. Time to take excursions to neighboring villages—Markdorf, Deisendorf, Uhldingen, Farm Haltenau—to know the lake and its rhythms, and to spend hours reading to one another in the library or in her tower room. Her writing talent seemed to overflow—the joy of their togetherness filled her heart and took form in words, fruits of the spirit of their love.

Heart pounding, she ran into the library, where he had promised to wait for her. But where was he? The candle on the desk had been snuffed out, his journal closed, pen at its side. The window was open, and she caught the scent of water. Where was he? Standing in the middle of the room, she felt cold, felt the blood draining from her veins. Letters and words surrounded her as if they were living things, and spirits of words she had not yet penned surrounded her. *My talent rises and falls with your love. Lebt wohl. Farewell.*

"Noooo!" The word was a plaintive cry of mourning.

Rachel awoke with a start, looking around the room. Emma stirred slightly in the bed next to hers. What had happened here? The dream had seemed so real. She had felt the excitement of one who was about to meet her lover, but he wasn't there. And the only recourse, the only comfort offered her, were black and white words on paper, penned words, printed words, immortal words. Annette's legacy.

But I'm not Annette! I can't turn my pain and disappointment into something of lasting beauty as she did. And resignation? How can I be resigned to something I don't understand? I'm just a normal person, a person who never knew love—at least until it found me in Westphalia. It found me, but why, if it was just going to leave as suddenly as it came?

She shook her head. So much for the truth of the grape, she thought ruefully. She'd had enough wine to make her giddy, to give her a crazy, mixed-up dream, and she felt more confused than ever. She lay back down and closed her eyes and fell into an immediate but restless sleep.

Emma awakened her some time later with a soft moan. "Rachel, it's so late. Are you feeling all right?"

Rachel mumbled something in German. Then she repeated the phrase. *"Lebt wohl."*

"What's that mean?"

Rachel sat up and rubbed her eyes. "It means 'farewell.' It's the name of a poem Annette wrote to Levin and his wife. It's beautiful, sad, and final, and I can't get it out of my mind."

"So you're still feeling bad. Me, too, but it has nothing to do with sad love affairs. You were right about the wine last night. I have a terrible headache, and my stomach is queasy."

Rachel opened her eyes wide. "But you said you'd go with me to the cemetery today. It's our last day!"

Emma sighed from her bed. "I'm sorry, honey, but I won't

be going anywhere for a while. Maybe later, but I can't promise anything. Can't you go on without me? I'll wait for you here."

Hands massaging her temples, Emma settled back into her pillows and Rachel got dressed and went to the dining room. She picked at her food, not too hungry after their large meal the night before, but thank goodness, she had no hangover after that wine. Best not to get into the habit anyway, though. From now on, she'd lay off the alcohol, *vino veritas* or not. She finished her cup of coffee and rose from the table.

It was a cool morning, with few people in the streets. Shopkeepers were just beginning to ready their stores for the day's business, sweeping their entryways, rolling up their awnings. Most of the other tourists were probably still sleeping or relaxing with their morning coffee.

Walking down a shady alleyway, Rachel wrapped her long green sweater more tightly around the cotton T-shirt and jeans she wore, grateful for the warmth of the wool. It was heavy enough to provide protection against the cold but light enough to carry when it was no longer necessary. And with no buttons and its wide shawl collar, it was easy enough to shed, she thought, remembering when she had last worn it. Midsummer Night at the Hidden Lake. It had slipped so easily from her shoulders when Michael took her hand, when they danced their way into love. She shivered, pulled the collar up around her neck, and continued her walk down the street.

Entering the cemetery, she wondered which way she should walk. The promotional literature about Meersburg boasted that the graveyard was final resting place of two of its most famous inhabitants—Annette von Droste-Hülshoff, and Franz Anton Mesmer, the Austrian physician who had cured hysterical patients with hypnotism, or what he called animal magnetism. She smiled, wondering if there was a connection between the two. Perhaps that was it, she thought—she and Annette had both been mesmerized by magnetic, charming young men.

She strolled among the graves, reading the names on the markers—Heinz, Elfriede, Gertrud, Dagmar, Karl. Who were you, she wondered. How did you live your lives? Were you happy? Who were your loves?

And then she heard it—the poet's voice. Gentle, comforting, without a touch of grief. "Life is so short, happiness so rare." Rachel followed her instincts, led by the sound, the feeling, the warmth. And soon she stood in front of a grave and read the words: *Annette Freiherrin von Droste-Hülshoff, 1797–1848.* And below, *Ehre dem Herren*—Honor to the Lord. The cold, hard marble testified to the outlines of a life: name, dates, and a reminder of the poet's religious convictions.

Suddenly Rachel was overcome with sorrow. She spotted a bench, dropped herself down on it, and wept. Why, she wondered. Life, death, and the time in between—what was it all about? Why was there so much heartache and confusion? Why love someone, only to lose him? She reached into the pocket of her sweater, looking for a tissue, and her fingers closed around something smooth, round, and cool.

She drew the object from her pocket. Small, perfect, the shiny blue globe, the little crystal ball that Michael had given her that magical Midsummer Night. As she clasped it in her palm, she could feel it becoming warmer, and its warmth flowed from her hand throughout her body. She opened her fingers slowly and looked down at the sphere. As she gazed at it, the color changed from a shadowy blue to a glistening iridescence. The full spectrum of the rainbow shone in concentric circles. Then the surface became smoother, silvery, glassy, mirror-like.

Rachel saw the reflection of her face, then watched as the image changed, not into the image of a living person but a suggestion, a personification of the numinous presence of Spirit.

The light around it became stronger, almost blinding. Rachel closed her palm and her eyes simultaneously and fell back onto her seat. Her left hand, enclosing the little blue ball, was still warm. She turned her palm upward on her knee and saw a soft blue light emanate through her fingers. As if of their own volition, they released their grasp and began to unfold outward like the petals of an exotic flower. And as she watched, its five petals parted in gentle supplication, revealing the crystal sphere at its center.

Perfectly round, the sphere rested in the palm of Rachel's hand, but its contours became gradually less defined. It lengthened ever so slightly, became elliptical, like a precious drop of dew born of the morning's mist, then a tender, quivering teardrop, expression of the heart's pain and of its joy. Then again it became round, now a shimmering, dancing bubble poised in its trajectory to float up and away, into the ether.

Breathless with wonder, Rachel gazed into the depths of the sphere, and all at once she knew herself as a person not of form and substance, but of spirit, and she felt herself become a part of everything and everyone that had ever lived and loved. And she felt Michael's presence, without specific form but as a distillation of spirit, and in that moment she knew that all her worries and insecurities were illusion, nothing more. Their earthly bodies were vessels placed in time and space, each containing an eternal spark of the divine. As all other beings in the physical world, they were offered the gift of transcendence to the ethereal plane through love.

Rachel let out her breath slowly. Finally she knew, she

understood. Michael had given her the gift of love. "Refuse not the gift . . ." the strange old woman had admonished her that day in the café.

Given a magical gift by her *Amme*—her nursemaid—the child called Nettchen grew up believing in the power of love. The love of the woman named Annette for the man she considered a soul mate became a transformational force that imbued her immortal poetry. And it was through that poetry that she was able to reach out and touch a kindred spirit from another time and place.

"Annette, thank you. I understand now," Rachel whispered reverently. Gently she placed the crystal sphere into her pocket, then she rose and held out her arms to embrace her surroundings—the verdant garden, the blue sky, and the spirits of all of those who had passed to another realm.

Rachel walked through the grounds in prayerful contemplation, but as she left the cemetery, her mood became exultant. She could hardly wait to get back to the hotel to tell Emma about her experience.

Rachel burst into the room, where Emma sat reading a novel.

"Well, from the look of you, I wouldn't exactly say you've seen a ghost, but something must have happened at that cemetery. You look like a different person!" Emma exclaimed with a smile.

Rachel dropped down next to her on the bed. "Em, you wouldn't believe it. I don't know how to explain it, but it was an epiphany. Suddenly, I understood what Annette has been trying to say to me."

"Did you have a . . . conversation with her?"

"No. But I heard her voice repeating the same phrase she has always said when I have heard her, telling me that life is short and happiness is rare. I knew that meant I was supposed to appreciate life, but now I know it's more specific than that. I've always been afraid of love, afraid to give myself over completely to it, except for the children, of course. But now I see that love is a gift, a precious gift, and that it is the only thing that can take us beyond our earthly concerns into eternal life."

"That sounds mighty close to theology for someone who has basically rejected religion," remarked Emma. "Are you saying this was a spiritual conversion, that you believe in God all of a sudden?"

"It *was* a spiritual experience, though I'm not sure I can classify it yet. Maybe I never will. But I know that I'll never forget it. I see everything differently now, even so-called unrequited love."

"And how do you explain the spirituality of that, then? One person loves, and the other one doesn't. What's so grand about that? Isn't it better to have two people in love at the same time?"

"Of course it is. But real love transcends circumstances. I've been feeling so sorry for Annette, but some of that grief was misplaced. She acknowledged her love for Levin, even if he could not return it, and was able to transform that love into a gift that enriched the world of others."

"Well, I know her writing has enriched your life. But can you really say that all of a sudden you're over the grief you've been carrying for Michael? I don't get it."

"I don't either. But I'm sure that all of that will be solved if I'm meant to find the answers. What I need to do now is go home and take care of my real-life concerns—keeping custody of the kids and finding a job—and Michael must do what he has to do to live his life. But I know now that what he said to me was real. He meant every word. He does love me."

"But don't you miss him? Don't you still want him?"

"Yes, I miss him. I'll always miss him. But I'm glad we were together, even briefly. And if we are meant to be together again, then we will be, somehow, someday."

"Just one more thing. I'm curious about—how did this all come about? You said you heard a voice, but how did you connect it to love and come to this kind of peace?"

Rachel smiled. "Remember I told you about that night at the lake with Michael? I told you he gave me something, a special memento? . . . Well, I reached into my pocket and found it again today, and, almost like a crystal ball, it showed me the truth I needed to know."

She reached into her pocket again and withdrew the little sphere. Here in the hotel room, away from natural light, its glow was diminished, but it still had a deep blue luster.

"It's beautiful, Rachel, but I fail to see its magic. It's almost like one of the kids' marbles, though bigger of course. And if it's like a crystal ball, why can't I see my future in it?"

"You're not supposed to see your future. You're supposed to see into yourself. And there's another connection, something I forgot to explain. Remember I told you about that old lady in black who spoke to me in that outdoor café one day?"

"Yes. She told you to go marry Kurt, right?"

"No, that's what I *thought* she meant at the time. She told me that I should accept the gift. That there was someone who loved me. I assumed that it was Kurt, but it was really Michael. And here's the weirdest part. I think that old woman was Annette's *Amme*—her nursemaid—Frau von Plettendorf!"

Emma frowned. "Let me get all this straight. Annette speaks to you, but she doesn't really talk. And this lady talks directly to you, but she's a ghost. Why in the world would you assume that some gabby old lady was Annette's nursemaid?"

"Because of the gift. She loved the little girl, little

Nettchen, so much, she wanted to give her something to hold, so that she would always remember the power of love."

"She was supposed to remember that her nursemaid loved her?"

"Partly that, but also the many stories of long-ago times she'd told the little girl, especially the legend of the Hidden Lake. And that legend is that it once was a magical spring with life-giving waters, with magical bubbles, like this one, that would float to the surface to be picked up and treasured by people who would understand the message of love."

"I'm still not convinced that your old woman was the nursemaid, but I'll accept the story about how this marble got to Annette. But how did Michael get it to give it to you?"

"Through Levin, a family relation. Annette gave it to Levin because she loved him and thought he would understand its message."

"But did he understand?"

Rachel smiled. "That's exactly what I asked Michael when he told me the story. No, he probably didn't understand. Levin appreciated Annette's talent, and did love her in his own way, but never really comprehended the depth of her love for fantasy and her romantic spirit. To him this crystal sphere was probably nothing more than a pretty piece of glass. But it was passed down through his family, given to the firstborn sons, until it landed with one who *could* understand."

"And that, presumably, was Michael."

"Yes. He knew I was confused about spiritual matters, knew I could not trust in love, and knew also that the only way for me to learn about it was to experience it myself. That's why he gave it to me, so that I would look inside myself and know."

"Unbelievable, and yet it makes an odd kind of sense. And

it's certainly a profound connection to your poet, too. It's as if all this was meant to be, as if this *was* your reason for coming to Germany. It gives me the chills."

"Well, I hope it makes you happy, too, as it does me."

Rachel's inner joy buoyed her through the difficult days ahead when she returned to the reality of her solitary life in Münster. She attended the remaining days of classes and began the process of extricating herself from the world she had come to love during the past months. She went to the foreign students' office and officially ex-matriculated from the university. She closed her checking account in the city. She gave away bulky items she had accumulated during her time there—toys and housewares—and even found someone to buy her bike, though she refused to part with it until her very last day.

Geoffrey lent her his car, and she drove to the post office, sending boxes of books to Julie's address in the States, since she wasn't sure where she would be living when she returned, and provided that address for mail forwarding as well. That accomplished, she was about to leave the window when the clerk called her back.

He handed her a registered letter, "Frau Simmons, this is for you."

Rachel walked outside the entrance and opened it. Finally, someone wanted her! The letter from the principal of the Waldorf School offered her the teaching position, complete with a generous salary, benefits, and tuition for her children! It even included a contract. She marched back into the building, purchased a stamped envelope, inserted the hastily signed contract into it, and sent it on its way.

She marveled at her good fortune as she finished packing her bags back at the apartment. Sadly, only one more night remained for her stay in Germany, but everything was going well in her transition. She had no promises from the attorney, Harmon, but the lawyer was reasonably confident she would have no problem retaining custody of Lisbeth and Chris when she returned home. Brent had backed down when he found out that she was returning to the States and had even promised to have the children at the airport to greet her.

Still no word from Michael, but the peace of mind she had found in Meersburg stayed with her. Michael had given her a precious gift, and they had shared something rare and special, so she held that close to her heart.

She had made her farewells and offered her thanks, sending parting gifts to all those who had helped her—a rare edition of *Faust* for Kurt, leather driving gloves for Geoffrey, and an antique cut-glass decanter to be delivered to the Obregón's country address. Just one thing remained on her list of things to do before her departure—a final visit to the House in the Rushes. She jumped on her bike, making sure she carried a water bottle and a granola bar for the long ride.

Conditioned by her many excursions, she wasn't at all tired when she arrived. Here, especially here, was where she always felt the spirit of the poet, her friend Annette.

It was a glorious summer day, with the roses in full bloom, infusing the air with their delightful fragrance. Rachel strolled through the gardens, her footsteps crunching on the gravel path. Here were the little cherubs representing the four elements. She smiled as she remembered her conversation with Michael about them. Leaving the path, she headed toward the little bench under the trees.

With Michael, she had sat on this bench where Annette had waited day after day for her love to come to her. And here Rachel had received her first kiss from Michael, the kiss that changed her life forever. She thought back on their moments together: the way he tilted his head with interest, his enthusiasm when engaging in metaphysical discussions, his blue eyes, broad smile and the cleft in his chin, and the five o'clock shadow when he neglected to shave. She remembered the warmth and fragrance of his breath, of his skin, and the taste of him. She felt again his beautiful, strong hands, his muscled body. The delicious combination of boyish innocence and manly ardor, and the evidence of wisdom beyond his years. Michael, Michael. And for the first time, she said the words aloud. "I love you."

How good it felt to give voice to what was in her heart. No matter if there was no one to hear the words. The very expression of love was a celebration of wonder, a celebration of life. So she said them again, merely three little words, yet a world of feeling, and rejoiced.

A honeybee droned behind her, birds chirped in the tree above, and a bright yellow butterfly flitted before her. She laughed with delight, and then she heard another sound. Footsteps approaching.

A figure came down the path, but she could not see who it was—the flash of sunlight in her eyes blocked her vision. Still, she rose from the bench, and as she did, she felt herself change. She became physically smaller, more delicate, her hair no longer loose but arranged tightly atop her head, her jeans and cotton shirt replaced by a long dress with a tight bodice and full skirt.

"You've come back," she said with a sigh of wonder.

"My love, my little mother," he said, his voice full of tenderness. She closed her eyes in bliss and felt him take her into his arms, and they were one, beyond time, beyond place, for all eternity.

Then Rachel felt herself changing back into her accustomed form and clothing, and she opened her eyes. Michael!

It was unmistakably Michael. He was really here, and he held her in his arms.

"Michael! I . . . I thought for a moment you were someone else. That *I* was someone else."

"I know, my love, I felt it too. Just for a moment, we were Annette and Levin."

Her mind spun with questions. How could they become other people? And, a more mundane concern, how and why was Michael here now, after such a long and unexplained absence?

"My dearest love, how concerned you must have been," he said. "I tried to contact you. I called so many times, but there was never an answer, not even your machine. And I had to leave quickly."

"But why? What was it that scared you so? Was it meeting your White Lady after waiting a lifetime for her? Was the reality just too much?"

"Of course not! My leaving was not to escape you. I wanted nothing more than to make contact with you. But it was my father. He died suddenly the day after you and I were together. I took you back into town and I was preparing to go to the office to finish some work for Kurt, but something told me to go right away to my parents' home, so I did. I saw my father and talked with him in the garden before he had his fatal stroke."

"But I didn't know. Oh Michael, I'm so sorry about your father. Are your mother and Paul and Anna all right? Why didn't you write if you couldn't reach me by phone? Maybe I could have helped."

"I tried, Rachel, I tried. I gave Kurt a note to give you, but Elke admitted to me yesterday that she took it, and she even told me about her lies to you. She was right about one thing— I did go to Spain. It was my father's wish to be buried in his homeland. But I did not go to be with another woman, as she claimed. I stayed for a while to be with my family and to investigate a business option with my sister and her husband."

"Why would you do that? You're not a businessman, Michael, you're a scholar!"

"I know that, but I wanted to prove to you that I could be a good husband and provider, so I explored the possibility of setting up a branch of their import-export business in the States."

"You mean you would have gone into business just for me? But, Michael, I don't want you to become something you're not, just to fill some misguided ideal of what a husband should be. You need to be yourself—and that's something you actually taught me!"

"I do know that," he admitted, "but I wanted to prove to you that I could be responsible and earn a good income for our family. I delved into the business, poring over the books, making appointments, arranging contracts, and so on. But then one morning I was sitting on the veranda of my sister's home, and something happened to change my mind. I heard a buzzing in my ear, and I followed the path of a little bee to a blue flower at the edge of the garden. The bee hovered above it, then flew away, but I was captivated by a tiny dewdrop that glistened on the edge of a petal. I knelt down in front of it, and right before my eyes, the flower opened, and I saw your face. Then I knew that I had to return home, that you were ready to accept me for myself, and that you finally had faith in our love."

"It's true, Michael. I didn't tell you at the time, because I couldn't accept it myself. But it's true, so true. I do love you."

He kissed her tenderly, causing her heart to flutter like the little butterfly of delight that had heralded his arrival.

"Remember I told you that things would work out if you would just trust in me, in love? I hurried back to Münster as soon as I could, and I got here early this morning. I went to your apartment right away, but you weren't home. So I went to Kurt's office and there I saw Elke, and I began to understand something of what had happened. And then came a stroke of good fortune through our mutual friend, Kurt. He contacted your university and arranged a doctoral fellowship for me in comparative literature."

"Michael, that's so perfect! I don't know why you fought it so long. With your father's legacy, as well as your own interests, it's just natural for you to become a professor!" Then the second aspect of his pronouncement hit Rachel. "Wait a minute. You're going to be at *my* university? In the States? I can't believe it!"

She threw her arms around him in her excitement, covering his neck with countless kisses, but stepped back when she sensed that Michael's demeanor had become quite serious.

"Please sit down for a moment, Rachel."

She did as she was bidden. Then he knelt before her, took her hands in his, and gazed into her eyes. "I love you, Rachel, beyond words. I cannot offer you riches, but I offer you my life. I want to be your partner, your soul mate, friend and guide to your children, and father to our own. I want to be your husband. Now I'm asking, with all that I am, will you marry me?"

"Michael, oh Michael, yes!" Rachel gasped.

"I know it is customary to offer an engagement ring, especially in your country. I hope this will be pleasing to you." He let go of her hands to reach into the pocket of his shirt. "You remember my father's ring, the one he wore on his little finger? My mother gave it to him, and now to me. I'd like you to have it. You could have it reset, if you wish."

He slipped the ring on the third finger of her left hand, and when she extended it to get a better look, the diamond shone in the sunlight, reflecting all the colors of the rainbow. "It's perfect as it is," she replied.

She stood up then and pulled him into an embrace that sealed the covenant of their love. Home. Right here, with her head against Michael's chest—this was home, no matter where in the world they might be.

Hands clasped, they walked through the gardens of the moated country estate for the final time. At the parking lot, before she loaded her bicycle into Michael's car, Rachel turned back to look at the House in the Rushes.

"Thank you," she whispered to the spirit of the poet. "You were right. Life is short. Too short to be consumed by worries, to let concerns over age or imagined security cloud what is true and real. And what is true and real is love—that and only that."

And she heard Michael's voice behind her. "Thank you, dear Nettchen, for bringing my White Lady to me, for allowing us to redeem the love that was denied you in your lifetime."

The last rays of the sun shone on the house, lending it a golden, magical aura, as if the spirit of love in the house and garden gave its blessing to the couple. And the breeze carried the whisper of a woman's voice: "*Lebt wohl.* Farewell."